LAST THINGS

*Also by Ralph McInerny
in Large Print:*

Leave of Absence
Abracadaver
Savings and Loam
Rest in Pieces
Easeful Death
Judas Priest
The Basket Case
A Cardinal Offense
Desert Sinner
Mom & Dead
Grave Undertakings
Irish Tenure
Triple Pursuit
Emerald Aisle

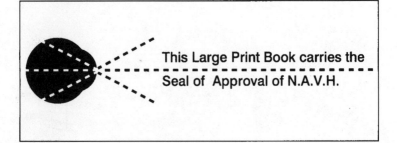

This Large Print Book carries the
Seal of Approval of N.A.V.H.

LAST THINGS

A Father Dowling Mystery

Ralph McInerny

Thorndike Press • Waterville, Maine

Published in 2003 by arrangement with St. Martin's Press, LLC.

Thorndike Press® Large Print Americana.

The tree indicium is a trademark of Thorndike Press.

The text of this Large Print edition is unabridged.
Other aspects of the book may vary from the original edition.

Set in 16 pt. Plantin by Liana M. Walker.

Printed in the United States on permanent paper.

Library of Congress Cataloging-in-Publication Data

McInerny, Ralph M.
    Last things : a Father Dowling mystery / Ralph McInerny.
      p. cm.
    ISBN 0-7862-5735-0 (lg. print : hc : alk. paper)
    1. Dowling, Father (Fictitious character) — Fiction.
2. Mothers and daughters — Fiction. 3. Women novelists
— Fiction. 4. Catholic Church — Fiction. 5. Illinois —
Fiction. 6. Clergy — Fiction. 7. Large type books.
I. Title.
PS3563.A31166L64 2003b
  813'.54—dc21   2003055968

To Richard John Neuhaus,
from first to last, and beyond

As the Founder/CEO of NAVH, the only national health agency solely devoted to those who, although not totally blind, have an eye disease which could lead to serious visual impairment, I am pleased to recognize Thorndike Press* as one of the leading publishers in the large print field.

Founded in 1954 in San Francisco to prepare large print textbooks for partially seeing children, NAVH became the pioneer and standard setting agency in the preparation of large type.

Today, those publishers who meet our standards carry the prestigious "Seal of Approval" indicating high quality large print. We are delighted that Thorndike Press is one of the publishers whose titles meet these standards. We are also pleased to recognize the significant contribution Thorndike Press is making in this important and growing field.

Lorraine H. Marchi, L.H.D.
Founder/CEO
NAVH

* Thorndike Press encompasses the following imprints: Thorndike, Wheeler, Walker and Large Print Press.

Prologue

The dead man was examined on the spot by the M.E. crew and by Dr. Pippen, assistant coroner. They had moved the body off the road where a horrified motorist had narrowly missed running over it. He had stopped, hesitated, but finally called the police, guarding the body from further outrage until they arrived. Of course they thought he had run over the man and had invented a fanciful tale of good citizenship to cover it. But the deceased had not been a hit-and-run victim. That had been determined before the body was moved to the sidewalk and examined more thoroughly.

Fussell, the motorist, was telling his story for the ninth time to the gathering media. He squinted at the lights the television crews trained on him but was enjoying the attention. In each version, he remembered more details.

"He was just lying in the street?"

"I nearly ran over him. I almost lost control of my car trying to avoid hitting him."

"How could you see it was a body?"

"At first, it was just something I didn't want to run over. As I swerved, I saw his face." He closed his eyes and shuddered.

His name and address were taken, verified. He was asked what he did for a living, did he live in the neighborhood, had he ever run over anyone, did he beat his wife? The reporters were bored with him by now and were anxious to talk to the medical examiners.

"Who's the dead guy?"

No one knew. The pack of reporters gravitated toward where the examination was in progress. This was the scene Phil Keegan came upon, having called Cy Horvath from the car. He got out and waded through the reporters, ignoring their questions, and headed for Pippen.

"Why did you say murder?" he asked her. It was she who had called him.

"Because that's what it is?"

"You looked at him?"

"I was the first one here, after the squad car. His identification was in this." She handed Phil a wallet. "And look." She showed him a baseball bat. She was wearing rubber gloves. "This was in the street."

"By the body?"

She shook her head, making her golden

8

ponytail dance. "It was thrown out too. It was back there, maybe twenty yards. I figure the car he was thrown out of was going south."

No wonder Cy Horvath spoke highly of Pippen. Why someone as bright as she was doing Lubins the coroner's work for him was a mystery. Was it for this that she had gone through medical school?

"The world is an emergency ward," was her answer to that. Quote, unquote, Cy.

"You sound like an eyewitness."

"I talked to him." She pointed the bat at a man who stood shivering and coatless on the steps of the house in front of which the body had been found.

Phil started toward the man, and Pippen came along.

"This is Captain Keegan, Mr. Sipes. Can we go inside? You'll catch pneumonia."

"A policeman?"

"Captain Keegan is chief of detectives." She took his elbow with her gloved hand and led him up the steps. The chief of detectives followed. "Just tell him what you told me."

Pippen turned to go back to the body, and Keegan listened while Sipes described cleaning the snow from his front walk, facing the street, when he first heard the sound of what turned out to be the bat bouncing off the icy pavement and then a thud that filled him with apprehension.

"I went down to the curb and looked out but couldn't figure out what it was."

"Did you notice the vehicle."

"It was a car."

"Not a truck, not an SUV . . ."

But Sipes was shaking his head. "A car. A sedan. Old."

"What make?"

"They all look alike now."

"You said it was old."

Sipes hadn't known what to do. He decided he ought to find out what had been dumped in the street. "I was pretty sure, but I didn't want to turn in a false alarm." He was going into the house for a flashlight when he heard the squeal of brakes as Fussell swerved to avoid the body.

Keegan turned Sipes over to Officer Agnes Lamb, who had just arrived. Cy was with Pippen and the group around the body.

The dead man's face was caved in from a blow and there was a contusion on the back of his head as well. From hitting the street? Pippen didn't think so. It was time to remove the body for a more thorough inspection in the morgue. The body bag was readied, and Cy and Phil huddled.

Pippen had identified the body so Phil had been able to give Cy the name when he called him. In the wallet taken from the body was a faculty I.D. card from St. Edmund College.

"I'll get on this first thing," Cy said.

"In the morning?"

"Okay, okay. I'll roust a few people out of bed."

"Half the campus police are former members of our department."

If Cy Horvath were capable of expressive reactions, that would have called for one. Phil, who from long familiarity could read the Hungarian map of Horvath's face, saw the slightest flicker in his eyes. This was Cy's equivalent of shouting Eureka and running naked through the streets.

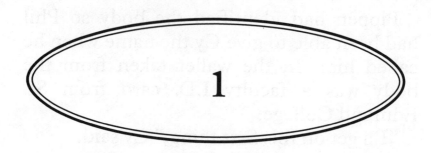

1

"You don't know me," she said as if he should. "I am Eleanor Wygant."

Father Dowling nodded. When Marie Murkin brought the visitor to the pastor's study she had given no indication what the call might be about. After identifying herself, the woman looked around the study at the four walls of books.

"You're quite a reader."

He shrugged. This too had seemed an accusation.

"I don't suppose you read fiction."

"Occasionally."

"Does the name Jessica Bernardo mean anything to you?"

"You think it should?"

"Not necessarily. She is my niece. She has written several novels."

"Have they been published?"

"They are highly thought of."

"But not by you."

"I didn't say that."

"Tell me about them."

"I read half of one and that was enough. I suppose all novels are like that now. She would call it honesty. Frankness. Showing people as they really are."

"And what does she think they really are?"

"Oh, I know people aren't saints. And I suppose a novelist wouldn't find it easy to write about a saint. But even we ordinary people have our redeeming qualities."

"What novels do you like?"

"Dickens." She waited for his reaction. "Jane Austen. Henry James."

This was a bit of a surprise. He would have thought she would mention the kind of edifying novel that was making a comeback in religious bookstores.

"Those authors certainly didn't write about saints."

"Of course not. But they didn't celebrate the faults of their characters as if it were good to be bad."

This was not the judgment he had expected from this woman. Eleanor Wygant was in her sixties. She was elegantly dressed, her silver hair beautifully groomed. But a perpetual frown had etched a censorious line between her brows, and her eyes were narrowed behind her rimless glasses. Father Dowling had

13

had his share of literary conversations in this study but never one that had begun like this. Experience suggested that this was merely an overture, a way of becoming less ill at ease in the presence of the priest. But it turned out that the real problem was connected with the overture. Eleanor Wygant wanted Father Dowling to convince her niece to give up the novel she had embarked upon.

"You may wonder why I have come to you. I am no longer a member of your parish, but the Bernardos have always been. I am a Bernardo."

"I see."

"Jessica simply must not write it, not the way I am sure she will."

"A writer is unlikely to take such advice from anyone."

"She certainly didn't take it from me."

"You've talked with her about it?"

"I pleaded with her. I begged." A sniffing sound. "I even tried to pay her not to write it."

"Tell me about Jessica."

"When she was a girl she talked of becoming a nun. She listened to me on that score."

"You talked her out of it."

"It was just a girlish fancy."

"Some girls have a vocation to the religious life."

Eleanor Wygant laughed. "Well, Jessica was not one of them."

"What is her new novel about?"

"The family."

"Ah."

No doubt Thomas Wolfe's family would have tried to head him off if they had suspected what his novels would tell the world of them. The autobiographical novel that stuck to self-revelations was one thing, but the inclusion of thinly disguised friends and relatives was seldom welcomed by the victims.

"It's not that we're that much worse than others, but why parade one's dirty laundry in public?"

"Are you sure that's what she intends to do?"

A vacuum cleaner suddenly roared into life, and for a minute or two growled away in the hallway outside Father Dowling's study but then subsided with a sigh followed by a listening silence. Marie Murkin would be miffed by the length of the visit and a conversation to which she was not privy.

"You would think that brothers had never quarreled before. My husband and brother-

15

in-law carried on a boyhood feud into middle age. I was almost surprised that they came to Joseph's funeral."

"Joseph was your husband."

"He has been dead fifteen years." Her lip trembled, and for a moment Father Dowling was afraid she was going to cry. The tap on the door was almost welcome. Marie looked in.

"Should I make tea?"

Father Dowling never drank tea. This, like the vacuum cleaner, was a ruse to free the pastor from a visitor overstaying her welcome.

"What a lovely idea," Eleanor Wygant said.

"Is there any lemon pie left?" Father Dowling asked.

"I have some cookies," Marie said.

"What kind?"

"Oatmeal."

Eleanor Wygant brought her hands together in almost girlish delight. "I love oatmeal cookies."

So did Captain Phil Keegan, which is why Marie persisted in baking them despite the pastor's indifference to what he ate.

"Are you having tea, Father?" Marie asked sweetly.

"Not this time."

16

"Why don't I serve in the kitchen then?"

"Just call when you're ready."

If Eleanor Wygant had any sense that she was getting the bum's rush from Marie she gave no sign of it.

"Dare I hope, Father?" She sounded like someone in the novels she preferred.

"Why don't I just say this. If Jessica cares to stop by the rectory I will talk with her about her new novel."

Some minutes later Marie led Eleanor off to the kitchen, where she would doubtless try to pry out of her the purpose of her visit. As Father Dowling found out after the visitor had gone, it turned out that she already knew a good deal about the Bernardo family.

"There's only one left in the parish. Of course the name doesn't ring a bell with you. Can they even be regarded as parishioners? You've never seen an envelope from them in the collection."

"That is a sufficient but not a necessary condition for being a parishioner."

Marie ignored this seminary jargon. "She comes to Mass anyway, the little woman in the green babushka, seven thirty on Sunday, most weekdays. Huddles in the back as if she's half ashamed to be there."

Father Dowling had a vague image of a little old woman in a green babushka. It was not his practice in saying Mass to keep eye contact with the congregation in the manner of an emcee. "How old?"

"About this one's age, Eleanor."

"Did you think she was a little old woman too?"

"How old do you think she is?" Marie asked.

"I've no idea."

"Add ten years. Some widows take better care of themselves than wives."

"I've noticed that."

Marie squinted at him. Her status had altered from grass to real widow, but she was the green babushka type nonetheless. "I hope I look half as good at her age."

Thin ice, this. As her employer Father Dowling knew the date of Marie's birth but that far-off event did not seem far-off in some of Marie's self-descriptions.

"I suppose having children has something to do with it."

"Nonsense. But about the Bernardos . . ."

The little old woman in the green babushka was Margaret, wife of Fulvio and mother of Jessica and two sons.

"One's a priest."

"Bernardo?"

"Some little order. He's on leave in California."

"And the other son?"

"He teaches at St. Edmund."

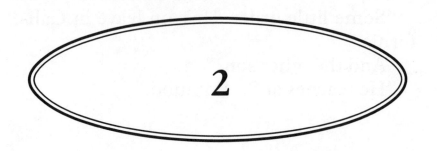

2

Once rival liberal arts colleges established by religious orders great and small had formed a chaplet around the city of Chicago, but if they vied for students they cooperated in other things, among them dances that provided opportunity for meeting the possible partner of one's life. Coeducation had come to these campuses late, during the tumultuous sixties, the decade in which they began the drift from their original moorings. It was not that they repudiated their religious past; it simply became less and less relevant as nuns and priests disappeared from the staffs, lay presidents were appointed, hiring was done on a basis indistinguishable from that of other lesser institutions, which now were enjoying a buyer's market as more and more people poured out of graduate school into a shrinking job market. In these circumstances Andrew Bernardo, with a mere master's and not even an ABD, all but dissertation with class work for the doctorate completed, might have been grateful for his tenured position at St. Edmund's, but in the manner of academics he engaged in pro forma grousing about the students, the salary, his class load, and the fact that he had to share an office with a colleague who seemed never to bathe. This necessitated keeping the window cracked even in the dead of winter and having a small air cleaner beside his desk whose steady hum had the added advantage of discouraging conversation. Foster was a slovenly giant who chain smoked and declaimed Shakespeare aloud at the least provocation, favoring the historical plays. No student visited him twice, if so often.

"Tell him to take a bath," Andrew urged Anne Gogarty, the chair of the department.

"You're as close to him as anyone."

"That's my complaint."

"It would come more easily from you than anyone else."

"It should be an official demand."

"It's not in the manual."

The faculty manual was a constant point of reference, the basis for grievances that could lead to the formation of a committee of the faculty senate and months of talk followed by inaction. Bathing by the faculty was not a requirement. That Foster was a philosopher, given to unintelligible mumbling about possible worlds' ontology, seemed only fitting. The man could not keep his own body clean, but he spoke of the universe as a personal possession. Several times Andrew had edged close to the sensitive topic.

"This room is so hot."

"It's that machine you insist on running all the time."

"That has a cooling effect. And it cleanses the air."

Foster lit a cigarette from the burning stub of another. Andrew never complained of Foster's smoking; the clouds of exhaled smoke did something to neutralize the effect of being downwind from his aromatic office mate.

"Do you ever exercise?" he asked Foster on another occasion.

"Not on purpose."

"You should, you know."

"What kind of a should is that?"

"How many kinds are there?"

A mistake. Foster launched into a lecture on the modalities of the deontological. Physical exercise seemed to be a mere hypothetical imperative. Andrew lauded the new wellness center that had been built by Alloy, the president, among whose achievements was to declare the campus both a smoke-free and nuclear-free zone. But faculty offices had been grandfathered, and Foster was free to puff himself to an early grave.

"The pool is magnificent," Andrew said. "Swimming is a marvelous tonic." The thought of Foster clouding the chlorined water of the pool was ambiguously attractive.

"I nearly drowned when I was a kid."

Was that the origin of his dread of water? "No one ever drowned in a shower."

"I thought you said pool."

"Who says pool says shower," Andrew replied boldly.

"Who is who?"

"The Marquis of Queensberry."

"You are being facetious."

That was as close as he had come to recommending personal hygiene to Foster. Of course Andrew had to meet his students elsewhere, usually at a table in the cafeteria. There he sat on the morning that he had received an early telephone call from his Aunt Eleanor.

"Jessica intends to write a novel about the family."

Jessica's small success as a novelist was the heaviest cross Andrew bore. He taught creative writing but had published only two stories, in quarterlies that had never made it through their first year. From sophomore year of high school he had dreamt of being a writer, but by senior year he had published nothing in the school magazine, the *Penna*, except one short essay on Scott Fitzgerald. Meanwhile, Jessica, two years his junior, dashed off sonnets, a verse play, and short stories that caught the attention of the *Chicago Tribune* because their older brother, Raymond, had sent them to the literary editor. She began to receive inquiries from literary agents. Andrew adopted a condescending attitude toward his sister's writing. She herself seemed to regard her own success as a bit of a joke. She had published a series of poems the first lines of which were taken from famous pieces: "Shall I compare thee to a summer's day"; "She lived among untrodden ways"; "Out of the cradle endlessly rocking." It seemed a species of cheating, trading on the achievements of others. The one beginning "Where the bee sucks, there suck I" was vetoed by the faculty advisor, an effete chemist who fancied himself a renaissance man and dismissed Hemingway as a primitive. Andrew longed to be a writer like Hemingway or Fitzgerald, a celebrity, his name on everyone's lips. Now he had to contend with the fact that the name Bernardo seemed owned by Jessica so far as writing went.

"You try too hard," she said to Andrew when she found an unfinished story of his.

"Writing should not come easily."

"It does for me."

Jessica was beautiful; even Andrew saw that. Thick yellow hair, an olive complexion, full lips, and almond eyes that mesmerized even in dust jacket photographs. She did not need fiction in order to be popular, yet she had never married. Sometimes he felt that she had been more affected by Raymond's defection from the priesthood than anyone, even their parents.

"I'd become a nun if I could find a convent that wasn't out of Boccaccio."

Hope flared up in him. If she had a vocation, perhaps to an enclosed order, she would put away her pen and fade from the field. He had come to believe that her success was the main cause of his writer's block. Jessica scoffed at the idea of writer's block.

"Just do it, for heaven's sake. It's just words on a page, one after the other."

He had pored over her novels in search of flaws. *Where No Storms Come*, her first, had been a bildungsroman, but in it she had invented a family as different from their own as imaginable. Her second, *We Waited While She Passed*, was set in a nursing home and drew on a summer job as a nurse's aide. He told her that in its way it reminded him of *The Poorhouse Fair.* She didn't know it. She claimed to read very little.

"Updike."

"What's Updike?" She gnawed on an imaginary carrot and gave an imitation of Bugs Bunny. Perhaps he was meant to be a critic, Edmund Wilson rather than Fitzgerald. He imagined a monograph on the fiction of the twenties and thirties but despaired at the thought that it had been done already a thousand times.

Across from him at his table in the cafeteria sat Mabel Gorman, a student whose prose had the polish of someone twice her age. She was an unlovely girl, thick black hair that rose wildly from her narrow head, a unisex body that seemed more limbs than torso. She sat sideways in her chair like a pretzel, legs crossed, hugging herself, blowing hair out of her eyes.

"I like your story," Andrew said.

Her smile was her best feature, toothy and full, radiant. "Thank you."

"I think you should submit it for publication." Andrew was the faculty advisor for *Scriptor,* the renamed student literary annual.

"I have!"

"You have?"

She had sent it to *The New Yorker*. Jessica's first published story had been in *The New Yorker*. It turned out that this was no accident.

"I didn't realize she was your sister."

"Bernardo is not that common a name."

"But someone so famous!"

His cross bit into his shoulder. It was cruel that even his own students looked past him to Jessica.

"That's a tough market to crack."

All his own submissions to *The New Yorker* had come back, in Thurber's phrase, like a serve in tennis. He had the sudden certainty that Mabel's story would be accepted. It was a soulful vignette about a young girl who continued to collect dolls into womanhood, the drama subdued, pregnant with suggestion, a story that clung to the imagination long after being read. Andrew had studied it, wondering what the secret was. Was he doomed to become the pupil of his pupils?

"Your class is the best I have ever taken," Mabel said, her smile coming and going uncertainly.

Students were given to unsolicited praise, usually when finals approached, but Mabel seemed to be speaking from the heart.

"What else are you taking?" Did he want to know what the competition was, in what field he was first? Mabel's smile disappeared.

"Do you know Professor Cassirer?"

"What do you think of him?"

Her eyes widened, she looked over both shoulders, she leaned toward him. "Is he crazy?"

It is a vice peculiar to the academic to elicit criticism of colleagues from students, but Mabel poured forth her view of Cassirer unprompted.

"Do you know he mentioned you in class?"

"Did he?"

"I looked up your stories and read them, just to spite him. I liked them." She might have said more, but she was honest. "I asked him what he had written. I looked that up too. It's all gibberish."

Mike Pistoia had suggested that anyone who did such violence to literature as Cassirer could be physically violent too.

"Andrew, he would hate us no matter how we voted."

"It's all bombast. Besides, what could he do to us?"

"Don't get me started. How's Gloria?"

Later Andrew would see his colleague's question as a warning. Now to Mabel Gorman he said, "So you don't think my

28

stories are gibberish."

"Oh no. I can see why you are such a good teacher."

This was heady indeed, cushioning the surprise that she was awaiting word from *The New Yorker* about her story.

Later in his office he wrote a line, "A sundial on a cloudy day," and stared at it. Like the opening of one of Jessica's early poems it seemed to cry out for a second line and a third. He would send it to *Poetry*. But the second line would not come. Foster was an oppressive presence. Andrew wrote another line, "Life in an olfactory," then pushed his notebook away and thought of Aunt Eleanor's call.

"So what?" he asked when she expressed her alarm that Jessica intended to base a novel on the Bernardo family. It seemed so unpromising a theme that he welcomed it. His impulse was to encourage Jessica rather than dissuade her.

"I talked to the pastor of St. Hilary's about it, begging him to intervene. Father Dowling."

"Are you serious?"

"Andrew, she must not write that novel."

"She's already written her growing up novel."

"But this will be about your parents. And your uncles."

"And aunts?"

Was Eleanor worried that some indiscretion of her own might come to light? Andrew smiled. Widowhood had turned Eleanor into a maiden aunt. She remembered everyone's birthday, sending a sentimental card. She was an obligatory guest for Thanksgiving dinner. She was dismayed that none of the Bernardos had married.

"Raymond's married."

"Andrew!"

Was that it? Did she fear Jessica would write of her brother the runaway priest? He was feeling better all the time. What a dead end Jessica was headed for. He agreed to talk to her.

"How is your father?"

"All right."

"All right! He has cancer."

"Prostate cancer. All men his age have prostate cancer. They usually die of something else."

"I wish he would go to Mayo."

"He prefers Miracle Whip."

"I don't understand you." Stupidly he tried to explain the bad joke. She made moist disapproving sounds into the phone.

At that moment Gloria emerged from the bathroom on a cloud of steam and Andrew crossed his lips with his finger. No need to shock Aunt Eleanor.

3

Fulvio Bernardo still lived in the huge house on Preswick in which he had raised his family and whose many rooms made it easy for Margaret and himself to avoid one another. Once this had been a neighborhood in which the newly affluent aspired to live, but with the westward expansion that had sent the white residents of Chicago fleeing, new roads had been built to accommodate their coming and going. As a result Fox River was now framed in freeways, and the once quiet neighborhood was assailed by the constant hum of traffic from all sides. But the Bernardos stayed on; Margaret because of St. Hilary's, Fulvio out of inertia. He was an old man with prostate cancer who spent his days contemplating the ruin of his life. His children had given him no grandchildren. Jessica seemed content to write silly stories. Andrew had never grown up and paid quick visits. As for Raymond . . . Fulvio groaned aloud. My son the priest. How proud they had been when Raymond was ordained. And then one day he had run off to California. Of course he had not told them of his plans. And he had never tried to explain. They never heard from him. It was Andrew who brought them the news, a note from Raymond too ashamed to write directly to his parents.

"It's all on the up and up," Andrew said.

"Running away?"

"Oh, he'll be laicized."

Fulvio had taken this to be a euphemism for the conjugal act and snorted accordingly.

"Then he can be married," Andrew explained. Margaret looked as if she were standing at the foot of the cross.

"Married!" Fulvio cried. "He's a priest."

"Not anymore."

"How can you stop being a priest?"

Fulvio had made his living coaxing plants and trees from Illinois soil to adorn the lawns of suburbia, but it was out of respect for his own father that he cultivated the tomato patch out next to the garage, fighting the blight and bugs, waiting for fruit that was all but given away in the market by the time his own was ripe. He might have been nurturing the memory of his father when he fussed away at the plants as the old man had done, as if his family would starve without his tomatoes. Fulvio had been more than successful in business, but he had never had the luck his father had. Oh, he had made money but look at his goddamn children. He had given them every advantage. Maybe that was the problem: all those years of Catholic education and it was doubtful any of them went to Mass anymore. Except Jessica, of course, her mother's child. Well, he had stopped going himself, out of spite, as a complaint against God. At Raymond's first low Mass, offered for his parents, Fulvio began to think of it as an investment. Now he was assured of endless Masses after he went, a daily commemoration by Raymond, standing at the altar. All his sins would be washed away. He had not wanted to hear what his son was doing in California, but Andrew had told him.

"Counselor! Who is he to counsel anyone? He should go to a monastery and do penance."

That was what fallen priests had always done in the past, a penitential stay with the monks while they got their moral houses in order. Now Fulvio punished God by staying away from church. Margaret begged him to go with her but he refused. She was a mother and could forgive anything, but Fulvio would never accept what Raymond had done. Did the boy know or care that his father had cancer?

When young Paul Rocco, the doctor, had told Fulvio the results of the biopsy three years ago it was like a death sentence, and he welcomed it, certain it would change everything. His children would rally around his sickbed; Raymond would come back, sorrowful and apologetic; Jessica would find a husband and have children; and Andrew . . . Marge had wept when she told him that Andrew was living with a woman, unmarried, no prospect of children, a goddamn pagan. But the prostate cancer had been treated as if it were a bad cold. Even Rocco downplayed it.

"Chances are you'll die of something else before it gets really serious."

He had had the operation, but another biopsy revealed that the cancer still lurked in his rear end, slowly eating away his life. Fulvio's father had died of prostate cancer, that was clear now when he knew about the disease, but his father had gone to no doctor and had borne his ailment in silence until it brought him low. He was dead within a week of the diagnosis. But not even Margaret regarded her husband as a man whose days were numbered. Fulvio had stopped taking his medicine, regularly renewing the prescription but flushing the daily dose down the toilet. The medicine didn't cure anything. There was no cure.

He stirred in the lawn chair he had put in the shade of an oak tree. The plastic ribbons stretched across the metal frame of the chair ate into the diseased flesh. Sitting there with the breeze rustling his tomato plants he would close his eyes and imagine the cancer consuming him. What the hell did he care? What did his children care? Margaret would mourn him, but she mourned everyone, attending every funeral at St. Hilary's as if she were a personal friend of the deceased. What else is being old but practicing to be dead?

There were voices from the house, and he opened his eyes to see Margaret and Eleanor coming across the lawn. It was too late to scramble out of the chair and hide in the garage.

"Well, don't you look peaceful," Eleanor said.

She had seemed a stranger ever since Joseph's death. She married Alfred Wygant, too good to marry another Italian. She was still smitten with Fulvio, but while he continued to respond, he had lost interest in her. Not that he let her forget their stolen moments. They had meant more to her than they had to him, but that is the way it was with women. And she had written him silly letters. Well, God is not mocked. Eleanor was childless. So she had adopted his children, helping to spoil them. She had bought a chalice for Raymond when he was ordained. Did she wonder what had happened to it? Maybe he had it in a trophy case in his counselor's office.

"I talked with Andrew this morning about Jessica's new novel," Eleanor said.

"I never read any of them."

"Fulvio, she plans to write about us."

"Us?"

"The Bernardos, you, Joseph. Even Alfred."

"What's there to write?"

Margaret went back to the house for iced tea, and Eleanor pulled a lawn chair next to his. "She has no shame; she will make us look like fools."

"Maybe we are."

"I don't want her to write about Alfred."

"I thought it was about the Bernardos."

"She wanted to pump me about the way he died."

Fulvio said nothing for a minute. "I am dying myself, you know."

"Oh don't say that."

"I have cancer."

"But they say prostate cancer can be controlled."

"So can breathing until it stops."

"Don't be morbid."

"How's your health?"

"Good."

"So you can afford to be jolly."

"I am not jolly. I am worried sick about Jessica. I shouldn't have to tell you why." She paused. "I spoke to Father Dowling about it. He agreed to talk with her."

"That ought to help."

"He is a very wise man."

Fulvio knew the pastor of St. Hilary's only by name. Margaret too sang his praises. There had been Franciscans in the parish when Fulvio still went to Mass, happy little elves always after your money.

"Has Jessica talked with you about it?"

Jessica had been here a week ago, sat next him as Eleanor did and talked about growing up and the benefit it was to have a family like theirs. It gave a framework to her life, she said. She seemed serious.

"Why aren't you married?" he'd asked.

She laughed. "I haven't met Mr. Right."

"There may be no men left by the time you do."

"Everything's different now."

"You can say that again."

"I mean young men. Young women too. Nobody believes anything anymore, nobody trusts the future, no one wants a family. Just an arrangement."

"Marry one and he'll want children."

"Even Catholics have lost any sense of what life is all about. They're like everyone else now."

"Do you ever hear from Raymond?"

"He asks about you."

"Did you tell him I'm dying?"

"You're not dying!"

"Will you guarantee that?"

"Daddy, what you have is bad, but it isn't terminal. I've asked. The medicine you take controls it. You have years ahead of you."

For a moment that prospect had stirred him. More time. But for what? To putter over his tomato plants and doze in the yard and wonder what had gone wrong with his children? Jessica was the best of the lot, he knew that, but a man puts his main hope in his sons and look what he had there.

"Tell me about your life," she had said. And he had, to his own surprise. He was flattered that she wanted to know, and once he had started he realized how little she did know. Did he think his children had inherited his memories too?

"Now I know where I inherited my gift for storytelling."

"Don't you believe me?"

"Of course I believe you. Who would know better than you?"

He told Eleanor that it was natural for Jessica to want to know about her family. "She paid someone to do our genealogy."

"There, you see. She isn't just interested in what you care to recall. She will make use of everything, records, newspaper stories . . ." A pause. "Letters."

Aha. "What do we have to hide?"

Suddenly Eleanor began to cry, for God's sake, right there in the backyard, with Margaret coming from the house with the iced tea.

"What did you tell her?" he asked.

Eleanor was trying to gain control of herself so that Margaret wouldn't see she had been crying. But Margaret was intent on the full glasses on the tray she carried. Besides, Margaret had never been curious, thank God.

4

"Did she tell you about her second husband?" Marie Murkin asked Father Dowling some days later, out of the blue. Or so it might have seemed to him, but she had been brooding on Eleanor Wygant's visit, all the more because Father Dowling ignored her leading questions.

"She's a widow."

"That's the point."

He dipped his head and looked at her. But she was not to be put off that easily.

"The Franciscans hushed it up, of course."

"All right, Marie, what is it?"

"The way he died."

"And how was that?"

"Suspiciously. He was healthy as a horse, and then he was dead, tumbling down the stairs in the middle of the night. She said he was walking in his sleep after taking an extra sleeping pill."

"She told you this?"

"She told Placidus." Father Dowling

frowned. He did not like her referring to his predecessor as pastor in this casual way.

"Who told you?"

"He wasn't as secretive as some people."

"So what is suspicious?"

"Why was he walking in his sleep if he took an extra sleeping pill?"

"You don't believe it."

"McDivitt told me he was drunk." McDivitt was the funeral director, a pink little man with snow white hair who was putty in Marie's hands.

"And you think she didn't want that known?"

"Within months she had sold her house and moved out of the parish."

"That is suspicious."

"And why didn't she recognize me the other day?"

"Ah, I understand. A housekeeper scorned."

Marie could have kicked herself for the clumsy way she had gone about it. How could he take her seriously if he thought that all it was was annoyance at being snubbed by Eleanor Wygant. No, not snubbed. Patronized. Practically ordering tea when Marie had given the pastor a way to get rid of her, taking up his afternoon with some nonsense about her niece's new novel.

"What's it about?" she had asked at the time.

"A nosy housekeeper. She wants to interview you."

Well, she had asked for it. Marie withdrew from the fray and brooded like Achilles in his tent. Not that she gave up.

"Was there ever an investigation of Alfred Wygant's death?" she asked the next time Phil Keegan joined the pastor for lunch after his noon Mass.

"Who is Alfred Wygant?"

"He was a very prominent man and you know it. His insurance business was one of the largest in Fox River."

"And he died. When was that?"

Marie had looked it up. "Seven years ago."

"And you expect me to remember if there was an investigation?"

"There was a coroner's report."

"How do you know?"

"I don't forget things like that."

"Then there would be a record at the coroner's office. Hire a lawyer and ask to see it."

"I was hoping you would look it up."

Phil turned to Father Dowling. "What is this all about?"

"Marie is afraid someone is going to write a book about her."

"Well, if they ever do, I'll read it."

But the seed had been planted. Phil Keegan might scoff like the pastor, but he was a policeman to the soles of his feet. Marie was sure he would take a look at the coroner's report on the death of Alfred Wygant.

The fact was that Marie had not recognized Eleanor when she came to the front door of the rectory. Of course, it had been many years since she had seen or even thought of the woman, and Eleanor had more reason to recognize Marie, having come to the rectory often. Marie remembered herself as having been an ombudsman between Eleanor and the flaky Placidus. You never knew what a Franciscan would do next, and your ordinary lay people had insufficient experience with priests to make allowances. It was when she called McDivitt to make sure Alfred Wygant got a proper send-off that the little undertaker, a faint scent of bourbon riding his breath, had confided in her about the condition of the deceased. How it all came back to her now. McDivitt had always preferred dealing with her rather than the Franciscans.

"He had a snoot full, that's for sure." This

44

was crude coming from the dapper little undertaker.

"Drunk?"

"Who's to say what *drunk* means," McDivitt said and slipped a peppermint into his mouth. On second thought, he offered Marie one. "These household accidents are always mysterious."

"In what way?"

"Wygant never drank."

"The widow told you that?"

"And the family. Of course they were interested in avoiding any talk."

"Of course."

"I suppose the autopsy would have measured the alcohol in his blood."

McDivitt had known he could tell Marie these things without fear they would go further. "I think he took a dive over the upstairs bannister."

"No."

"Sheer speculation of course. Based on a lifetime's experience."

Of people diving over upstairs bannisters? McDivitt was a gossip, no doubt of that, his character all twisted out of shape from simulating grief at the death of strangers. What were such people called in the gospel? They had laughed at Our Lord when He said the child was merely sleeping. She could

45

imagine McDivitt in that derisive chorus.

"If Jessica Bernardo calls I will see her," Father Dowling said.

Marie had already surmised that the niece was the cause of Eleanor's visit. Jessica the novelist. Marie had tried to read one of Jessica's novels, but it was not her sort of thing, and she told Father Dowling as much.

"Her aunt is of the same opinion."

"Of course I'm no judge. I understand they were well received."

"Do the Bernados strike you as a promising topic for a novel?"

Aha. Marie would have thought less of herself if she had not put two and two together. Eleanor had come to express concern about her niece Jessica. Jessica was a novelist. Now he wondered if the Bernardo family could inspire a novel. It was as plain as the nose on your face. Eleanor was worried that Jessica would stir up curiosity about the way Alfred Wygant had died.

But the moment of triumph was brief. How could Marie not sympathize with Eleanor's reluctance to think that her husband had ended his own life? A suicide presents the ultimate pastoral problem. Of course Placidus would have buried Judas Iscariot with a solemn high requiem Mass. What would Father Dowling have done? It was unnerving to think that in this he would have been indistinguishable from Placidus. But after all, what did anyone know for sure? The deceased deserves the benefit of the doubt if anyone does.

When the call came from the hospital telling her that Fulvio Bernardo had been brought in, having suffered a stroke, Marie exercised similar latitude. No need to tell Father Dowling that Fulvio had not darkened the door of a church in living memory. The call came from the son, Andrew.

"My father is in intensive care at St. Mark's. My mother wants a priest to see him."

Marie brought the word to Father Dowling, and within ten minutes he was on his way to the hospital.

5

Andrew took Jessica in his arms in the waiting room of intensive care, and she assumed the worst had happened. Andrew began to weep. She rocked him in her arms and wanted to whisper in his ear "It is the fate man is born for, it is Margaret you mourn for," but he might have thought she meant their mother.

"Where's Mom?"

"With him."

With him? "Where is he?"

He nodded at the open door. "But when did it happen?"

He didn't understand. "How is he?" Then she brushed past him and went into a room where her father dressed in a silly gown lay on the bed, her mother seated at his side, staring into nothingness. But Margaret's lips moved mechanically in prayer. She held a rosary. She looked up at Jessica as if surprised to see her. Jessica put a hand on her mother's shoulder and looked for the first time at her father. A bag of fluid on a stand dripped slowly into his arm, and he was wired to a device beside him that monitored his vital signs, conveying them to the nurses' station. His breathing was heavy and irregular. A nurse all in blue with a bag over her hair came in on little cat's feet.

"How is he?"

An enigmatic look. "It's serious."

Stupid question, stupid answer. Great vague thoughts invaded her mind. This was the hospital in which she had been born. Somewhere her father had been born, then lived into his eighth decade, and now he was dying. Birth, copulation, and death. Human duration seemed gathered in a point, the tenses that give life meaning gone. All flesh is grass. We have here no lasting city.

"Has Raymond been called?" she asked her mother.

"I think Andrew told him."

And? And then Father Dowling arrived. Her mother scrambled to her feet, all deference, but the thin priest with the aquiline nose eased her back into her chair. He went around to the other side of the bed and laid a hand on her father's forehead. A simple gesture, priestly. Immediately Jessica liked him. This was the pastor her mother gushed about. The priest leaned over the bed and spoke in her father's ear, and incredibly her father's eyes opened. He looked almost wildly at the priest and shook his head. A priestly nod. What had he asked him? Her mother stood and leaned over the bed.

"Father Dowling is here, Fulvio."

He glared at her, and she looked imploringly at the priest. If her mother's faith could have sufficed for two everything would have been well, but nothing had been the same for Fulvio since Raymond left. Her brother's defection had shaken Jessica as well. Did nothing last anymore? Marriages fell apart, priests went over the wall, nuns deserted their convents. "All life death does end and each day dies with sleep." Father Dowling went to her mother and led her into the corridor. Jessica took his place and reached for her father's hand, but what she grasped was the tube that admitted the contents of the plastic bag to her father's veins. She leaned over him.

"I love you, Daddy." Tears welled in her eyes. She felt ten years old, a little girl frightened at what was happening to her father. He nodded and made a kissing sound. She sobbed openly. She had never felt the equal of her brothers in his eyes — she was just a girl — but somehow she felt he loved her best. He was trying to say something.

"What is it?" She leaned over him, ready

for some great revelation, some message she had waited for all her life.

"Raymond."

She laid her hand on his forehead as the priest had done. "Raymond's coming."

Was he? What harm could it do to say so? The nurse was back with a doctor, and they shooed her from the room. She was almost relieved to go and hated herself for it. Andrew, dry eyed now, sat silently with their mother and Father Dowling in a little waiting room with pastel walls and inane pictures on the wall but over the door a crucifix. Jessica stared at it. Once the hospital had been staffed by the nuns whose order had founded it; now it was part of some national chain of nominally Catholic hospitals.

Andrew asked, "Should I go in?"

"A doctor and nurse are with him."

"They come and go."

Like Michelangelo. How professorial Andrew looked: blue sports jacket, open collar, chinos, and massive tennis shoes. She had stopped minding that he resented her success as a writer. His own stuff was impossibly self-indulgent, mannered, "look Ma I'm writing." Is that what he taught his students? Jessica had avoided writing courses like sin and took the bare minimum of

51

courses in English in which pompous young men treated fiction as grist for their critical mills. She had majored in chemistry and now worked in a pathologist's lab, testing tissue like that they had taken from her father some years ago. Did she ever think her findings related to someone waiting here for the bad news?

"He asked for Raymond."

"I left a message on his answering machine," Andrew said.

Her mother said to Father Dowling, "He hasn't been to the sacraments for years."

Good God. But the priest only nodded. "I'll talk to him again."

"It won't do any good," Andrew said. He might have been defending their father against what?

"We'll see. I'm Father Dowling."

She nodded. "Jessica."

"The novelist."

A little leap of pleasure. "How did you know?"

"Your Aunt Eleanor told me."

"Eleanor?"

He nodded. That was all. Why did she feel she could bare her soul to him? Because she was flattered he knew she had published novels? No, that wasn't it. There was a serenity about him she liked. She looked at

Andrew. "Did you call Eleanor?"

He hadn't. Should she? She wanted something to do. "I will."

"What for?"

"Andrew, he's her brother-in-law."

She went outside the waiting room and called Eleanor on her cell phone. "Daddy is in the hospital, in intensive care."

"Oh my God."

"He's being looked after." Intensively. "He's awake."

"I'll come."

"St. Mark's?"

"Of course."

Father Dowling had come out to talk to the doctor, nodding as the doctor spoke. He turned to Jessica, and she went to him as the doctor scampered away.

"He has had cancer for years."

"Is this his first heart attack?"

"Heart attack?"

"Didn't you know?"

She looked at him. "I didn't even ask. He has prostate cancer . . ."

She had assumed the cancer was his reason for being here. "He is stabilizing, they tell me. Is Raymond the priest?"

"The former priest. He's why my father . . ."

"Ah. Is he coming?"

"Yes." She said it firmly as if that committed her brother to come from California to be at their father's bedside. "If he is in danger," she added.

"If he were younger, they would operate." The priest knew more than any of them, made privy to it all in moments by the staff. Of course it would be easier for them to talk to a stranger. "Let's go in."

She followed the priest into the cubicle where her father lay. Her father's eyes tracked him to the side of the bed. In a slurred voice he said, "I don't believe in God."

"Well, he believes in you." Again the hand on her father's forehead. His lips moved like her mother's in prayer.

"I want Raymond."

As a priest? Was that the condition of his faith, that his son should regain his?

"I understand he's coming," Father Dowling said.

Her father smiled.

"You are not in immediate danger, but the prospects are not good."

The old man's eyes were fixed on the priest.

"I am dying?"

No need to say it, the priest's expression conveyed the answer. The old man's eyes

54

closed and then immediately opened as if he did not want to shut out the light.

"There's a chaplain on duty," Father Dowling said when they were again outside the cubicle making way for the fussy nurse with the bag on her head. "I'll make sure he knows."

"It wouldn't matter."

"His name is Fulvio?"

"Yes."

"*Lei parla Italiano?*"

She shook her head. "Neither does my father anymore. He's second generation. His father came from Palermo and wanted instant assimilation."

"Yet he named his son Fulvio."

"Bernardos aren't very consistent."

"Almost no one is. That's why we mustn't give up hope for your father."

He assumed she shared her mother's faith. Did she? Her life too had been changed when Raymond ran off to California with the nun he later married. The only thing worse would have been if her father deserted her mother.

After the priest left she got out her phone and put through a call to California.

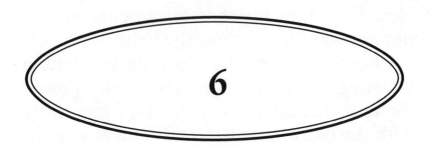

6

"Can you make the meeting this afternoon?" Anne Gogarty, the chair, asked when she heard that Andrew's father was in the hospital. "Appointments and tenure." Her tone was significant.

"He's improved."

"So you'll be there."

"I wouldn't miss it."

She took that for reassurance. "I need your vote."

There were five on the committee, the chair ex officio and four elected members. Andrew was the default member of every departmental committee, someone everyone trusted, or at least did not distrust. Everyone, that is, but Cassirer. And Cassirer was the main item of business at the afternoon meeting of the A&T. He had applied for early promotion to tenure after only four years on the faculty, his argument, scarcely disguised, that he was so manifestly superior to everyone else in the department that it was unjust that he should be untenured. All departmental committees were only advisory committees, their decisions going to the dean as recommendations. Holder, the provost, actually made the decisions, but as a matter of practice dean and provost merely endorsed the departmental committees. Alloy, the president, probably learned of promotions from the printed menu distributed at his annual dinner for the faculty. Cassirer had lobbied for votes like a candidate for the French Academy — minus the obsequiousness, of course — thereby solidifying the opposition. Anne wanted the slot for another woman, a reasonable enough objective in these days of affirmative action, not that Anne needed her gender for her position, and Mike Pistoia loathed Cassirer with all the passion of a lover of literature. Whenever Cassirer mentioned Foucault, Pistoia warned him not to speak like that in the presence of a lady. "With a name like his, he should talk," Cassirer retorted, out of earshot of Pistoia. Lily St. Clair leaned toward Cassirer, in every sense of the term, but if he was aware of her décolletage he gave little evidence of it. Besides, she was inclined to take the opposed position to Anne Gogarty as a matter of habit. Zalinski had a weakness for critical nonsense and was firmly for Cassirer."

"He infuriates the philosophers."

"Everything infuriates the philosophers."

"They don't understand a word he says."

"Neither do the students."

"The students!" Like Cassirer, Zalinski despised students. His notion of an ideal college was one in which students were on vacation, all books available on their shelves in the library, and he free to do the *New York Times* puzzle in the office he shared with Cassirer. A straw vote taken at the last meeting was two to two, leaving Gogarty with the deciding vote. Of course Zalinski passed this confidential information on to Cassirer, prompting an immediate visit on Cassirer's part to Andrew's office. He was driven back to the doorway by the presence of Foster.

"Can we talk?"

"You seem to be."

"I mean in private." Cassirer put his handkerchief to face and glanced at Foster.

They went to the cafeteria, where over coffee Cassirer said hoarsely, "My fate is in your hands."

"In what way?"

"My promotion to tenure."

"You have years before a decision need be made."

"Come on. You know I have applied for

early consideration. God knows I deserve it." There was a yellow fleck in Cassirer's right eye. He wore a bristly beard, the better to look older; and had a heavy gold chain around his neck.

"Is that a St. Christopher medal?"

"Ha. It's my sign. I am a Pisces."

"You realize I can't talk about the proceedings of the committee."

Cassirer glared at him. "Is that your position?"

"No, it is departmental policy."

"If you had any concern for the department, you would vote for me."

"I hope concern for the department will motivate us all," Andrew said, feeling prissy. He found himself enjoying this.

"I have just had another article accepted by *Theseus*. I will be on the program of the MLA. I have made St. Edmund's known to people who never heard of it."

"It is a small pond for a Pisces."

"In this job market one has to take what's available. Of course I don't plan to end my career here."

Was this meant to soften Andrew up, tenure merely as springboard to another job elsewhere? "You say you've applied for early consideration."

"Come on. You know I have. It has already been discussed. I know your vote can make the difference."

"Surely Anne didn't tell you that."

"Look, the committee represents the past. When did you get tenure, by the way?"

"After the usual number of years."

"And you don't even have a doctorate. That's my point. What has Gogarty published? What has Pistoia done to deserve tenure?"

"About as much as Zalinski."

"Exactly. All this talk about excellence, yet mediocrity is entrenched. My application should be a foregone conclusion."

Cassirer had an odd way of soliciting support, belittling those whose votes he needed. Andrew was thinking of Mabel Gorman's remark that Cassirer had ridiculed him in class.

"Tell me about your new article in *Theseus*."

Cassirer confided that he had exposed Saussure to withering criticism and offered an alternative to Derrida. One had to realize that a literary text was not about anything, not about the writer's ideas, not about the world. It was a thing in itself, without analogues, and must be spoken of only in terms of itself. He had hunched across the table, causing a faint olfactory memory of Foster, and the yellow fleck in his eye seemed to pulse like a harbor light.

"It's hard to explain in a few words."

"I think I get the idea."

"It's not an idea! That's the point. Criticism too is without analogues."

"Interesting."

"You're being condescending."

No wonder students hated the man. That was the objective basis for opposing his application for tenure. St. Edmund's was not a research university — its main task was teaching — and Cassirer's contempt for their students made Zalinski seem Mr. Chips.

"Can I count on you?"

"You can count on us all."

Cassirer sat back. "I understand. I threaten you, don't I?"

"Horst, I teach creative writing. I have published a few stories. My time is largely taken up with my students, some of whom are very promising."

He thought of boney little Mabel. "I am beginning to hate him," she had said with cold intensity.

Andrew said to Cassirer, "I haven't read the French authors who are your passion."

"I have read your sister's novels."

"I will tell her."

61

"They are quite good of their kind. You can tell her I said so."

"I will."

"I have not read your stories."

"I will lend you copies."

Cassirer shook his head. "I really don't care for fiction."

Then what in God's name did he do in his course on Victorian novelists? Unfortunately, Andrew already knew, from Mabel. Dickens was a pamphleteer, George Eliot repressed, Trollope a wordy joke. Students had wept in Anne Gogarty's office when they told the chair of Cassirer's comments on their enthusiasm for the novels assigned.

"We have to stop him now," she said to Andrew. "It's providential that he has offered us an early chance to cut him down."

"But he will still have his job."

"For another year."

Their tête-à-tête confirmed Cassirer in his surmise that Andrew would not vote for him. He went to Arachne, the dean, and to Holder, the provost, and said the committee was incompetent to judge his work. He demanded an outside review. He was told he would have that in any case. He meant a committee made up of someone other than his colleagues. Holder called in Anne Gogarty and asked if there was any chance

62

that insufferable young man would be voted tenure. She told him how matters stood.

"I will exercise my veto if he slips through."

"That shouldn't be necessary."

"I almost wish it were."

But Cassirer's animus was directed at Andrew. He found the issues of the defunct journals in which Andrew had published and analyzed his stories in class, as Mabel reported. ("I do hate him now." Dear girl. She would trouble no one's concupiscence, but she was brilliant.) Cassirer had hired a lawyer named Tuttle to represent him, and the little man in a tweed hat came to Andrew's office. He seem unfazed by the aromatic Foster.

"Nice room. Very homey."

"Cassirer hired you? What for?"

Tuttle fluttered a faculty manual. "To make sure correct procedures are followed. The days of academic confidentiality are over. There is the freedom of information act. There will be no secrets, no star chamber, justice will prevail."

Tuttle took some chips from the open bag on Foster's desk: Here was another sign of the times. Now disgruntled faculty regularly sued their institutions, often with success. But that took time.

"So what can I do for you?"

"Resign from the committee. You are prejudiced against my client."

"How can you possibly know that?"

The little lawyer pushed back his tweed hat and winked. "I told you there are no secrets."

"I suppose I could countersue for libel."

"Are you asking my professional advice?"

"Would you give it?"

"Not in the present circumstances. But if circumstances changed, let's just say you'd have a strong case. Is Fulvio Bernardo your father?"

"Yes."

"Wonderful man. I was sorry to hear about his illness."

Tuttle seemed genuinely sorry and Andrew warmed to the man. "He's a little better."

"Thank God for that. A man only has one father, you know."

"You really ought to tell Cassirer to let matters take their course."

"Now you're advising me."

"No charge."

Tuttle laughed. He did not seem a formidable opponent, if that is what he was. "I am anxious to get into academic law, it's a growing field."

"I'll keep you in mind."

Tuttle took off his hat and fished a card from it and put it on Andrew's desk. "You might let your colleagues know. Why do you have that machine running?"

"It records conversations."

Tuttle thought he was serious. He got up and went to study the air freshener. He looked at Andrew. "You're kidding, right?"

"Yes."

"That's quite a little breeze it puts out."

But Cassirer decided to take the fight to the enemy camp. He published an article in the student paper about tenured mediocrity, a mistake. Dozens of students, not all of them anonymous, wrote at length about Cassirer's incompetence in the classroom. Mabel Gorman wrote that he was simply the worst teacher she had ever had in her life. Word got to Andrew that Cassirer was sure Andrew had orchestrated the campaign. One night he went out to his car and found both rear tires were flat.

7

Phyllis drove Raymond to LAX from their home in Thousand Oaks. There was not much conversation because of the traffic and her faint resentment that he was going. Had she expected to be asked to accompany him? Unlikely. Someone had to meet their patients. The message from Andrew and then Jessica's call had filled him with dread, not because his father was on his deathbed but at the thought of returning to Chicago. Neither of them had been back since leaving, taking their own sweet time on a cross-country jaunt in a rental car and living high on the Order's credit card. They owed him, that was his attitude. He and Phyllis had become licenced counselors and made a good living giving bad advice. It was like hearing confessions without giving absolution. The trick was to convince the patient there was no sin. When Raymond decided to go to Chicago it occurred to him that it would give him relief from Phyllis's obsession with Julia.

"In a few hours you will be back there."

"You can't go home again."

"Do you still think of it as home?"

He touched her arm but she shrugged off his hand. They had become one another's patients. Physician, heal thyself.

"I'll cancel your appointments."

"You might take some of them."

"Julia?"

"If you'd like."

If he had been driving she would have started in on it, but they were nearing the airport now and she had to keep alert for the signs. The prospect of time away from Phyllis filled him with the same carefree madness with which they had run away together years before. It had been on the spur of the moment but a moment when they had already gone too far. Driving west over plains and through the mountains and finally to the Golden State had been like shucking the skin of the past. What a romp they'd had. They had driven away from all restraint. In motels they watched soft porn movies and frolicked like teenagers.

"You can just drop me off."

She made a face. "I'm sure you can buy a ticket for yourself."

She found a space near the United entrance and he leaned toward her to kiss her cheek, but she turned to him and gave him a passionate kiss.

"Be good."

"At a funeral?"

"Call when you get in."

He hopped out. She had popped the trunk, and he removed his bags, then ducked down to smile in at her. She stuck out her tongue, then smiled. He turned and hurried inside.

When his turn came and he told the girl he wanted a ticket to Chicago, she asked his name.

"I don't have a reservation."

"And you want to fly today?"

"I have to."

She clacked some keys and gave him a figure.

"Ouch."

She looked sympathetic but then he was giving her the full benefit of his professional smile. "If you didn't have to travel today . . ."

"My father is dying."

"Oh." Lips rounding in sympathy. "But that's different." There was what was called a compassionate exception. He huddled over the counter; they were coconspirators now. She gave a figure half of the previous one. "I'll try to get you into first class."

"How much more is that?"

She smiled. She was doing it as a favor. Only there were no seats in first class. She was more disappointed than he was. Rhonda.

"You've been wonderful," he said when he handed over his credit card.

"How long will you be gone?"

There was a definite note of invitation in her voice. "Do you live in L.A.?"

"I'm in the book." She slid her card across the counter, and he put it in his hankie pocket and patted it. Another professional smile. He was both flattered and shocked. Were lovely girls like Rhonda so readily available? But it was Julia he thought of.

Rhonda had put him in a window seat in the row with the emergency exit, lots of leg room. He was buckled in before he remembered that he hated to fly. It was as if he were daring God to take his life. Fulton Sheen had scoffed at those who feared to fly. Did they think God was only on the ground? But it was the fact that he seemed to have a freer hand in the air that disturbed. For a mad moment he wished he was going by car, reversing the flight he and Phyllis had made years ago. He sat back and closed his eyes and almost immediately fell asleep. Phyllis had given him a Dramamine before they left the house. When he awoke they were aloft, going counterclockwise to Chicago, into the past, to his father's deathbed. He hoped that he would not arrive in time, dreading to face the old man invested with all the authority of the dying. He had not so much as talked with his father on the phone since his desertion. Desertion. Away from Phyllis he could call a spade a spade. He closed his eyes, and their conversation about Julia played in his mental ear.

"What's going on, Ray?"

Out of the blue. "In what sense?"

"Julia."

"She is a perfect pagan."

"She wants you."

"Oh, come on."

"And it's mutual."

"Phyl."

Their quarreling consisted of falling into a routine where the lines they spoke were not their own but ones borrowed from patients and their own responses to them. Phyllis was obviously annoyed but could not show it.

"Get mad," he advised her.

"There's no point to that."

"So what do you propose?"

"Get it out of your system."

It angered him that she thought she could issue such a pass to him, a furlough from fidelity. And he had been true to her, in his fashion. Over the years they had devised a common personality that was built around their practice, the present, the avoidance of the past.

"Just use her?"

"Do you really want to do anything more?"

Using shared professional tricks on one another, they seemed to have lost the capacity to communicate. What else was their practice but the issuance of passes? Therapy consisted of permitting people to do what they wanted without the pang of guilt. Usually it took several sessions to find out what the supposed problem was. His response to Julia, twenty years younger than himself, made him a type he had often dealt with. As Phyllis was dealing with him. The patient was finally asked if he disapproved of what he was doing or wanted to do. A negative answer seemed called for.

"Then why are you here?"

Therapy was aimed at discovering whose opinion the patient feared if not his own: that of a spouse, a child, a parent. His father. The flight attendant arrived with her trolley, and he asked for tomato juice, then changed it to a Bloody Mary. Phyllis was trying to manipulate him as they both manipulated patients. He would be indebted to her for allowing him to indulge himself with impunity.

On the phone Jessica had told him that Aunt Eleanor was at the hospital. She had given him a chalice when he was ordained, a beautiful full cup with scarcely any stem and a wide octagonal base. He had rented a safety deposit box in Chicago and put it there before going. Why of all the ties that bound him to the past he should refuse to sever that one he didn't know. Its value? What is the market for used chalices? No, it was more than that, a sign of which was that he had never told Phyllis about it. He paid rental for the box annually, lying to her that it contained papers.

"You should transfer them out here."

"They're family stuff."

He did feel that he was flying into the past, the great jet a time machine that negated the years since he and Phyllis had left. She had been in campus ministry. It began when they chaperoned a student dance, wearing civvies of course. She asked him to dance.

"But I don't know how."

"I'll bet you're a quick learner."

"I never went to a dance," he told her.

"I did. I entered after my junior year in college." The convent. The fact that they had both taken vows in obscure Orders was a bond between them, and as they discussed her reasons for wanting to leave they became his own. Somewhere in an abstract world he must have imagined what it would be like to step back from the life that was his, but it was with her that he had first put it into words. Everything he knew told him the danger of what he was doing; retreats and spiritual reading should have been enough to make him turn away, to stop seeing her. But from the outset she had put him in the role of her confidant, her spiritual advisor, because of course he asked whom she had spoken with about her doubts.

"No one else."

"But you should; you can't just walk away."

"Of course I can. So many others have. Haven't men left your Order?"

Quitters, that is how in his heart of hearts he had thought of those who left, who applied for laicization, who for one reason or another claimed they had made a huge mistake. But now the Church herself made it possible to leave, to start over. He found himself beginning to sympathize with those who left as if they alone were serious enough to think the thought and say the word. And act. Within hours, holding her in his arms, her voice sweet as Eve's in his ear, he could feel the resolution of a lifetime begin to dissolve. Later, alone, in his single bed in his celibate room, he had stared at the play of lights upon the ceiling and trembled with fear. He resolved never to see her again. It was insane to think that a warm body against his own and her subversive chatter could undo what he had built up over so many years, the very self he was. When sleep came he had prayed for strength and was certain his prayer had been answered. In the morning, at the altar, saying Mass, all his actions seemed incredible, unfamiliar. He lifted the bread in his hands and bent to say the words of consecration, and they stuck in his throat. *Dear God, I believe,* he had prayed, *help thou my unbelief.* The efficacy of what he did was not dependent on his mood; he was a priest. He managed to say the words. *This is my body.* And then he took the chalice Aunt Eleanor had given him and whispered the words of consecration over the wine. But when he raised the chalice he had the dreadful thought that it was still only wine.

Incredibly, within a week his faith was wholly gone. He saw Phyllis at every opportunity; they exchanged tales of those who had left, nuns, priests. How easy it seemed. They were both young; there was still time for another life. They began to fantasize about California.

"Let's go," she said.

In answer he showed her the keys to the car and the Order's credit card. It was as if the decision had already been made by his blood.

At thirty-eight thousand feet he relived it all, and it was as if for the first time he dared think about it, review the steps, see himself as if from some great height. He had two opposed sets of criteria with which to judge himself: those he had acquired during the years of study for the priesthood — the prayers, the conferences, the advice of directors — on the one hand, and on the other those he had adopted with Phyllis. He was condemned by the one set and exonerated, even liberated, by the second. Flying across the country he was returning to the setting where the condemning criteria seemed to have their habitat, where his father awaited him, dead or alive, and the family that must regard him as a traitor.

The pilot began to draw their attention to the scenery over which they were passing, a tour bus guide. Those on the right of the aircraft could see below them the Grand Canyon; later those on the left could see where the mountains gave way to plains. A jolly mindless voice dedicated to making their trip more enjoyable. Raymond would have given anything to be back in Thousand Oaks sparring with Phyllis about Julia. The final hour was the worst as they slowly descended toward O'Hare and the city came into view and rose slowly to meet them. He had the feeling that he had left a Technicolor world and was reentering a world of black and white.

8

In any profession there are bottom feeders, lowly creatures who live off the leavings of those in the water above them. Doubtless there is often resentment down there at the bottom of the tank, but among the lowly are some who are happy to be in the tank at all. Such was Tuttle's position, and attitude, in the legal profession of Fox River, Illinois. His path through law school had not been easy, though he had attended the Calhoun & Webster School of Law, not the most eminent institution of legal instruction in the Midwest. On the other hand, admission was largely a matter of paying the fees. Tuttle's father brought him to class the first evening, riding the bus with him from the South Side and hugging him proudly before he passed through the portals of the school, in fact a revolving door that resisted the shoulder and made entrance a hard-won success every time. There were tears in Tuttle senior's eyes. He himself had dreamt of being a lawyer, but it was not to be. He had shuffled through his mail route in those years before carriers were equipped with vehicles, mace, and seasonal uniforms. But the pension was a godsend, enabling Tuttle senior to send his son through Calhoun & Webster. Although it was a night school, Tuttle studied all day long, living at home, the saving realized more than offsetting the daily carfare to class. The law had not come easily to Tuttle. But when he flunked a course, he simply took it over again and either that time or the next passed. He flunked many courses. In a sense, he might have been called the most thoroughly educated lawyer in the region. His father's support had never wavered. When Tuttle himself grew despondent, his father was there to cheer him on. Eventually, he graduated and gladdened his father's heart that his son was now indeed a Bachelor of Law. That gladdened heart soon gave out as if the goal being reached he now could lay his burden down.

Tuttle opened law offices in Fox River, hoping to find less competition in the little town to the west of Chicago but part of the greater metropolitan area. He had lettered on his door Tuttle & Tuttle in commemoration of his father. Few Chinese could rival Tuttle's ancestor worship. The memory of his father could bring a tear to his eye, and a day did not go by that, prompted by the name of the firm, he did not breathe an Ave for his father. Fox River proved to be rife with lawyers, as what town is not, and Tuttle carved a place for himself slowly. He would not touch divorce cases, this scruple inherited from his father and honored unquestioningly. Besides, divorces were notoriously messy. Hanging around the courthouse, drinking the vile but free coffee in the pressroom, making acquaintances if not friends with the resentful members of the media, he also formed a real friendship with Peanuts Pianone, a police officer who owed his appointment to the influence of his family, in several senses of the term, and who spent the day napping in various places about the courthouse. Peanuts would never have made the force on the basis of an examination; there was one school of thought that claimed he could not read — false — and Captain Keegan, when asked, said that Peanuts was on a roving assignment. He and Tuttle roved together, and from time to time a client came Tuttle's way, some poor devil helpless in the municipal court and ripe for representation. Occasionally bigger things came to Tuttle, but he was ever on the qui vive for his main chance.

When Professor Cassirer called Tuttle's office he and Peanuts were enjoying fried rice and chicken wings. It was their pleasure to have such snacks brought to the offices of Tuttle & Tuttle, a pleasure less frequent now that Hazel had established herself as his secretary, but today she was indisposed and home with the flu. The office was a fourth-floor walk-up in a non-air-conditioned building that had somehow survived urban renewal. The rent was risible, and the manager not a stickler for timely payment. Tuttle was masticating noisily when he answered the phone.

"My name is Cassirer. I am a professor at St. Edmund's, and I am seeking legal representation."

Tuttle suppressed a chuckle, assuming that Tetzel in the pressroom was playing a practical joke.

"Who recommended you?"

"The yellow pages. I chose your name by the *Sortes Virgilianae*. I would like an appointment."

Something told Tuttle this was not a prank. He looked around his office. No need to ask how it would seem to Cassirer.

"As it happens I have business near St. Edmund's. Are you free this afternoon?"

"I am. Do you know the student center?"

"I will find it. Two o'clock?"

"Wonderful. How will I know you?"

"I will be wearing a tweed hat. Irish tweed."

He hung up, tilted that tweed hat to a more rakish angle, and looked at Peanuts. "A client."

"Too bad."

Peanuts assumed that he avoided business the way Peanuts avoided police work. But Peanuts was on salary.

"Do you have a car?"

"I can get one."

"On second thought, I'll take mine." Arrival in a squad car might send the wrong signal to Cassirer. "Give me a few bucks for gas."

"I paid for the Chinese."

Tuttle flourished a piece of paper. "I am keeping exact records. My ship may be about to come in."

"What ship?"

"A manner of speaking."

No time to expand Peanut's command of the King's English. Tuttle was a stranger to professional optimism, fish regularly slipped his net, but the call from Cassirer was different. His thoughts lifted to his sainted father, whom he had consulted about continuing the ad in the yellow pages.

The saving that cancellation promised had its attractions in this time of drought, but the paternal voice had suggested keeping the ad. He could take it out of the rent money.

He found the student center, and Cassirer found him, confronting him as if about to demand his I.D.

"Tuttle?"

"Cassirer?"

They shook hands. "You're young to be a professor, aren't you?" The beard was clearly an effort to add gravitas, but it gave him a mad-bomber look.

"I have always been precocious."

Cassirer led the way to a cafeteria and pushed a tray along as he impressed on Tuttle the utter confidentiality of what he wished to discuss. Once mugs of coffee were on the tray and Tuttle had made a half-hearted attempt to pay, Cassirer led him to a table for two in a far corner.

"How much do you know about academic tenure?"

That quickly, the moment of truth. "Tell me about it."

A stroke of genius that, as Cassirer was primed on all occasions to lecture. It was a trait that would enable Tuttle to seal their relationship. Cassirer assumed that Tuttle knew what Cassirer knew, and since the young man did all the talking this fiction was sustained. Cassirer laid a copy of the faculty manual on the table.

"You will want to study that. The usual way is for people to wait until they have been turned down for tenure and then sue. I plan a preemptive strike. Of course my job is good for another year whether or not I am granted tenure, so the risk of suing after the fact is less, but I cannot be passive in this matter. You probably have heard of Foucault."

He heard of him then. Gradually Tuttle discerned that Cassirer was not speaking of a Chinese friend. Tuttle nodded through the unintelligible narration, which led finally to the heart of the matter. Cassirer had put himself forward for tenure before the stated time, and he was now sure he would be turned down.

"This will be a monumental injustice. I have means of learning what goes on in the committee. I have identified my principal enemy." He leaned forward and mouthed a name. Then he said it audibly. "Andrew Bernardo."

"So what's the plan?"

"I want to sue Bernardo, the dean, and the provost. Their names are in the manual.

The sooner we file the better."

"You want to sue on the basis of what you have learned about the committee's proceedings?"

"It sounds weak when you put it like that. I don't have to tell you this, but the lawsuit is a means of putting pressure on them. Of course they will want to avoid court and wish to settle. Usually that means money. I am not interested in their money."

"Payment of money is a powerful admission of guilt."

"Oh, I'd take it. But what I want is tenure now."

"You must really like this place."

"I hate it. It is a monument to mediocrity." He pushed a copy of a newspaper across the table. "There is a piece of mine in the student paper you will want to read. The orchestration of response to my article is a public matter. Of course Bernardo was behind it."

"What's his motive?"

"Jealousy. I tell you frankly that I am both the youngest and the most distinguished member of my department. For me to be denied tenure would be a crime against the intellect."

So phrased, there was no local, state, or federal statute that covered the crime. But

Tuttle knew that he was on to something. Rumors, newspaper stories, bits of information gathered from God knew where had acquainted Tuttle with the litigious atmosphere on college and university campuses.

"It would help if I could meet Andrew Bernardo."

"Good! Stop by his office. Shake him up. I want them to know I mean business."

And so Tuttle had visited Andrew Bernardo in his office, where a whirring machine made everyone speak in a high voice. Foster, his officemate, was a genial sort, reminiscent of Peanuts, and Tuttle liked Andrew as he had not warmed to his client. Cassirer was someone who would put mother love to a trial. Tuttle had met his share of egoists, but most of them were in the pressroom and their self-estimate was at variance with general opinion. Cassirer, he was sure, was as good as he said he was, but the fact that he kept saying it was off-putting. Andrew on the other hand was affable, diffident, more like Tuttle's notion of a professor. And the son of Fulvio Bernardo.

The imminent death of the young man's father appealed to all Tuttle's devotion to his own, and he felt a genuine sympathy for him. And there came to him the conviction that this campus was a fertile field for his talents. He would study the faculty manual, he would become an expert in academic procedures, and he would make his name known so that the disgruntled would find their way to his door.

9

Death, judgment, heaven, and hell — The Four Last Things — how they pressed on Father Dowling's mind as he drove away from the hospital. Cronin, the hospital chaplain, a stolid humorless man whose life was lived in the misery of others, had not filled Father Dowling with confidence. Cronin's thinning hair was cut close to his domed head, and he listened to the account of Fulvio Bernardo's refusal to see a priest with no visible emotion.

"It happens all the time."

"What do you do?"

"Pray that they come around. Some do. You have to realize that they are usually drugged or in pain, either way not the best circumstances to think clearly. People are what they are by the time they come here. Deathbed conversions you can count on one hand."

"You'll talk to him?"

"But will he listen?"

Driving to the rectory, he prayed for the

old man. The defection of his son the priest was at the bottom of it according to Jessica, and he was on his way from California. Father Dowling prayed for Raymond too, wondering what he could possibly say to his dying father.

That evening he was having dinner with Amos Cadbury at the University Club in the Loop and was unsure he would be good company for the lawyer because of the events of the day.

"Eleanor Wygant tells me she has been to see you," Amos said.

Father Dowling smiled. "I should have guessed you would know her."

"Her late husband, or I should say her latest husband, Alfred Wygant, was a dear friend." Amos frowned over his glass of Barolo. "His death came as a decided shock to me."

"And when did you see Eleanor?"

"Just yesterday. I look after her affairs, and she stopped by the office. Widows like to fuss about their holdings."

"Is she comfortable?"

"Oh yes." Another frown, a sip of Barolo. "Not as comfortable as she might have been, but no need to worry. I oversee her investments, and the market has been good to her."

"I saw her today at the hospital."

"The hospital!"

"I suppose you know Fulvio Bernardo? He has been in intensive care." Father Dowling told the lawyer of Bernardo's stroke.

"And of course Eleanor would be there. Her first husband was Fulvio's brother. The Bernardos continue to be her family. She had no children by either marriage, poor thing. Is it serious?"

"Very."

"God bless him."

Something in Amos's tone caught Father Dowling's attention. "That sounds grudging."

"Then God forgive me. I never really liked the man but *de mortuis nil nisi bonum*." Amos's Notre Dame education often put in such an appearance.

"Oh, he isn't dead yet. I called the hospital before coming here and learned that he had been transferred out of intensive care."

"One of the Bernardos was a priest."

"Tell me about him."

"Have they informed him?"

"He is on his way from California."

"This is exceptionally good wine."

"I gather he wasn't diocesan."

"Oh no. An Edmundite. The Order of St.

Edmund. They are said to be an old order, not quite medieval, but they have never amounted to much in this country. St. Edmund College was founded by them."

There are many contingencies in any vocation, one of the main ones being the priest who first discerns that a boy may be destined for the priesthood, in Raymond's case an Edmundite named Bourke.

"Father Bourke is still alive, a veritable patriarch." Amos sighed. "Think of what a man that age has had to witness." The remark might have been autobiographical. "In any case, he was the reason young Raymond opted for the Order of St. Edmund. His departure was a surprise and a shock. I'm on the board there, you know."

"I didn't know."

"For my sins. It is a sad thing to see the way we have dismantled our own institutions. I stay on to slow the process, not very effectively, I am afraid."

"I know the college is there, of course, but little else about it."

Amos over brandy developed the pathology of the once Catholic college. The Second Vatican Council, providential as it no doubt was, had effects it could scarcely have envisaged. The urge to renew and update — aggiornamento — was taken by many to be an invitation to jettison the past. The Edmundites, whatever their lack of success in the country at large, had flourished in the Chicago area. Their seminary was on the grounds of the college; indeed the college was in its way an outgrowth of the seminary, thought of at first largely as a source of new vocations but soon opened to young men at large. The curriculum expanded, accreditation was won, the faculty enlarged. In the wake of the Council it was the college that wagged the tail of the Edmundites, soon eclipsing all else. And becoming increasingly secular.

"Priests became rarer and rarer on the faculty, lay professors were hired, soon the standards for hiring became increasingly like those of any secular college. Today it boasts of its academic excellence, and in a sense this is justified, but at what an expense has it been bought. Raymond Bernardo was not the only Edmundite priest to abandon his calling. There was for a time a hemorrhage. It seemed to have subsided, and then he left, a blow to Father Bourke. The seminary was closed years ago."

"No vocations?"

"That is not a problem confined to the Edmundites."

"Indeed not. You knew Raymond Bernardo?"

"Only in the way you know a youngster. And then he was assigned to the college after ordination and further studies."

"What did he study?"

"Psychology."

"Ah."

"The witchcraft of our times, Father Dowling. Freud, Jung, Reich, the whole lot as far as I can see needed exorcism rather than therapy. It has made mincemeat of the law, of course. The assumption is that a criminal act cannot be freely performed but is the result of some obscure mechanism that need only be righted. No matter the harm that has been done to society and the demands of justice. The courts have become the anteroom to the counselor's couch. But I am raving."

Father Dowling chuckled. Passionate as Amos's words might be, his precise elocution and modulated bass voice seemed the very organ of rationality. "Bishops too have fallen prey to it. A battery of psychological tests must be taken before one can enter the seminary."

"Raymond Bernardo was named spiritual director of the Edmundite seminary on campus. He changed the title to spiritual counselor."

"How long after ordination was he laicized?"

White brows rose over Amos's dark rimmed glasses. "That would suggest that he left in an orderly way. Not at all. He commandeered one of the order's cars and credit cards and went westward with a young nun from campus ministry. Bonnie and Clyde." Amos closed his eyes. "A dreadful movie I once saw as captive on a flight from Rome."

Amos did not know if young Father Bernardo had ever applied for laicization, once easily had for the asking but after the unbroken flow of men from the priesthood made more difficult.

"He married the nun?"

"God knows. The Reformation seems almost innocent compared with recent years. Luther and his nun, the vulgar talk at table, German earthiness, but at least it was accompanied by a sense of sin. No one could think less of Luther than he thought of himself. Of course he thought his actions did not matter since he was not truly free. God would throw a cloak over his corruption; that was salvation. I suppose psychiatry is a version of that but without the sense of sin and without redemption. Sanity consists in accepting the actions we do not freely do."

"You are becoming a philosopher, Amos."

"I am an old man who is heartsick at the spectacle of the times."

"A man named Rosmini wrote a book called *The Five Wounds of the Church*."

"Only five?"

"It brought him under a cloud."

"The Church has become St. Sebastian now, more wounds than one could count. Sometimes I fear some great calamity will befall us for what we have done to the Church."

Amos did not know if Raymond Bernardo had ever repaid the Order for the expensive westward journey he had taken with his bonny nun. "I was told he considered it just recompense. Occult compensation, as it used to be called."

Father Dowling's degree was in canon law, a subject in which Amos was well read. Once men took degrees *utriusque legis,* in both civil and church law. Amos was the latter-day equivalent of such a dual doctor, trained in the one, an autodidact in the other.

They ended their evening in the club library, where Amos could smoke his cigar and Father Dowling light his pipe.

"You say the college is flourishing?"

"On its altered terms, yes. The question

is, why have Catholic institutions if they are so little different from secular ones? But of course there is a bull market in college students and government loans to encourage young people into debt and fill the coffers of the colleges. I will not bore you with some of the nonsense that has entered the curriculum."

"You mentioned Eleanor Wygant earlier. She came to me quite upset with the prospect that her niece plans a novel about the Bernardo family."

"Jessica. She is the best of the lot, a very gifted young lady. I cannot say that her fiction is my cup of tea, but it shows obvious talent. And her reviews have been magnificent."

"So she has been successful."

"Not financially, of course. Few novelists could live on what they earn from their books. She is a lab technician at Sorensen's Labs. Once pathologists worked for hospitals; now they establish their own laboratories and profit far more handsomely from their work. Not that Sorensen himself has touched a slide in years. That is him over there."

A round little man sat in a leather chair frowning at the financial page, a cigar emerging from the exact center of his mouth, which was stretched in a grimace of pain. Amos rose.

"Come, Father. I will introduce you."

And so it was that Father Dowling made the acquaintance of Eric Sorensen in the library of the University Club. The little doctor managed not to stare at Father Dowling's Roman collar.

"I am Missouri Synod. Our ministers have stopped wearing those."

He meant the collar. Amos said, "I mentioned Jessica Bernardo to Father Dowling, then looked up and saw you, Eric. I thought the two of you should meet."

"Ah, Jessica. I love her novels. I wish all my employees wrote novels. It gives one great insight into their minds." He rolled his cigar in his fat fingers. "I sometimes think of writing a novel myself."

"Better not, Eric. It will give your employees insight into your mind."

Sorensen laughed.

"Jessica's father has fallen seriously ill," Father Dowling said.

"Fulvio," Sorensen said deliberately as if there were dashes between the syllables.

"Don't get started on him, Eric," Amos Cadbury said. "Father Dowling and I are leaving."

Handshakes all around. Amos's car came

round, and he took Father Dowling to his rectory where, enjoying a final pipe in his study, the pastor of St. Hilary's reflected on the connections between what might have seemed a random group of people. Before going to bed he called the hospital and learned that Fulvio Bernardo had slightly improved and was now in a room out of intensive care.

10

Thunder, Jessica's agent, called before she went to work, and even his bored tones could not conceal his excitement.

"I think this is your breakthrough novel, sweetheart. Diurno loves it. How soon can you get me a one-pager I can get a contract on?"

Jessica's enthusiasm for the literary life, never high, had suffered from the events of recent days. It is a sobering experience to stand at one's father's bedside in intensive care and see the digital monitoring of his vital signs wink in green and red while fluid drips into his veins from a plastic bag. How evanescent everything seemed.

"They like it?"

"Diurno likes it. Meaning he is eager to sign a contract."

"How did you describe it?"

"I? You did. The saga of a Midwestern Catholic family, from order to chaos, from rules to what the hell, disintegration. But with tears."

"That was my description?"

"I paraphrase, of course. You deal with me; I deal with publishers. I know Diurno's mind, such as it is. The man is a cash register. I doubt that he has read half a dozen books in his lifetime. He knew a man who turned down *Gone With the Wind* when the novel was only the whisper of a breeze in the mimosa. For him novels are one page long."

"So what do you need?"

"Drama. Gut-wrenching episodes. A dying fall."

She thought of her father. Suddenly her great idea seemed an exploitation of her family, of real tragedy. Raymond was at the heart of it, but how could she make Thunder or Diurno understand what it meant for a man to abandon the priesthood, destroy his parents' pride, flee to California, and join the fruits and nuts? She promised to send the one page.

"Fax it. When can I expect it?"

"Give me a deadline."

"What time is it there, nine o'clock? How does noon sound?"

"You're kidding."

"I have never been more serious in my life. I nurtured you, sweetheart. I loved your first two novels, you and I and four thousand buyers. Plus two hundred reviewers, which is the important thing. They were the prelude; this novel is the main act. Think big. Noon, okay?"

"I'll try."

"Succeed."

He hung up. Jessica had difficulty thinking of what she wrote as a commodity, but of course that is what it was for Thunder and even more for the cash register Diurno. They thought in terms of dust-jacket hype. Had Thunder actually read her novels? His only suggestion was to soften the religious motif. "This is a neopagan age, sweetheart, like it or not. I speak as a lapsed Catholic."

"I didn't know that."

"I don't mention it in *Who's Who*. What's the point? Nobody is what he was."

"I am."

"Sweetheart, that is your charm, your strength."

"This novel could be pretty religious."

"I'm counting on that," Thunder said with breezy inconsistency. "I want you to put the fear of God into us backsliders."

She called Sorensen's and said she wanted to take the morning off. The reaction made her think she could have asked for a week and gotten it. Then she sat at her computer and stared at the screen, but all she could see was the monitor above her father's bed in intensive care.

The phone rang. It was her colleague Walter. "Is anything wrong?"

"No."

"I heard you had called in sick."

"My father is in the hospital."

"Is there anything I can do?"

Dear Walter — gifted, dumb, unimaginative Walter — who tried desperately to understand that her writing was more important to her than her work in the lab. For Walter Sorensen's lab was the world; the slides he worked on *rerum natura*. Make-believe was a distant childhood memory. Their work determined what surgeons would do, what physicians would tell their patients, whether flesh and blood people would live or die. Walter never forgot that.

"He's better now. They've moved him into a room out of intensive care."

"He has prostate cancer?"

"This was his heart. They don't think they should operate."

She had the feeling she was inserting her father into a carefully calibrated category for Walter's benefit. That was unfair.

"Take the day, Jessica. I will cover for you."

A good part of her relation to Walter was avoiding becoming beholden to him. He was too good for his own good, too good for her. She had the sense that he was the kind of man she should love, but all she could muster was a profound admiration.

"Thank you."

"I would do anything for you."

"I know."

She could tell him anything. She had told him about Raymond as well as about the academic squabble Andrew was involved in at the college because of a bumptious colleague named Cassirer. "Apparently he has hired a lawyer."

"Are professors insured against that sort of thing?"

"You would think it the most peaceful life in the world, wouldn't you?"

"I'm surprised you weren't attracted to teaching."

And compete a second time with Andrew? No thanks.

She hung up, full of the tranquillity talking with Walter always gave her. She began to plink away on the keys of her computer. She thought of Raymond, coming home at last, to be with his dying father. What a drama that would be. Fulvio had never forgiven his son for what he had done. He could not begin to understand how a man could be so unfaithful to his vows.

"I will go to Mass when Raymond is the celebrant."

That was his position. He was punishing himself in the hope of shaming Raymond into repentance. Did Raymond even know that their father had stopped going to Mass, that their mother wept and pleaded but always got the same answer? He would go to Mass again when Raymond was back at the altar.

"It would kill your father if you wrote about the family," Aunt Eleanor had said.

That might not be necessary. What had struck Jessica was the intensity of Eleanor's concern. Did she really care that much for the family she had married into? Uncle Joe had died and Eleanor had married Alfred Wygant, much to her father's disgust.

"What does he have but money?"

Uncle Joe had been the black sheep of the family, dependent on her father. When he died there had been an insurance policy worth five thousand dollars.

"I'll take care of Eleanor," Fulvio had said, the prosperous brother asserting his authority. But she had married Alfred Wygant. When Alfred died, Eleanor had considerably more than five thousand dollars.

A call came from Leonard Bosch, literary

editor of the *Tribune*, Chicago, not Fox River. "Sorry about your father."

"He's somewhat better."

"Good. Is this a bad time to talk about my suggestion?"

"Yes."

Leonard wanted her to do a column for the Sunday book section or if not that to agree to be a regular reviewer. "You are a local asset, Jessica. You have to accept that. And I have an obligation to be sure our readers know it."

"Andrew would be the one to write a column."

Silence. And then, "What I like about the Bernardos is that they stick together."

Was that true? Raymond had gotten Andrew the job at St. Edmund's not long before he left. It seemed a compensatory gesture. No, that wasn't fair. Andrew knew so many things she didn't; he loved literature. Too much. His writing was impasto, spread with a knife, overwritten, aimed at God knew what reader. Whom did one write for, after all? What reader did she herself imagine when she sat at her computer and followed the fortunes of imaginary people? Only they did not seem imaginary. Not real, more than real. She wrote for them, her characters. That seemed the answer to her question. Andrew wrote for critics.

She typed a title on the screen: *Last Things.* And stared at it. What were The Four Last Things? That was something she felt she had known but now could not remember. Whom could she ask? She smiled, remembering Aunt Eleanor's plea. She found the number for St. Hilary's and dialed it.

"Father Dowling? Jessica Bernardo."

"How is your father?"

"Better."

"Thank God."

"I called to ask you a question."

"All right."

"What are The Four Last Things?"

A pause. "Death, judgment, heaven, hell."

"Wow."

"Why do you ask?"

"I am planning a novel I want to call *Last Things.*"

"Is this the one Eleanor Wygant spoke to me about?"

"I suppose."

"And that is the theme? She said it was a family novel."

"I wish I had never told her about it."

"She wanted me to talk you into dropping it."

"No!"

"I think I'll stop by the hospital this morning."

"Maybe I will see you there."

Thunder and Diurno could wait. But suddenly she began to type, and the story idea was all about Raymond and how what he had done affected his family. Of course that was the story of the Bernardos. Jessica wrote swiftly, acknowledging what her brother's defection had meant to her, knowing what it had meant to her parents. Was Andrew unaffected? How could he be? But he probably saw it in turgid Graham Greene tones. She finished the page and printed it out and faxed it off to Thunder with scarcely a change.

Then she called Andrew and told him she was going to the hospital.

"I am meeting Raymond's plane. I'll bring him there."

11

O'Hare was LAX without sun or half-dressed people. Raymond felt that he was not dressed properly for late October, a pale green jacket, yellow shirt, black trousers, and loafers. No familiar faces, but then only passengers were admitted into these long ganglia that led out to the flight gates. Everything seemed larger than he remembered, not that he had flown much in the old days. It was always more attractive to take one of the cars and be in complete charge of one's destiny. He smiled as the memories came back. Once he visited a high school in Indiana . . . He stopped, and grumbling travelers went around him like a rock in a stream. He got out of the traffic, entered an uncrowded waiting area, and sat. The trip he remembered had been a recruiting one, talking with boys about the priesthood as a possible vocation. He looked at the people going by and realized that the world was full of people whose only contact with him had been as a priest. The full importance of this return came home to him. In Chicago he had been a priest; in California he was a counselor. Two worlds that could not overlap before, but now anyone, not just his father, could look at him with double vision, seeing both the priest that was and what he had become. If it had been possible he would have retraced his steps to the plane and asked to be taken back to Los Angeles. He rose and continued slowly to the baggage claim, where Andrew awaited him.

The two brothers looked at one another across a gap of nearly ten years. What did Andrew see? Raymond saw a paunchy, tweedy academic trying to disguise his little brother. In a moment they were in one another's arms.

"How's Dad?"

"Better."

His heart sank. "How much better?" The question sounded as if he were asking if he had made this trip in vain.

"He's still in the hospital." Andrew looked away. "He won't be coming home again, ever."

"What exactly is it?"

They stood away from the carousel where passengers already stood three deep although no bags had yet appeared.

"He had a heart attack, a mild one, and if he were younger and stronger they would do open-heart surgery because of all the clogged passageways. I don't know what I'm talking about, you understand. Jessica can explain."

"How is she taking it?"

The question seemed to surprise Andrew. Jessica was just their sister, beautiful and smart and all that, but a girl. Andrew must have felt that way toward her too. They had learned it from their father.

"Calmly. How else?"

"We talked a bit on the phone. Her voice is very much like Mom's."

Are people just reassembled pieces of their forebears? What else do we mean by DNA? But the idea is that each combination is unique. Raymond could see traits of his father in Andrew, and of his mother.

"You look more and more like Dad," Andrew said.

He had stepped back as if to get perspective. He nodded in agreement with himself. "When I first saw you I thought, my God, it's Dad. It's no one thing, just the way you walked in here."

Was he flattered or offended? Once his father had been a hero to him and vice versa. He was the oldest, lucky or successful in most things, better at tennis than baseball, and with a vocation. From the time Father

Bourke first asked him if he had ever thought of the priesthood it seemed that he had thought of little else all along, subconsciously. Of course he had been an altar boy at St. Hilary's, but the Franciscans all looked like bit players in a farce, with their sandals and cinctures and floppy cowls, always looking as if they needed a shave. And they all looked as if they talked to birds. St. Francis had always seemed a wimp to Raymond; it was only later that he read about him and knew better. But his followers had always been a scruffy crowd, and in the States they had become affluent beggars. Raymond could see that his father liked Father Bourke when he first came to the house.

Fulvio put on his wop persona, getting out the wine, talking about his tomato plants, but his cool business eye was appraising this strange priest who had interested his son in the Edmundites.

"You want to kidnap him, eh?"

"I don't think Raymond should do anything until after high school." That was half subversive, as he admitted later; he should have been helping fill the preparatory seminary on the Iowa border, but the attrition rate there was high and the staff not the cream of the order. "He can enter the seminary on the campus grounds. After his novitiate, of course."

Father Bourke had ticked off the stages to the priesthood: a year as a novice, which was devoted to the spiritual life, acquiring the outlook of an Edmundite and future priest, then college with two years of philosophy, after which theology began.

"Nine years!"

Father Bourke smiled. "How old would you be then, Raymond, twenty-five?"

"Twenty-six."

It was all settled on that first visit, but Father Bourke came by regularly after that, and he and Fulvio got along like a house afire. With jacket and collar removed, in his shirt sleeves, Father Bourke would play pinochle with Fulvio in the back room that was alive with plants.

"He's a man as well as a priest," was Fulvio's verdict.

Belatedly, Raymond asked Andrew about their mother. Bags had begun to slide down a chute onto the moving carousel, and passengers elbowed one another to get a look at the passing luggage. Carts had been wheeled up, and ankles were run into by eager passengers when they spied their bags. They would let it thin out before claiming his suit bag.

Andrew looked solemn. "Dad shagged the priest out of the room."

What could he say? His mother had written him a long letter, telling him Fulvio's reaction to his leaving. There had not been an accusative note in it. It had always been her role to be understanding, forgiving. Isn't that what mothers are for? She had always been a background figure, busy in the kitchen, off to Mass in the morning, the salvation of them all. Fulvio had never been a devout man, and Raymond was not about to take the blame for his present attitude toward his religion. Did he think his father had lost anything? A terminal provides a hectic sample of the race, all the anxious jostling people, each one the center of his own universe. How many of them really believed that a benevolent God knew them all by name and listened to the secrets of their hearts? It was all a great consolation, no doubt of that. Raymond himself sometimes missed it. Every civilization had some version of it. Of course Christianity was different. Once long ago a man had lived in the Middle East who had died the death of a criminal, and the events of his life were the key to human history. Christ died for our sins, conquered death, would return in triumph to judge us all, separating the sheep

112

from the goats. A billion crucifixes carried that message.

"How is Mom taking it?"

"I think she hopes you can bring him around."

My God. He looked away. Where did Andrew stand on all this? Andrew insisted on carrying his suit bag, and they headed across the street jammed with shuttle buses and cabs to the parking garage, where Andrew's ten-year-old Honda awaited. The trunk door squeaked when he raised it and stuffed the bag in with his golf clubs.

"Do you get out much?"

"Just to the college course."

"Just? As I remember, it's a pretty good nine-hole course."

"It's been expanded to eighteen. We have a golf team now."

"St. Edmund's has a golf team?"

"You wouldn't recognize the place."

To Raymond's surprise, Andrew began to talk shop, some silly quarrel in his department about a young man demanding tenure.

"I'm on the committee. He hates my guts."

"Will he get tenure?"

"Over my dead body."

Andrew got them out of the great echoing

parking garage and into the traffic headed for the interstates.

"It's odd to be back."

"The first time."

"Yes." Andrew must know that, unless he thought he might have slipped in without telling the family.

"It sounds as if you're doing all right in California."

"Tell me about the changes at the college."

Raymond realized he was not elated at all the alleged improvements Andrew spoke of. He had shut the door of his mind completely on the place since leaving it, avoiding any news of it, needing to pretend that it didn't exist. Nostalgia and remorse were dangers still, and he and Phyllis were watchful of any signs of them in one another so they could be nipped in the bud. Their life was in the present and such future as lay before them, period.

"There aren't many Edmundites left."

"Oh."

"I mean on the faculty. Of course all the administration is lay now."

That seemed stupid. How could you control an institution if you delivered it into the hands of mercenaries? An old loyalty to the Order surged up in him, and he resented the thought that the Edmundites had become a disappearing presence in the college they had founded. And again Andrew adverted to the quarrel raging in his department. Obviously it was much on his mind.

"Cassirer knows nothing of the past of the place. Most of my colleagues know nothing about that. I suppose things are different over in Hurley House" (the residence building of the Order).

"They haven't given that away?"

Andrew laughed. "I sometimes see old Father Bourke."

"A good man," Raymond said, closing that off. "How's your writing?"

"So so."

"Jessica still at it?"

"Oh yes. She's planning a new novel. Ask her about it."

"That sounds mysterious."

"She has Eleanor all in a snit. Apparently it's to be the saga of the Bernardos, suitably disguised of course, and Eleanor is terrified."

"Eleanor! Why should she care?"

But something in the way Andrew had brought it up alerted Raymond. It occurred to him that he himself might figure prominently in the saga of the Bernardos. As for Eleanor, he thought he could guess the cause of her uneasiness. An old anger at his father flared up. Had discovering his father was a womanizer eased his own way out of the order? That made as much sense as his father's blaming him for his loss of faith.

"Eleanor has become our guardian angel. She was one of the first to the hospital to see Dad."

Raymond glanced at Andrew, but his brother seemed not to intend anything special by the remark. But mention of Eleanor had brought back the crushing event of his life, when he had learned that his father was not the paragon of family virtues he had always imagined. They stood vulnerable to one another, Raymond and Fulvio, but neither of them could occupy the role of judge.

12

Father Dowling had two remarkable assistants in Marie Murkin, the rectory housekeeper and general busybody, and Edna Hospers, who directed the center for seniors the parish school had been turned into when the demographics of the parish made a school no longer viable. Even if there had been a sufficiency of students, there were no longer nuns to teach them for a song, and it would have been a great financial burden to keep up the parish school. Of course, he would have done so if it had made any sense. Once he had tried a meeting with both women together and once had been enough. Marie had a sense of turf that was formidable; Edna had been hired to run the center, and she intended to do so. For Marie, it was intolerable that any parish activity escaped her watchful supervising eye. Civil war had threatened. Marie was reined in; the center was Edna's, and that was that. After a few days of icy silence, Marie emerged smiling from her kitchen. "Live and let live, I say."

"Is that Mark or John?"

"Murkin." And she went back through the swinging door into her kitchen like a figure on a clock.

Now he met his lieutenants singly, Marie first, in his study, then Edna, in her office in the school.

"The Franciscans killed the school," Marie said.

"Not even Franciscans can produce children at will, Marie."

"I should hope not."

"What is this about painting the house? How do you paint a brick house?"

"The trim, Father. It has been years."

"I don't remember its ever being done."

"Exactly."

"So what do we do?"

Marie tolerated the pronoun. She had already made provisional plans.

"A professional painter would cost an arm and a leg. They would put on a crew, make a great production of it, be here for weeks."

"What's the alternative?"

Marie took a folded sheet from her apron pocket and laid it on the desk. He opened it. It was a computer printout announcing that students from St. Edmund's College were available for work of all sorts: snow removal, lawn care, baby-sitting, companions for the ill, house painting. The name of Rudy Berg was in caps with a phone number in even larger type.

"It looks year round. Except for the painting. That must be in summer."

"Of course it is. And they do a land-office business. I checked. We have to get on their list early."

"Student painters," he mused.

"Just my reaction. I checked that out too. They painted three houses in the parish, and I spoke to the people and went to look at one place."

"How did you know they had done that?"

"I called them."

And she had arranged for Rudy Berg to come by later in the day. He was faced with a fait accompli, and didn't mind it a bit. He had no independent views on house painting and was not anxious to acquire any.

"Have you signed the contract yet?"

"He'll bring it along."

"You got an estimate?"

"He will adjust it when he looks at the house."

"Well, that's settled."

"If you agree."

"I'll talk to Rudy."

"Good."

On the walk to the school from the rectory there was a junction with another walk coming from the church, and there, in a little wooded area, a grotto had been built. By one of the Franciscans, though Marie was reluctant to give credit. There was a little knot of seniors in conversation and one old man on the kneeler before the Madonna, beads in his hand. The center gave a chance to the retired in the parish to get together, sometimes say their prayers, and lie about their grandchildren. The conversation stopped, and three old ladies bobbed their heads at Father Dowling like schoolgirls. He bobbed in return and continued to the school.

In what had been the school gym a variety of games were being played: shuffleboard, darts, always a risky venture, and cards, with one table for the truly serious bridge players. More bobbing to the pastor as he went through. Up the wide staircase that had known the feet of hundreds of children, some of them now among the elderly in the gym, to Edna's office, once the principal's office.

"Father Dowling," she said, rising from her desk. "You're right on time."

Edna was an admirable woman, a wife and mother of three, whose husband, Earl, had run afoul of the law and was in Joliet. He and Edna would be old before Earl got out, their children grown, one of the sad facts of life that apparently no wishing could make go away. Earl had been convicted of manslaughter, but it was arguable that he had been guilty only in intention and not in fact. But he accepted his fate, feeling it just, and Edna had responded to Father Dowling's suggestion that she start a center for seniors, a therapeutic suggestion, with enthusiasm and success. The results had been far beyond anything he had imagined, and the position had brought Edna and her family back into the mainstream of the parish.

"Do you need any painting done around here?"

"Watercolors or oils?"

He laughed. "They will be painting the rectory next summer."

"No need of anything like that here." She paused. Her hands were flat on her desk. "I would like to add a little summer help here though. Someone to supervise the trips to the mall and help generally."

"Sounds reasonable."

"I thought Janet?" Janet was her daughter.

"Perfect."

Edna smiled and shook her head. "You've

been so good to us, Father."

"I think the benefit has gone in the other direction. How does she like St. Edmund's?"

"Why do they teach them about computers when kids already know all about them? It's the same thing in high school. Carl teaches the teacher. Now Janet says she wants to major in computer science. I suppose it's a practical choice."

"I hope she's learning some other things."

"She hates English."

"That's a shame."

"You should hear her stories. She has a fanatic named Cassirer and is trying to transfer out of the class. Anyway, I was thinking minimum wage, forty hours a week, is that okay?"

"Can't we do a little better than minimum wage?"

"Maybe later. Why don't we see how she does?"

"And it will be nice for you to have Janet here."

"Yes. To keep her out of harm's way."

She said nothing more, but it seemed a generic expression of parental concern. "I did take her to see her father."

Earl had been adamant that he did not want his children to see him as a prisoner, but Janet had been equally adamant. She had a right to see her father.

"How did it go?"

"Fine. You would have thought they had seen one another a week before instead of years ago. She is very much like him. I guess that explains it. Now the boys want to go."

"I was in prison and you visited me." But this was even more fundamental than that. The Hospers seemed to be benefitting from their adversity.

"How much longer?"

"Five years at least," she said in a small voice.

"Is there anything I can do?"

"You already have."

"Would you want me to look into it again?" He could drive to Joliet and talk with the chaplain, his classmate, and find out what chances he thought there might be for a parole. If he put Amos Cadbury on it . . .

Rudy Berg was six feet tall with a fat and happy face and enormous blue eyes. On his T-shirt was emblazoned Hire A Student and beneath that, Boss The Future Bosses. He wore baggy pants and sandals that seemed to have stirred old memories in Marie. But she was sticking by her man.

"This is Rudy Berg, Father."

A two-handed shake, and he dropped into a chair. "I've looked over the house, Father. And I think my estimate was a little high."

Behind him Marie beamed. Had she assisted his rethinking?

"Tell me about your group."

"We're all students at St. Edmund's; this is our second year. I'm contracting for more jobs every day. I'll be part of the crew here."

"So what year are you in?"

"I'm a junior. Major in accounting."

"I thought St. Edmund's was a liberal arts college."

"Oh, it's grown way beyond that in recent years. Far more practical than it was."

"And that's good?"

"If you hope to get a job, it is."

Father Dowling's own college years had been devoted to Latin and Greek, history and literature. If he hadn't become a priest what would it have prepared him for?

"When can you start?"

Rudy had a little notebook whose pages he flipped. "Mrs. Murkin has talked me into bumping you to the top of the list. Middle of May?"

"How long will it take?"

"Three to four days."

Marie said, "I've also talked with Rudy about the grotto."

"I'll go take a look at it. Can't say what that would run."

Marie said she had become concerned about the rocks that made up the grotto. Were they stable? The original cement holding them in place might have to be replaced. It sounded like rebuilding, but perhaps she was right.

"Let me know what you think."

Another warm handshake.

"Isn't there a contract?"

"I'll bring it Monday."

He shuffled toward the door. One of his sandals became loose, and he had to work his foot into it. "I don't work in these," he said apologetically.

"No one ever did," Marie said.

13

"The eagle has landed," Andrew had told Jessica, calling from the house, where he had taken Raymond. "He's with Mom."

"I thought you were going to take him to the hospital."

"He wanted to talk to Mom first. And since Dad is better . . ."

She thought of the page she had sent off to Thunder. How fair was it to write a novel that would be so clearly based on her brother? The fact is, Raymond was a stranger to her. When she grew up he was always away at school, studying for the priesthood. Summers he came home, but the difference in their ages made him seem an adult. And she was affected by her parents' near awe of the son who would become a priest. In retrospect, it seemed to her that Raymond had condescended to them. She and Andrew were children to her parents, but Raymond was treated almost as their senior. After his novitiate year, his visits home were much briefer but all the more festive because of that. An occasion. Raymond, the soon-to-be Edmundite priest.

Of course she had attended the college, and there was made aware of Father Raymond, already a big man in the Order, mover and shaker in the Edmundite part of the campus. He taught a course in the seminary, but his main task was supervising the training of the young men. She had felt a real if distant pride in him. From time to time, a professor would ask if she were any relation to Father Raymond Bernardo, and she benefited from his status. But in chemistry the Edmundites were less of a factor, and her teachers probably had only a vague notion of the relation of the college to the Order that had founded it. She loved the precision of lab work but from time to time would return to the sort of thing she had done in high school. Stories and poems came so easily she was sure they were no good. Andrew's reaction indicated otherwise.

"I didn't know you were working on these."

"Work? I just wrote them."

"Oh sure."

He never did believe how easily writing came to her. She began her first novel in senior year, a conscious balance to her major.

When she sent it off to a publisher, cold, she was ready for rejection, but she got a telephone call from the enthusiastic publisher.

"Look, this is your first book. You need representation. Can I suggest an agent?"

He suggested Thunder. "I wouldn't change a thing," Thunder said emphatically. "The book has freshness, naïveté, feeling."

"Are they really going to publish it?"

"They are. And you are going to write another and another and another and become famous. What exactly do you do? For a living? Or are you independently wealthy?"

"I work in a lab."

"A lab?"

She had just been hired by Sorensen's Lab but had not actually started. She wanted a little time after graduation to just vegetate. "A pathology lab."

"My God." But he was delighted. It would make unusual dust-jacket copy. "Just don't write any murder mysteries."

"I don't think I could."

"Don't even try. You have a real talent. I don't often gush like this."

He gushed in very blasé tones, and she developed an image of him that was shattered at their eventual meeting. He was five and a half feet tall, bald, with his glasses propped atop his head.

"Are you a mind reader?"

It took a minute, then he laughed. "Use that."

"I just did."

"In a story, in a story. It only counts if you write it down."

The novel appeared and did well, in the phrase, very well locally. She was taken up by the *Tribune*, and Leonard Bosch asked her to lunch. He was full of unwelcome advice. Quit the lab, get a fellowship to a writer's congress, start making the rounds of writers' meetings. He arranged for her to talk at the public library and covered it, as he put it, as if she were from out of town. She had no intention of quitting Sorensen's. What her first novel earned her would not have supported her for half a year, living lean. It was best to regard income from writing as a bonus.

She had found a message from Thunder on her phone when she got back from the hospital last night, leaving a number she was to call no matter when.

"Why isn't he here?" the old man demanded when Jessica told him Raymond had arrived.

"He wanted to be fresh."

"Ha."

"Daddy, it's jet lag. He flew all day against the clock."

"Does he think I'm not going to die?"

"Oh, don't say that," and Margaret tried to take him in her arms and he let her. Yesterday when her mother tried to do that he had pushed her back. He was still on IV, that was the excuse: She might dislodge the needle. Jessica found it cruel of him not to let her mother show her affection. Bernardos did not hold back but fought and cried and made up, living in the upper registers. At least that was true of her father. Was it true of her? She found that she did not want to see Raymond when her mother suggested she come to the house. Not yet. Was she reluctant to see the model of her proposed novel? She called the number Thunder had left. He sounded drunk.

"Bingo, my dear. Not that I am surprised. I was about to tell him I would not take less than fifty when he offered eighty."

"Eighty thousand!"

"Nonrefundable too, by God. A year ago he would have said who cares about a Catholic priest. Now it is hot."

The newspapers were full of clerical scandals, and Jessica did not know what to make of them. Whatever Raymond had done, he had not caused scandal of the sort that interested the media. The massive advance Thunder conveyed in tones of triumph seemed thirty pieces of silver. But she managed to sound delighted. He went on, congratulating himself for predicting this was her breakthrough novel. He didn't need scandals to see the importance of her story.

"When can you finish it?"

"I haven't really started it."

"Quit your job, write full time; there's no risk now."

"How soon does he want it?"

"He is begging me for a sample. No samples. Let him wait. You want to show me some early chapters, fine. I can use them to get started on foreign rights and the rest of it."

"Six months?"

"Can you do that?"

"If I can do it at all, I can do it in three months."

"You're wonderful!"

She did not feel wonderful when she hung up. She had just received unimaginably good news, and it was almost a letdown. For a possible novel she was being offered the moon. There was no one she could tell, certainly not Andrew; it would kill him. She knew how equivocally he reacted to her writing success when everything he touched turned to lead. She didn't want Raymond to know of the novel at all. Whatever happened with her father, he would go back to California and revert to his status as mythical presence in their lives.

She called Walter, and he assured her that everything had gone well on her day off.

"Oh good. It's nice to feel indispensable."

He was full of apologies; he hadn't meant that. She could have kicked herself for teasing him.

"My father is slightly better."

"Jessica, if you want to take tomorrow off . . ."

"No, no. There's no need."

"I've said it before. I'd do anything for you."

She wanted to cry at the one-sidedness of it all. Why couldn't she fall in love with good, old, dumb, smart Walter? She did not tell him of the good news Thunder had given her.

At the hospital Dr. Rocco had looked in at her father, and Jessica went with him into the hall.

"Is he out of danger?"

"Well, I'm returning him to intensive care."

"Is that an answer?"

He looked at her. How often did he have to give bad news? "I don't think he will leave the hospital alive."

She gasped. "How long?"

"I could give you a web site where you could look up prognoses. All predictions are averages in such cases. But take the best case, and it is bad."

"Does he know it?"

"He seems to be looking forward to it. Your father is a strange man." He looked down the hallway. Messages punctuated the air; there was the odor of medicine and of the sick. "Is he a religious man?"

"In a sense."

"Your mother is a saint."

"Yes, she is," Jessica said, after a moment, knowing it was true. Her mother lived the life she had as well as she could, and what more was there than that? Now, in her apartment, staring at the summary she had sent off to Thunder, she felt that the mother's part should be enlarged. Her mind began to work, and she switched screens and began to type.

There had been another message on her machine, from Eleanor, but she had forgotten it in the excitement of Thunder's news. Eleanor was someone else she could not tell her good news. Imagine, going to Father Dowling and asking him to stop her from writing a novel. Fortunately the pastor of St. Hilary's was too sensible a man to do anything of the kind.

She wrote for several hours with no sense of time, and afterward she was keyed up. She poured a glass of white wine, got into her pajamas, and turned on the television. Immediately she muted the sound; the schoolyard snickers of the late-night talk shows made her feel old. She searched the channels. No movies old enough to be called classics. She turned it off and sipped her wine.

She was thirty-one years old. She could never quite believe the age she was. She still felt like a girl. On the other hand, she felt ancient. Writing involves a kind of omniscience about one's characters that gives the illusion that one understands real people. Was there a single one of her friends or acquaintances she really knew? Does anyone understand anyone? If Raymond should try to explain to her why he had done what he had done, would he become intelligible to her? Only Andrew, in a long-distance call to California five years ago, had gotten anything like an explanation from Raymond:

Do you know the history of the last Tsar and his family? They were groomed for roles that ceased to exist. That is what the priesthood seemed to me. You've seen all the changes. It isn't the cruise I signed on for. And it will get worse. But the truly upsetting thing was that I ceased to believe in what I was doing when I said Mass.

"He lost his faith?"

"What else was he saying?"

That was the first time Jessica had been shocked by what Raymond had done. When Dr. Rocco had asked if her father was religious the answer she almost gave was that all Bernardos are religious. If her father had really lost his faith he could not have reacted as he did to Raymond's defection. He would have seen it as Raymond apparently did, as a shrewd career move. Now Raymond advised clients on a basis he could believe. As a priest he would have had to act as a hypocrite. That made running away with a pretty nun almost an imperative. But what Jessica found she could not comprehend was losing one's religious faith.

When she checked the messages on her phone — she had just let it ring while she worked — there was an angry call from Horst Cassirer. She erased it.

14

Eleanor could not find out whether Fulvio had prepared for death, arranged his papers, letters, burnt things. He just looked up at her from his bed when she asked.

"Are you worried?"

"Why should I worry?"

"You wrote such beautiful letters."

"You didn't keep them!"

"Do you think I would just toss them in the wastebasket?"

"You're saying that to annoy me."

"And what are you doing, coming to my deathbed with annoying questions?"

"You have to think of others."

"At the moment that is difficult."

"You're not serious about the letters."

His smile was almost a leer. "Wait and see."

"I know you destroyed them."

"Then you have nothing to fear."

What an infuriating man he was. He always had been. And yet it was with Fulvio that she was in love when she had married

Joseph, second best, a substitute. She wanted to be a member of the Bernardo family. They were everything she had always wanted: alive, always venting their emotions, fertile. All but Joseph as it turned out, but she had no children by Alfred either, so maybe the fault was hers. How different things would have been if she'd had children. She and Joe would have formed their own family circle and not been drawn into Fulvio's like bit players.

"Are you pregnant?" Fulvio would ask shamelessly in the first years of her marriage, and Eleanor's blush was his answer. "Maybe you ought to buy a manual."

"Stop it."

"Stop wishing that my sister-in-law should have children? Maybe I should show you how."

Her indignation was feigned. His vulgarity fascinated her. No, she told herself, not vulgarity. Fulvio was alive, vital, full of animal spirits. Joseph, a pharmacist, seemed to wear a white coat even when he took it off, measuring out their lives in precise doses. She was awkward with him in bed because he was awkward. But he was supposed to lead. It was like dancing.

"A vertical expression of a horizontal desire," Fulvio said when he swept her around the dance floor at family gatherings. They were usually held at the Vesuvio, owned by some cousin or other, giving them the run of the place, all stucco and bright paint and checkered tablecloths with candles in lamps. And wine. The wine flowed and Eleanor felt giddy.

"Are you pregnant?"

"It's this dress."

"You would have to prove that."

She was not herself when she was with him, or she was herself, which was probably truer. Joe didn't dance and urged her to stand up whenever Fulvio asked. Margaret was equally complacent, content to be a matron, smiling at the good time her family was having. She sipped one little glass of wine all evening.

"Maybe you're not getting enough," she said boldly to Fulvio.

"A man never gets enough." His expression warned her that Margaret was out of bounds in their kidding, if it was kidding. He held her so very tight when they danced, and she was aware of him against her, urgent, manly. A woman wants to be taken, swept off her feet, all the clichés. Joe drank mineral water and would give a lecture on its medicinal properties. When Fulvio brought her back to the table, he gripped her bottom as he stood there talking to his brother. What could she do, make a scene, accuse her brother-in-law? Everyone would think she was mad. Of course Fulvio was playful, and he was the head of the family.

Summer, when they all went together to the lake, was the dangerous time: far too many for the bedrooms, bodies sprawled everywhere. And during the day, on the beach, she was conscious of Fulvio's interest in her body. She had thought of him when she bought that bathing suit.

"You're not pregnant," he said.

He had a little boat and loved to sail. Joe never went near the water, reading on the porch, smoking his pipe, content to be by himself. Of course she should take up Fulvio's offer to teach her how to sail.

"He's the best sailor in the family."

"You should see my dinghy," he said, when she effused about the little boat. She knew she should not go out with him. There was an island, far out on the lake, that was his destination in the little boat. On their way there he was all business, tending to the sail, putting her at the tiller and expecting her to understand and execute his orders. It was silly to be concerned about so absorbing an occupation, and there was the family back there on the shore. What could happen?

What could happen did happen, on the island, out of sight of the cabin, though it would have taken binoculars to see anything from that distance. As soon as they pulled the boat up on the sand of a little cove everything was predestined. This was an assignation, and it was far too late to protest. He laid a blanket on the sand, and then he laid her on the blanket and she closed her eyes, turned off her conscience, and knew what she had not known on her wedding night or any night since. He kissed her eyes afterward and patted her behind.

"Don't get pregnant."

"I thought that was the idea."

Years of deception began, years of humiliation. Once she had succumbed his manner changed; nothing overt, it was just that he no longer wooed her and of course took her for granted. A woman who has been unfaithful once will do it again. If the woman was Eleanor, this was true. Why? Fulvio lost much of his magic once she had yielded to him, but what he gained was the elemental fact that with him she became fully a woman. But she did not become pregnant. She half hoped she would and lured a puzzled Joe off to bed several times as an insurance policy. Any child would look like a Bernardo and that was enough. But for all his joking about her getting pregnant before they had sailed to the island, she was unsure what Fulvio's reaction would be. It was never put to the test. Eleanor attributed it to a psychological bloc on her part, however physically abandoned she was with him. And she wrote him letters.

Stupid, girlish, long letters that she needed to write more than he needed to read, if he ever did read them all the way through. It was a compulsion, as if she wanted to have the case against herself down in blue ink on pink paper. How many letters had there been? Dozens. Eleanor froze in embarrassment now at the thought of anyone finding them. It was largely the thought of Jessica finding them that had taken her to Father Dowling. But she could not even learn if they were still in existence.

"I worry about your mother," she said to Jessica.

"She'll be all right."

"That's easy to say. Remember, I've been there before. Twice. A widow is never ready for all the practical decisions she has to make. Your mother never took care of the checkbook, did she?"

"No."

"Fulvio paid the bills."

"I guess so."

"And then there are insurance policies, burial plots, monuments . . ."

"Eleanor, we will help her, Andrew and I."

"You have about as much experience as she does."

"So what's the answer?"

Eleanor paused. "Oh, you're probably right. She'll do just fine. She always has. But someone should find out if your father has all his affairs in order, to make it easier for her."

"I'll ask him."

"If you'd like I could make an inventory."

"Now?"

"I've been there before."

"That's the last line in *Huckleberry Finn*."

"What a curious girl you are, Jessica."

"Girl?" Jessica squealed, and kissed Eleanor on the cheek. "I am in my fourth decade."

"You are not!"

"I am thirty-one."

"Well, put it that way, for heaven's sake, if you have to mention it at all. And don't forget my offer."

"Offer?"

"The inventory."

15

Andrew had let Raymond know what the problem was. "He refuses to see a priest. Imagine Mom's reaction to that."

The hospital chaplain had dropped by after Father Dowling had struck out.

"He ordered him from the room. She's counting on you."

"Me."

"A big reconciliation, you know."

The reunion with his mother had been easy. He took her in his arms, and wordlessly they were reconciled. No questions, no accusations, her son was home in a moment of crisis, and she thanked God for it. He hadn't remembered how cluttered the house was with religious bric-a-brac, statues, paintings with vigil lights flickering before them, his mother's rosaries everywhere. Or was it just the absence of such things from his own place, his and Phyllis's? Entering the house in which he had been raised, sleeping in his old room that night, everything he had been seemed to return. Of course he believed all these things. Lying in the dark, on his back, he raised his right arm and tried to make the sign of the cross, but his hand would not move to his forehead in order to begin. Was this superstition in reverse? Recent years seemed less real than memories of his boyhood. It was in this house that Father Bourke had made such a great impression on his father, as he had earlier on Raymond.

I shouldn't have come. Now that he was here, the urgency had drained from the whole scene. Andrew all but apologized for the panicky message he had left on the machine.

"You'll have to go," Phyllis had said when they'd listened to it several times as if seeking for some escape clause.

"Would you?"

"I have no living parents."

"You have me."

"Yes, Daddy."

There was always the erotic to fall back on. What was their creed except pleasure now, pain never, be positive, and don't think about dying? Had sex once seemed the meaning of it all? The difficulty was that the pleasure principle demanded variety, impermanence, no binding ties. No, that

145

wasn't true, not for real people. "If sex were all, then any hand could make us squeak like dolls the wished for words." He had often used that line of Wallace Stevens's with patients. He and Phyllis were bound together by what they had fled, but the power of that to haunt had lessened; hence Julia, maybe. Did Phyllis think he needed a new load of guilt in order to find her his indispensable cohort?

When he came down in the morning, his mother wasn't there. Gone to Mass. My God, it's Sunday. Would he have gone with her if she had asked? He told himself he would have. But she would have gone to communion and expected him to. Or would she? What exactly did she imagine his status was?

"We can go see Dad after breakfast," she said, when she bustled in, taking the green babushka from her head. He imagined that the smell of the church clung to her.

"I'm starved."

"You should have made your breakfast."

He hugged her. "I wasn't complaining of the service."

"You'll have to drive."

"You still don't drive?"

"What's the need?"

"When you have me for a chauffeur, none

146

at all. The house doesn't seem to have changed a bit."

"I hope not." She put on coffee, began bacon and eggs. "I want it to stay just as it was when you kids were here."

"I was always away at school."

"That isn't how I remember it."

Again he took her in his arms. My God, how good she was. Not even her expression betrayed what she must think of him. What he could too easily imagine they all thought of him now that he was back in the gray world of Fox River. Was there really less color? It was the sense of being shut in, indoors.

"How I've missed you, Mom."

It just came out, and it seemed the first genuine thing he had said in years. I love my mother. I love this self-effacing little woman, busy in her kitchen, whose heart I have broken and who will not break mine by letting me know it. He spoke into her hair.

"I didn't know how to explain."

"Would I have understood?"

"I could have tried."

"You must hug your father and speak like this to him."

As if it could possibly be the same. "I'll try."

"He'll make it hard. Raymond, he hasn't

147

been to church in years."

"Because of me."

"What kind of a reason is that?"

She wouldn't blame him even for that.

"Will you talk to him, son?"

"Why else am I here?"

The family car was ten years old and had twenty thousand miles on it. Keep it another ten and it would become a classic and double in value. He had to follow her directions, and since she never drove they were hard to follow.

"I never pay attention when your father's driving."

The hospital looked dingy, no place you'd want the ambulance to take you from a tollway accident. He left her at the front entrance while he parked the car. She waited for him and took his arm as they went inside.

"He was so rude to Father Cronin, the chaplain."

Raymond had not known many local priests who were in the archdiocese of Chicago. His clerical circle had been Edmundites, and they had never been big for ecumenical relations with the secular clergy. There was no reason to think he would know Cronin. He didn't know Father

Dowling either. They just went up to the room, no need to get permission, and then they were there.

He followed his mother in. His father was in a bed placed almost in the center of the room, lots of space on both sides, windows at head and foot, on the wall a crucifix behind which was stuck a dry piece of palm. A Catholic hospital. But the art of medicine is neutral, areligious. He realized he was looking into his father's eyes. He put his hand on his father's arm and patted it. His mother stepped back. He was being examined now as he had not been by his mother. She left the room.

"Well, you look good."

"I wish I could say the same."

"I'm a goner."

"I don't believe it. If you do, maybe you shouldn't have thrown the chaplain out."

His father's eyes fixed on him. Waiting.

"Talk to him, Dad."

"Why?"

"Just talk to him."

"That isn't why he wants to see me."

"Do it for Mom."

"Not for you?"

"Do it for yourself."

"Do you mean that?"

The time had come to lie, but he found

he just couldn't, not even now. It had all slipped away, the creed dissolving article by article, repealing the early councils, receding into past quarrels that no longer made any sense to him. It was unreal. He had not thought of it, not really, for years, but it seemed part of the gritty atmosphere of Fox River. Still, he could remember believing here as he could not in California.

"Have you ever heard of Pascal's bet?"

His father did not encourage him. He told him anyway. Either Christianity is true and accepting it gains you eternal bliss, or it is not true and you will never know it. "You can't lose; that's the idea."

"That argument should have kept you here."

"Let the chaplain talk to you. Whatever happens, happens. For Mom."

The first try at a smile, and he realized his father did not have his dentures in. How it robbed him of authority, made him old. The hand with the tube stuck in it moved on the sheet. How gray his skin was, stubble on his face, hair just sprouting from the head, a pattern of freckles on the skull. Memento mori. This is how he would look one day, even in California.

"Are you in any pain?"

"Why don't you give me absolution, Ray?"

The request shocked him. The old man wanted him to act the role of priest.

"You want to go to confession?"

"Only to you."

"You never did that before."

"Things were different before. You can't refuse me. I am a dying man."

"Priests are getting in line to see you."

"You're my priest."

"Are you sorry for your sins?"

For a moment the old man looked frightened. Was he counting on being refused? Raymond felt a slight advantage. "Let me get the chaplain."

"No!"

"You want a stranger as your confessor, not your son."

"You've become a stranger."

"You had no trouble recognizing me."

"I have thought of you every day." Tears filled his eyes and ran down the side of his face. Raymond wiped them away. Here was a small sign of the pain he had caused, the knife he had slipped between his father's ribs. How had he learned that his son was gone, off to the West Coast with a nun from campus ministry? What a cliché it seemed. Had they called and asked for him and learned like that? It seemed awful that he had not told them and had no way of knowing how they had gotten the news. The Order could have put out a bulletin claiming the car was missing; they could have stopped payment on the credit card. That would have been scandal enough to make the papers. But everyone had been so damned good about it, everyone but himself. He leaned over the bed and kissed his father's forehead. As he lifted slowly away the eyes stopped him.

"Judas," his father whispered.

16

Father Dowling, in his study, picked up the phone and called Cronin, the hospital chaplain. He was paged, and when he came on seemed to be speaking in an echo chamber.

"Roger Dowling. Any luck with Fulvio Bernardo?"

"Nope. The son Raymond has been in to see him." A pause but not silence, crowd noises, garbled announcements. "Nothing doing there either."

"Did you talk with him?"

"The son? No. Mrs. Bernardo told me. That was yesterday."

He thanked the chaplain and left him to his busy rounds. Men like Cronin were what made the whole thing work, priests going about their jobs, doing what they could. But Cronin seemed to have had the hope drained out of him.

But there were more proximate concerns for the pastor of St. Hilary's. It seemed a morning to telephone chaplains. He put through a call to Joliet and got Mike Dolan's answering machine. After the beep he said who was calling and that he would like to talk with Mike about Earl Hospers. Almost immediately, Mike came on the line.

"Roger, how are you?"

"Is this still a machine?"

His classmate laughed. "I use it for caller I.D."

"Avoiding bill collectors?"

"No, parole officers. I dread hearing that one of the boys has misbehaved and is being sent back to serve out his full sentence. What about Earl Hospers?"

"Mike, you must know that technically he is innocent."

"He wouldn't be here if he weren't. All my boys are innocent."

"Tell me his status."

"He is one man I would really like to see leave here. Prison is not exactly a school of virtue, you know, but I think he has really become a better person for being here."

"So what about parole?"

"The board expects me to plead for the applicant, of course. And I could be eloquent in Earl's behalf. But he has the nutty idea he should serve the time he was given."

"That's pretty hard on his wife and kids."

"Well, it's no picnic for him either. Have you talked to him about it?"

"First I wanted to have a better idea of what's possible and what I might do."

Mike Dolan sounded more like a lawyer than a priest during the five-minute disquisition that followed. Earl had never gone before the board, which in its way was an advantage. There was no previous refusal.

"He needs a good lawyer, Roger. But there isn't much point if Earl won't play ball."

"What if I came down and had a talk with him?"

"Anytime. I'll set it up."

"Today?"

"You are serious, aren't you?"

All the more serious because he felt he had been delinquent in the matter. He told Mike he would be there in a few hours.

"I'll skip my nap."

He said the noon Mass and afterward asked Marie to make him a sandwich.

"A sandwich!"

"To eat on the trip."

"The trip? Are you leaving?" In Marie's eyes danced the dreadful possibility that the bishop had called, Father Dowling would be reassigned, the Franciscans would return.

"No, no, it isn't that. I'm going to see a classmate."

Her manner changed. Marie often expressed concern for what she considered the excessive solitude of the pastor. How could he explain to her that there was nothing he preferred to the parish? His assignment there had been widely regarded as consignment to Siberia, all the bright hopes of his ecclesiastical career dashed when he had crumbled under the pressure of the marriage court and had sought solace in drink. Eventually that had led to the stay in Wisconsin, where his pride was put to the severest test. Did he really belong there among the other casualties of the priesthood? Learning to answer that question affirmatively had been the beginning of his recovery. When he emerged and had his interview with one of the auxiliaries, the sense of humiliation returned, but he almost welcomed it now.

"St. Hilary's in Fox River is open. The Franciscans have been running it, but they are pulling out."

"Fox River."

"Do you know it?"

"Not yet."

Bishop Brizec beamed. "So you'll take it?"

"Gladly."

"Roger, I can't tell you how sorry I am that things have turned out this way for you." The bishop's face was a mask of anguish as he thought of himself in Roger's shoes. Once it had been tacitly understood that Roger was destined to be in such shoes as Brizec wore, an auxiliary, putting in a few more years in Chicago, then a diocese of his own. Now Roger felt that he had escaped that fate.

Within months in Fox River he had shed the notion that he was in exile and disgrace. St. Hilary's provided all the scope he needed to fulfill his priesthood and save his soul.

So content with his lot had he become that it almost took an effort to get into his car and set off for Joliet. Even a day away from the rectory, other than on his monthly day of recollection with the Athanasians, seemed a species of desertion. But he was on parish business, not on a lark. There was a four-lane highway dropping southward like a plumb line from Fox River, and the drive took scarcely an hour, but it was long enough for him to ponder the different lives his classmates led. Mike Dolan had been a very good student but begged off when the prospect of further study was offered him after ordination. He had been assistant here and there, and when the time came that he was eligible for a parish of his own, the chaplaincy at Joliet opened and he applied for it.

"They thought I was crazy," he said to Roger, when they spoke of this.

Roger had been let through the gate, parked his car in the parking lot, and been escorted to Mike Dolan's office.

Roger Dowling had assumed that Mike would want to indulge in a little clerical gossip before they got down to business, but to his surprise Earl Hospers was with the chaplain.

"I'll leave you two," Mike said. "We can talk later, Roger."

Earl rose and shook Father Dowling's hand. "I can't thank you enough for what you've done for Edna and the kids."

This was not the woebegone young man who had stood trial. Mike had said that Earl had become a better man in prison, and Father Dowling believed it. Physically he was trim, and calm resignation occupied his deep-sunk eyes, the wisdom of one who was expiating his sins.

"There's something else I'd like to do. I want you to apply for parole."

"I'd be turned down."

"How do you know that?"

"Because I should be. This isn't as bad as it sounds."

"Isn't it? Your family needs you, Earl. It's worth a risk. There's nothing to lose."

"I don't want to beg."

Roger Dowling smiled. "Is it all right with you if I talk to a lawyer about your case? Mr. Amos Cadbury."

"Cadbury? How could I afford someone like him?"

"He may be more reasonable than you think. Do I have your permission?"

Earl looked out the window at the expanse of sky beyond, at freedom. "My permission? Father, there isn't anything I wouldn't do for you."

How easily it was settled. They talked for half an hour, Father Dowling describing the great job Edna was doing in the center.

"Janet will work with her next summer."

Earl's eyes grew moist as they talked of the wife and children from whom he was separated.

"About a parole, Father. I don't really expect it."

"We'll see."

"I don't want Edna to get her hopes up."

But Edna too had toughened and grown during these awful years of separation.

"She can handle anything."

There were tears in Earl's eyes. "She is the best thing that ever happened to me. When I think what I have done to her . . ."

"You must know that she does not blame you."

"That's the hardest part."

Afterward Mike Dolan wanted to hear about St. Hilary's, but he had another interest as well. "What do you know about the Athanasians, Roger? I'm told Marygrove is a good place to make a retreat."

"It's where I made mine last year. And intend to again this year."

"I thought they were dead in the water."

"Don't you believe it."

"Maybe it was the Edmundites."

17

Jessica came to the hospital on Sunday straight from Mass and stopped in the restaurant off the lobby to pick up a roll and container of coffee before going upstairs. She met Raymond in the hallway as he was coming out of her father's room. He looked stricken.

"Raymond?"

He stared at her a moment before recognizing her, and his expression changed into a California one. She hesitated but he did not, taking her in his arms. He said as he held her, "That was bad."

"What happened?"

"Later."

If ever. "How like Dad you look."

"Do I?" He stepped back. "You look just like you."

"Come on, you didn't recognize me at first."

"Jet lag."

They found their mother in the waiting room, sitting with her eyes closed, a rosary in her hands. When she opened her eyes and looked at Raymond she saw at once that her prayers had not been answered.

"He's being stubborn, Mom. That's all."

Of course she knew better. "What did happen?" Jessica asked.

"He wanted me to hear his confession."

"Could you do that?"

"I told him I'd have to get in line; there were several others before me."

"They won't be able to do a thing," Margaret said. She got to her feet. "I'll go in to him."

"I'll be along in a minute, Mom," Jessica said. When they were alone, she asked him, "Could you do that, hear his confession?"

"Technically."

"Do you lose the power or what?"

"Something like that. The exercise anyway."

"Then do it, Ray. For Mom."

He smiled at her. "It doesn't even require that I believe in what I am doing."

"Ex opere operato."

"How on earth did you know that?"

"I'm researching a story."

She almost hoped he would ask about it, but he only said, "We have a lot of catching up to do."

162

"I want to hear all about California."

"Not all."

"What you do, how you live, everything like that."

"My favorite subject."

"Do you have pictures of Phyllis?"

"No. Does that sound awful? We've never been apart. I do have her photograph on the desk in my office."

"What's she like?"

"What have you heard of her?"

"That she was a nun. And you were a priest."

The expression he had worn coming from her father's room was back. "Raymond, I didn't mean . . ."

"I know. Everyone is so damned kind. Except Dad."

Leaving together as they had spared him and Phyllis experience of the shock they had caused. Was this the first time he had confronted anyone who thought he had done something awful?

"Is that coffee?" The container had cooled in her hand.

"I got it downstairs."

"Come with me so I can get some."

"Didn't Mom feed you?"

"That has to be a rhetorical question."

They went down in the elevator in silence.

This was so different from being with Andrew; with Andrew she always felt a little edge of resentment. Raymond was such a different kind of brother, tall, good looking, tan. And dressed about a season off for Chicago.

The cafeteria had been almost empty when she stopped there; now they had to get in line, no skipping places just for coffee.

He leaned toward her and whispered, "Everyone is so fat."

"I'm not."

"No, you're not. You've become a beautiful young woman."

No flattery, just an observation. She found that she liked him. Of course she felt sorry for him, too, having seen what the visit to her father had done to him.

Eventually they got coffee, he paid, and they took a little table that looked onto the parking lot and the entrance to Emergency. Half the customers in the cafeteria wore hospital garb. Outside were smokers, all in hospital garb.

"I'm surprised they allow it."

"You don't smoke?"

"Not for years. Do you?"

"Only when lit." A stupid remark, a blush spread over her face, and she frowned at the smokers out in the cold, killing themselves in stages.

"In the seminary in those days, everyone smoked. I suppose it was like the service."

"Do you miss it?"

"Smoking?"

"All of it."

"You ask very direct questions."

"And fail to get an answer."

"What story are you writing that required you to find out about *ex opere operato?*"

"Oh I don't want to talk about me. I want to hear about California."

He decided she meant it and proceeded to describe the house in Thousand Oaks, the offices he and Phyllis had, their clientele.

"What are they, crazies?"

"No. Normal enough. Full of self-loathing and guilt."

"From what?"

"Usually sex."

"It sounds like hearing confessions."

"Well, it isn't *ex opere operato,* no inevitable results."

"So what do you tell them?"

"What they want to hear, mainly. Sometimes I think Phyllis and I are charlatans. There are many who would find it odd that we should be telling others how to live their lives."

"Doesn't a priest hearing confessions feel that way?"

"But he's not acting in his own name."

"So hear Dad's confession. You can do it. It would be such a relief to Mom."

"Jessica, it's just his way of blackmailing me. It's a bargain. He goes to confession and I . . ." He made a face. "What a godawful conversation to be having when we haven't seen one another in years."

"Did you miss us?"

"You don't forget your family."

"That sounds as if you tried."

"I did. I had a lot of forgetting to do."

"Have you ever regretted going?"

Again he made a face. "You'll end up writing a book about me."

"Did you ever read my novels?"

"Yes."

"Well?"

"The dust-jacket praise is deserved. I marveled at your ability to tell a story so movingly."

She definitely liked him.

"Are we going to spend the day here?" he asked.

"Andrew will come at noon, then you and I can go."

"Mom?"

"She'll stay of course."

166

"Andrew went on and on about academic politics at St. Edmund's."

"Trouble in paradise."

He laughed. "That's what we called our residence there. Paradiso."

During the next several hours Jessica fluctuated between wanting to abandon her novel and being determined to write it. Being with Raymond made it a more vivid idea. If he hadn't come home, if she hadn't had the chance to talk to him, her character would have been very different, black and white. *Tout comprendre est tout pardonner.* Would he go out to St. Edmund's and see old friends? The thought seemed to alarm him. "They might be more unforgiving than Dad."

"Are you in touch with any of your old friends in the Order?"

"No."

What an odd man he was. Was it possible simply to walk away from one's life, to tell no one he was going, never contact his family or his friends? How could one escape the memories that brought the past into the present willy-nilly?

"Latin was one of my favorite subjects," she said apropos of nothing, and everything.

"It lost its significance in the Church, but I loved it too."

"Horace?"

"Livy was more to my taste. My teacher for Horace was a bore. He seemed always to fear we would catch him in a mistake."

"Maybe it's because I've only read him on my own. It's not just the odes; he is a collection of pithy phrases."

"Such as?"

"*Dimidium animae meae. Non omnis moriar.* Are you testing me?"

"Jessica, if there is one thing I am sure of it is that you would not pretend."

But she felt she was pretending with him. It was undeniably moving to be reunited with the older brother she had never really known, but it was equally undeniable that she was studying him with an eye to her novel. He was forty-one, he had been gone almost a decade. How long had he been active as a priest, half a dozen years?

"I count all the years, from the time I entered the novitiate."

"What happened?"

He looked at her. "I don't want to shock you."

"You won't." Was there some lurid story to be told?

"I lost my faith."

"How do you mean?"

"It was as sudden as some conversions. Gaining and losing faith have a lot in common. One day while saying Mass I realized that I did not believe that the words of consecration made any difference. What was bread and wine before was still bread and wine."

"Just like that?"

"That is how it seemed to me then. It still does. Maybe things led up to it, but I don't think so." He tipped his head. "Phyllis came after, not before." But he looked away when he said it.

"But what you believed was a miracle already. You couldn't have been surprised at what consecration means."

"The Eucharist is so central to it all that if belief in it goes everything goes. Losing faith in it destroyed my sense of the priesthood, and with the priesthood go the bishops who ordain and the apostles from whom they descend and the whole tradition of the teaching Church. I had a greater sense of its coherence when I lost it than when I had it."

"And you couldn't pretend?"

"Could you?"

"No."

"That's why I can't do what Dad asks. Even if I thought he was sincere about it, I couldn't do it. Of course if it's all true, then what I believe or don't believe would not vitiate the deed. But you know that."

What a nice smile he had. "What did Dad say when you refused him?"

Again the abject expression he had worn when he came out of their father's room.

"He called me Judas."

18

"Can your father receive visitors now?" Gloria asked, her pretty mouth a pout, avoiding his eyes.

Andrew looked at her. Only those we know can be such strangers. Gloria was miffed that, at this critical moment, he had excluded her from the drama of his father's illness. Did she expect him to show up at his dying father's bedside with her on his arm? Apparently she did. She had never met his father. On the one occasion she had come with him to his parents' home, only his mother had been there, and the consideration she had shown Gloria told him that she had guessed their secret. Secret? Of course it was a secret, and suddenly a source of shame.

"So you are in the same building?" his mother had said, when she had asked Gloria where she lived.

Gloria glanced at him, and he gave a little shake of his head. But then he caught his mother's eyes and saw that she was not deceived. How must what the world had become strike her, men and women living together without benefit of clergy, their cohabitation having nothing to do with the biological purposes of gender? He had wanted to erect a buffer between this self-effacing, good woman and the mores of the time. Her son the priest had deserted his vocation and gone off to California with a nun; her only daughter worked in a pathologist's lab, wrote novels the old woman could not understand, and showed no signs of settling down and marrying. That he himself added to the cross she bore filled him with a desire to flee, but of course she insisted they must have something to eat, wait for his father, pretend that Gloria was just a friend of his who happened to be with him when he stopped to say hello to his mother.

That had been two months ago, and nothing had been quite the same between him and Gloria since.

"Why didn't you tell her?" Gloria had asked with that prelapsarian innocence that explained in large part her attraction for him. His residual conscience had no counterpart in her; he had never detected the slightest indication that she regarded their living together as in any way at odds with the way things ought to be. How had he drifted into their arrangement? *Drift* seemed to be the right word; he could recall no agony of decision when the practical advantage of their sharing an apartment had arisen.

"She wouldn't understand."

"Andrew, she knows."

"Did she say something?"

"She didn't have to."

"So what's the point?"

"Are you ashamed of me?"

This was in the car after they had driven away from his parents' house. For answer, he had turned the car around and headed back to the house.

"What are you doing?"

"If you want me to tell her, we will."

"Oh, don't be silly."

"Are you ashamed of me?"

Her question, redirected, made her laugh. She took his arm and moved closer against him.

"Let's go home, you idiot."

Victory of a sort, but from that visit she had understood what he really thought of their living together. That a man should find irresistible the prospect of having a live-in girlfriend was no mystery, but that a woman whose body was the perpetual possibility of pregnancy should agree to it was something else.

"Let's get married," he said.

"Married!"

She had received tenure the previous spring, she was a member of the faculty senate, her rewritten dissertation was scheduled for publication, and she had already cannibalized it for a number of articles in historical journals. She had defined herself as an academic, and living with him was sufficient concession to the urges of the flesh. It was clear as could be that she had no intention of having children. Even if she had, the category of single parent would have been sufficient for her. Graduate school and academic politics had made her a foe of bourgeois standards. Her contempt for the past and its vision of life was odd in an historian. What could marriage add to what they already had? Did she imagine the two of them growing old together, sharing a bed and campus gossip, busy with their separate careers, living happily ever after? But the future seemed as uninteresting to her as the past.

He thought these thoughts and hated himself for them. He was trying to heap on her the guilt he had felt when his eyes met his mother's. He knew how those old eyes would view the life he led. And he knew he shared her judgment on it.

174

"Sometimes I think I am exploiting you."

"I don't know what you mean. I thought it was mutual."

"Mutual *exploitation?*"

"That's your word."

She had no counterpart of his mother. Her own had engaged in serial matrimony, something Gloria professed to despise.

"She has no notion of herself except as attached to a man."

Which meant that Gloria's attachment to him was only incidental to what she was. The one thing they had never discussed before he moved his things into her apartment — hers was larger than the one he'd had and there was no question which could accommodate them both — was an exit strategy. In theory, at least, marriage ruled out an exit. Divorce would have been easier than any decision to move out of her apartment. Their apartment.

The following weekend they had flown to New York, where she was to read a paper at a meeting of historians and they could avail themselves of the excitement of the city. Such flights from the ordinary were the seasoning of their lives, sharing a hotel room more illicit than their shared apartment in Fox River. His parents' ignorance of their living together was something else they couldn't talk about, like Horst Cassirer, whom Gloria professed to admire. The visit to his parents' home had been a revelation to her, and she saw how he regarded their life together. He knew this, not because she said anything, but because she hadn't. Until her question about visiting his father in the hospital.

"Would you like to come along?"

"I don't know. What do you think?"

He ostensibly gave it thought. "Maybe later. If he continues to get better."

She seemed relieved. She did not really want to visit a dying man in the hospital.

Aunt Eleanor had met Gloria, and it was clear from the outset that she understood and, being Eleanor, had to let him know that she knew.

"Of course your parents don't know."

Andrew just smiled at her.

"It would kill them."

He was damned if he would discuss it with her. Eleanor's status in the family was in one way clear and in others obscure. Her marriage to Uncle Joe had made her one of them, and her remarriage hadn't weakened her obvious assumption that she remained a Bernardo. They all joked about Eleanor; she had become a caricature of the maiden aunt despite her twice widowed status. She seemed to regard herself as the guardian angel of the family. So it was not surprising that she fussed about how Margaret could possibly cope if something happened to Fulvio.

"I've talked with Jessica about it, and it was suggested that someone ought to make sure that everything is in order. Of course you're no more practical than your mother, Andrew. I myself am perfectly willing to put order into his papers."

"That would be up to my mother."

"But what do you think?"

"I am sure that Dad's affairs are in apple pie order."

"Isn't that an odd phrase? You have to understand that I have experience in such matters. I have been through it twice."

"You want to check out his financial affairs?"

"No, of course not. I was thinking of his papers. Letters, that sort of thing. It is unbelievable how things accumulate."

"I'm sure my mother would appreciate any help you could give her."

Eleanor squeezed his hand. "I will tell her you said so. And, Andrew?"

"Yes."

"I wouldn't burden your parents with any revelations about Gloria."

For years, Andrew had resented what Raymond had done, seeing what it did to their father, but in some ways he was glad to have his older brother fall off his pedestal. Raymond had always been the standard the rest of them fell short of, but his defection had changed all that, at least with his father. He was certain his mother would say nothing to his father about Gloria, but even if she had it would not have figured as high on Fulvio's scale of disillusionment. He might in his way approve. The old man had always had a flirty manner, pawing ladies, even Aunt Eleanor. Had there ever been anything more?

When he met Raymond's plane, when for the first time in years they had talked, Andrew resolved not to let his brother know about Gloria. It wasn't that he thought Raymond would be shocked. It would be worse than that. He would no longer be able to generate in Raymond the uneasiness he sensed on the way from O'Hare. The fact that Raymond had wanted to go home, to see their mother first, obviously postponing the confrontation with Fulvio, made it clear that Raymond recognized his own role of pariah. He did tell Raymond about Cassirer, babbling away like an idiot, wishing he could shut up about it.

It was at Raymond's suggestion that he had applied for a position at the college, and it was clear that the way had been smoothed for him by his brother. The Edmundites still had clout in the college then, and the suggestion that hiring Andrew would be smiled on by the order weighed heavily in his favor.

"I don't have a Ph.D."

"No boasting, please."

But if that hadn't mattered to Raymond it mattered to him. From the beginning he felt at a disadvantage, and his desperate efforts to publish fiction had been meant to be an ex post facto vindication of his appointment. His miserable publication record had increased his sense that he was the benefactor of academic nepotism. Cassirer had spoken more truly than he realized when he said that Andrew felt threatened by his younger colleague's self-esteem. However overblown it was, it was not without an objective basis. And Cassirer was a bone of contention between him and Gloria, who was a stickler for academic protocol.

"You didn't have anything to do with the students writing those things in the *Monitor*, did you?" Gloria asked.

"Good Lord no. You must know what the students think of him. They wouldn't need any prompting to respond to his ridiculous piece."

"Ridiculous?"

"Don't you think so?"

"Andrew, he has a point. The deadwood on the faculty resent someone as ambitious as Horst. It is a mediocre bunch."

He felt included in the bunch.

"He won't take no for an answer. I've heard he has hired a lawyer."

Andrew had not told Gloria of Tuttle's visit to his office. Nor that Cassirer considered him the major foe of his application.

"How will the vote go?"

He cocked his head. "If I violated the confidentiality of the committee he would have reason to complain."

"Someone already has. He knows the outcome of the straw vote."

"Have you talked with him?"

"He talked to me."

It occurred to him that Cassirer could easily discover their living arrangements, which, technically speaking, ran afoul of the faculty manual. For the first time, Andrew realized how vulnerable he might be if Cassirer decided to deploy the full artillery available to him. When he mentioned the possibility to Gloria, she fumed.

"I wish he would make an issue of it. We

180

could get a lawyer of our own and fight it. It is ridiculous that the college still insists on these medieval notions while pretending to be a bona fide academic institution."

"That's not a battle we need."

"Andrew, it's not just us. The point should be made for the entire faculty."

"Would you want us discussed in the faculty senate?"

Her eyes sparked. "I would love it."

19

Anne Gogarty scheduled the meeting of the Appointments and Tenure Committee of the English Department in a seminar room in the library, an unusual venue, but Cassirer's campaign to intimidate the committee was unprecedented, and it seemed wise not to gather in the office of the chair in the Arts & Letters Building.

"He'll call it a rump meeting when he hears," Andrew said to her.

"Well, the subject is an ass."

Any pretense of neutrality had long since deserted the little committee that held Horst Cassirer's fate in their elected hands. Anne had told Andrew of the provost's eagerness to get rid of Cassirer.

"Does Holder feel threatened?"

"We all do." A little cupid smile. Anne was the kind of girl he should have: bright, feminine, serviceable good looks. Of course she was married and had two children. With a shock he realized that she reminded him of his mother, an updated version, but nonetheless. Gloria was a lot more like his Aunt Eleanor, and a lot less.

Lily St. Clair entered, avoiding everyone's eyes, her unlipsticked mouth a severe line in her hawklike face. She joined Zalinski on the opposite side of the table to Andrew. Zalinski had been ostentatiously reading student papers since sitting down, groaning as he did so, and making savage marks on the pages he disdainfully flipped through.

"They don't know English," he cried.

"Well, whose fault is that?" Anne said, squaring the papers before her. "We're the English department."

"My God, it's their mother tongue."

Lily seemed inclined to take this as an assault on her gender, but let it go. Mike Pistoia, hunched shoulders, bald, wearing a baggy corduroy jacket, looked in, looked around, entered. When he sat next to Andrew, Anne called the meeting to order.

"First, I'll distribute the external reviews. They are all quite favorable."

"Of course," Lily said.

Zalinski dropped his student papers on the floor and took his copies of the letters. Andrew too began to read them. Someone from somewhere called Rowan University asserted that Horst Cassirer was the white hope of criticism in the United States.

"They were in graduate school together," Lily murmured.

A second letter was from the editor of *Theseus*, praising the pieces of Cassirer's he had accepted for publication.

"He could scarcely trash them," Pistoia observed.

"No one could trash them," Zalinski said.

It was agreed that Horst Cassirer was a formidable scholar and that his work was recognized as superior by his peers in his chosen specialty.

"There are, however, three major criteria for promotion; scholarship is only one. The other two are teaching and collegiality."

Anne had laid the grounds for the subsequent quarrel, which went on for an hour and a half, Lily and Zalinski arguing that scholarship trumped the other two, Pistoia reminding them that St. Edmund's was not a research university but a college whose principal task was the instruction of its students. Cassirer's hapless record as a teacher could not be ignored. Letters to the student paper from his indignant students in response to Cassirer's screed were part of his dossier.

"An orchestrated campaign," Lily said, looking meaningfully at Andrew.

"Odd. That is Cassirer's phrase. He

seemed to know all about our last meeting, incidentally." And Andrew in turn looked meaningfully at Lily. Anne reminded them of the confidentiality of their considerations, and Lily made a little impatient noise. Of course there was much other evidence of Cassirer's classroom performance and treatment of students, and Anne went through it in a dispassionate voice. There was an eloquent letter in the file from Mabel Gorman describing Cassirer's contempt for students and the literature he was supposed to teach.

"So he's a lousy teacher," Zalinski conceded. "But he brings distinction to the department."

Andrew wondered about the wisdom of telling the committee of the visit he had received from Tuttle representing Cassirer and conveying unveiled threats of legal action. He and Anne had discussed this and left it an open question whether this card should be played. Andrew kept his peace.

Pistoia said, "As a colleague he makes Attila the Hun look like St. Francis."

"That is completely subjective," Lily said. "I find him very . . ." She hesitated, searching like Flaubert for the mot juste. "Congenial," she finally said and Pistoia laughed. It was Lily who brought up

Cassirer's intention to litigate.

"We should be aware that what we are doing cannot remain private. Of course I acknowledge the confidentiality of our proceedings." She glared at Anne. "But if lawyers get into it, everything will become an open book."

"Lawyers?" Pistoia said.

"Lawyers. I have reason to believe Horst has already engaged legal counsel. He may not wait for us to act."

All academic hell broke loose. Anne and Lily sparred and jabbed, Lily defending the right of any faculty member to demand that the hitherto sacrosanct records of the college be brought into the light of day, Anne wanting to know if she were willing to deliver her responsibility over to a judge who could not possibly understand what was at issue.

"I think anyone would understand what is going on here."

"And what is that?"

"You intend to railroad Cassirer," Zalinski said. "This meeting is a perfect example of what has gone wrong in academe. Here we are, what we are, presuming to thwart the career of a young man simply because his superior talents threaten us. Well, I for one want us to promote people better than myself."

"No feat that," Pistoia said.

Anne tried unsuccessfully to regain the role of umpire of the discussion, but her own judgment on Cassirer was plain, and her exchange with Lily had removed all doubt. When she tried to bring the matter to a vote, Zalinski slapped the table.

"I will refuse to vote under these circumstances."

"When you could lose?" Pistoia asked.

Anne said, "You cannot let down your colleagues who have elected you to shoulder this responsibility."

"Our colleagues!" Lily said. "You are more concerned for the deadwood in this department than for its future."

"I will record your complaint."

"Do so. I will put it in writing."

"For the judge?" Pistoia asked.

"For the record!"

"You're remarkably silent, Andrew," Zalinski said in surly tones.

Andrew replied that he was willing to concede Cassirer's scholarly accomplishments, obscure as he found them, but he thought him woefully inadequate in the other two categories.

"The lawyer Lily mentioned has called on me already."

"Of course he would," Lily said. "Your silence today cannot conceal that this is all your doing."

"Mine?"

"Doesn't it bother you that you lack the ultimate credential of the professor? I wonder what Gloria would make of this discussion."

"I'll ask her."

"Confidentiality," Pistoia purred.

"Lily makes a valid point," Zalinski said. "I mean this quite impersonally, Andrew, but you represent the past of this place. We all know how you came to be on the faculty."

"And how was that?"

"Nepotism!"

"Please," Anne said. "Let us exhibit a little collegiality."

"I cannot exhibit what I do not feel."

"Are you calling into question my status as a member of this committee?" Andrew asked hotly.

"I think you are a perfect representative member of this committee."

"You seem to have picked up some of the more charming traits of Horst Cassirer."

"I would rather have a competent curmudgeon as a colleague than . . ." His eyes were wild, but some vestigial trace of decorum stayed his tongue.

A stunned silence followed Zaliniski's incomplete sentence.

Anne dealt slips of paper around the table. "Let's vote."

Lily said, "Maybe we should postpone it until tempers cool."

"Let's vote!" Pistoia said.

They voted. Unsurprisingly, it was three to two against granting tenure to Horst Cassirer. Zalinski leapt to his feet when Anne announced the result, stooped to pick up the student papers he had dropped, and headed for the door. Lily followed on his heels.

"We have struck a blow for Western civilization," Pistoia said with satisfaction. "You say his lawyer called on you?"

"In my office."

"Was Foster there?"

"It didn't faze him a bit."

"The odor of sanctity," Pistoia said.

Anne thanked them for coming and got to her feet. Then she sat down again. "What a rotten place this is becoming."

"Lilies that fester smell worse than weeds," Pistoia said and, turning to Andrew, "but not perhaps worse than Foster."

"I would prefer a competent unbathed office mate to . . ."

They adjourned on a note of laughter.

"Is it true?" Gloria asked in shocked tones when Andrew stopped by her office.

"You've already heard about our vote on Cassirer?"

"You turned him down?"

"Was it Lily?"

"Andrew, I agree with her. If this college cannot accommodate someone with Cassirer's credentials it is doomed to mediocrity."

"My own credentials were questioned."

"That was uncalled for."

"So Lily told you that as well."

"Andrew, what possible difference can it make to you if Cassirer becomes tenured? Your job is safe. You do what you do; he does what he does."

"And the students?"

"Frankly, all this concern about the students strikes me as a little forced."

"Gloria, you saw the student letters."

She looked away. "I assured Lily you had nothing to do with that."

"You sound doubtful."

The fact that the execrable Cassirer could come between them seemed a revelation of the nature of their relationship. That night it was silent in the apartment. Gloria had her study, he had his, and they worked that night on separate islands no common water seemed to lap. Later, he put a video in the VCR and watched *From Here to Eternity*. When Pruitt settled into the apartment of the girl with whom he had formed an attachment, he said, "This is like being married."

"It's better," she said. In his own case it had become worse.

20

Amos Cadbury, now in his late seventies, was still a daily presence in the firm he had founded although he himself supervised only the work of his old clients as they dwindled and departed, one by one, and their estates had to be looked after. Sometimes he thought that he would be kept alive until he had seen the last one through probate, and then his own summons would come. Meanwhile, he was hale and hearty and had devised a number of mental exercises to chase away the thought that he was living in one of the later chapters of the Apocalypse. His knowledge of history was narrow in scope but profound, confined to the great crises in the Church. No previous one could possibly compete with the present dissolution. The apparently terminal illness of Fulvio Bernardo brought back memories of one of his departed clients, Alfred Wygant.

Many lives end on an ambiguous note, no doubt of that. An orderly dignified exit was the exception rather than the rule. Too many old friends had ended in Alzheimer's or dementia, there but not there when he visited them, thankful he had power of attorney and could fulfill the will they had expressed when their will was still amenable to reason. Amos loved the precision of the law and the illusion it gave of imposing rationality on the messiness of life. In this very office he had gone over Alfred's affairs with his widow, Eleanor. And Alfred's fears about Eleanor's affair with a man he would not mention, but whose identity, of course, Amos guessed. Eleanor was still a handsome woman, but in her second bereavement she had taken on what Amos regarded as a classical beauty. If only she wouldn't frown.

"He has left you amply provided for."

"You can tell me everything. I am practiced at this."

Joseph Bernardo. Her first husband. She had swept her second into the bosom of the Bernardo family, an equivocal blessing. Alfred too had sat across this desk.

"Tell me about Fulvio Bernardo, Amos."

Alfred had prospered in insurance, playing a role that Amos in his darker moods compared with that of a bookie. Bet your life; enrich your heirs. But where would his own practice be without such

193

concern for a future the client would not see?

"He turned a modest little nursery into a chain of garden stores in the Chicago area. He has done very well. His son is a priest."

"What does he know about the market?"

"The stock market? As little as anyone else, I suspect."

Amos was a loyal and patriotic citizen, but in the deeper recesses of his heart he despised what was called "the market." In the commodities market in the Merchandise Mart men who had never seen a farm bought and sold wheat futures, sow bellies, all sorts of things they never came in contact with, driving the price up and down, their activities light years removed from the activity of growing wheat and raising hogs and all the rest. Yet their speculations vitally affected the prospects of the farmer. And was Wall Street any better? Half-mad dealers dashing about, frantically buying and selling the shares of companies they knew only through their books. The plants, the employees, the product — these in their reality were incidental to the buys and sells of the traders. He knew the replies to these doubts. Without capital the entrepreneur could do nothing, and the market furnishes that capital. Amos had a soft spot for the entrepreneur, the inventive risk taker who alas paved the way for the managers and traders and accountants, the soulless parasites. What money of his own that was not in tax-free municipals was invested directly with such enterprises as Fulvio Bernardo's chain of garden stores as silent partner. It turned out that the analogy was all too relevant to Alfred's visit.

"He knows his own business, certainly."

"This is something else."

Amos never got clear on what "this" was, possibly because Alfred himself did not understand it. Insofar as he did grasp the idea it had to do with opening the Bernardo family business to investors but keeping it in the family, not going public. Alfred would be an officer of this new entity, his investment getting him onto the ground floor of the enterprise. Fulvio knew the nursery business, and Alfred as a businessman had reason to be confident in that, but Amos with great obliquity and indirection suggested caution. Alfred never spoke of it again, and Amos had been relieved. It had sounded like a way to buy off his rival for Eleanor's affection. Only after his death, as he went through the grim task of closing Alfred's account with this world did Amos learn that his mild demur had had no effect.

"I urged him to go in with Fulvio," Eleanor explained. "The man has a Midas touch."

The interval between her marriages had created in Eleanor the illusion that she was a practical woman. Nearly a million dollars of Alfred's money had been turned over to Fulvio over a period of several years. The record of outgo was clear. There was no record of earnings.

"It was in the formative stages," Eleanor said. "They both agreed to let their money ferment."

"Ferment."

"Taking money out prematurely would weaken the prospects."

The prospects of what? It was Bernardo's chain that had received the money. In return, Alfred had been given receipts.

"Was there a written agreement?"

"Amos, they were practically relatives."

Never do business with relatives or the Church was an axiom to which Amos subscribed, at least in part. One did not do business with the Church in any case. His own services were always pro bono where the Church was concerned.

Despite the fact that Eleanor seemed quite at ease with this odd arrangement, Amos took the liberty of speaking with

196

Fulvio on behalf of his client.

"It's all right, Mr. Cadbury. Not that it is the sort of deal I would normally have made. Mine is a family business. But he wouldn't let me say no. At least his wife wouldn't."

"Eleanor?"

"Eleanor."

"I am engaged in wrapping up his affairs, and I must confess I don't see what Alfred received in return for a considerable amount of money."

"He became a partner. A silent partner."

"Sharing in the profits?"

"What else does *partner* mean?"

"I can't find any record of income from Bernardo Garden Stores."

"That surprises me. Alfred was a pretty astute businessman."

"I always thought so."

"And now it will go to his wife."

"Eleanor."

"Eleanor."

There are decisions a lawyer makes that do not give his mind rest even with the passage of years. He should have demanded an audit. When he mentioned it, Eleanor was horrified.

"That would sound as if I think he cheated Alfred."

He told himself afterward that he had

simply respected the wishes of his client, but Eleanor understood the arrangement between Alfred Wygant and Fulvio Bernardo even less than Amos did. But he had let it go. Nearly a million dollars! Did he think that Bernardo had cheated Alfred? In any case, there was still a handsome amount for Eleanor. But, ever since, Amos felt he had let down his old friend Alfred Wygant. Hadn't the normally level-headed Alfred ever raised the question to Fulvio Bernardo? One thing was clear: He would have had to do so without Eleanor's support.

Amos shook away such troubling thoughts and turned his mind to Father Dowling's request that he look into the possibility of a parole for Earl Hospers. The strange events that had led to Hospers's trial and conviction were easily recalled. The body of Sylvia Lowry was found in the freezer in her basement. There had been several suspects — the son, the son-in-law, and a charlatan from Chicago — but eventually evidence that Earl Hospers, a television repairman, had carted off the meat from the freezer and dumped it had led to his arrest. He denied killing Sylvia, but the only palpable evidence pointed to him. He had been tried for manslaughter and been in prison in Joliet ever since.

Amos called in young Nordquist, who dealt in criminal law, not a busy sector in Cadbury & Associates. Nordquist, a tall and gangly fellow with stiff blond hair, entered the office uneasily, as if he feared a dressing down.

"What do you know of paroles, Harry?"

"Paroles?"

Amos explained Father Dowling's request and told Nordquist he wanted him to look into it.

"Yes, sir. Was he a client of ours?"

"Earl Hospers. No, Sylvia Lowry, his alleged victim, was."

"Alleged?"

"Not legally of course. He was tried and convicted. But he has paid a great price already, and if there is any chance of getting him released, I would like us to bring it about."

Nordquist seemed delighted with the assignment. No doubt he was not overemployed in the firm, and this chance to try his skills was welcome.

"Keep me posted."

"Yes, sir."

On Amos's desk was a notice of a meeting of the trustees of St. Edmund's for that afternoon. Here was a duty that had seemed only a duty in recent years. The newer appointees to the board had little conception of what the college had been, but then the president and provost seemed equally uninformed or perhaps simply disinterested. For them the college was a possibility without a past, something they were ushering into the wider academic world. The watchword was *excellence*, which seemed to mean being guided by received opinion. Once meetings had been presided over by an Edmundite, and the officers of the college were also members of the order. Trustees were there to help these good priests fulfill their mission. In that Amos had found satisfaction. Of late he felt that he was colluding in the abandonment of that mission.

He thought of Raymond Bernardo, Father Raymond as he then was, addressing the board on a long ago occasion, insisting that the mission of the college would never change. An impressive young man, his manner more reassuring than his message, and yet he was within months of his personal defection. And now at last he had returned to be at his dying father's bedside. What thoughts must come in such a setting? To them both?

21

"How's it going?" Phyllis asked over the phone from Thousand Oaks.

"As bad as I feared."

"What do you mean?"

"My father used what might have been his dying breath to condemn me."

"Oh, Raymond."

"My mother could not have been sweeter."

"Well, good for her."

"It's not that she approves."

A sigh bounced off a satellite and settled warmly in his ear. "Have you seen anyone else?"

"My brother and sister."

"Have you been to the college?"

"Of course not."

"You should go there, talk to people. We can't let them sit in judgment on us."

He had found this suggestion more alarming than the confrontation with his father. But the anticipation had been worse than the event, horrible as that had been.

Judas. How that word had pierced his soul, as his father had meant it to do. Andrew had mentioned Father Bourke. Would his old mentor react in the same way?

On Monday and Tuesday he made sure that his mother was in the room when he saw his father. The old man was neither better nor worse, but Dr. Rocco had no intention of moving him again from intensive care, not liking the less vigilant nursing his patient would receive in an ordinary room. So there continued to be the little winking digits registering his father's condition, transmitting their readings to the nurses' station. On Wednesday, he left his mother with his father, which is where she wanted to be, and got into the car and drove. The horse knows the way. Almost without thinking he drove to the college.

Once he would have been able to go through the gate and simply drive around, but now there was a guard on duty, checking cars for the windshield sticker that authorized their entrance. A visitor's parking lot had been created across the street from the entrance, and Raymond pulled in there and found a place. After he turned off the motor, he sat in indecision. He could have driven more or less anonymously around the campus, but to walk was to run the risk of recognition. He thought of Phyllis and what she would say if he expressed fear of walking onto the campus that had been the setting of their meeting and where he had so swiftly and easily exchanged the role of confidant for that of lover. And he thought of telling her casually that, yes, he had visited the campus, walked around, seen this and that. He got out of the car, crossed the street and walked through the gate.

In early November the trees were already stripped of leaves, and this made all the new buildings immediately visible. He walked purposively, as if he had a destination, feeling at once a stranger and back in familiar territory, however much the campus had changed. Students seemed to be going in all directions at once, almost all of them wearing backpacks. Once the main road he walked along had been a long avenue leading to the community buildings, the community residence, the seminary, the magnificent Gothic church. When the college was founded, its buildings were put on the land closer to the road. Now there were twice as many buildings as before, their architecture the bland functionalism that characterized the rapidly expanded campus. Everywhere there were signs with arrows pointing to this building or that, many of the names unknown to him. His fear of being recognized vanished. You can't go home again because home has become unrecognizable. Unlike his parents' house, which seemed frozen in time, the campus had altered beyond recognition. He was almost surprised when he saw a building that had been there in his time.

Classroom buildings, faculty offices, a new library, a dining hall expanded out of recognition and residences for the fraction of students who lived on campus, a computing center. A student center was now the target at which the main road aimed and now as midday approached was the destination of many of the hurrying students. How bundled up and unimpressive they looked, students at a lesser college, wanting the credentials of a degree rather than any sentimental identification with the school. He walked around the student center, and suddenly he was in the past.

In the tower, bells suddenly began to toll deliberately, their throaty sound a monotone save for slight variations, a two-bar staff without sharps or flats. But the sound of the bells seemed to emerge from deep within himself as well as from the tower. How many years had his life been measured by those sounds riding the air of the campus? He had not heard them for years, but they were as familiar as his own voice and seemed to fill up the interval of their absence from his life. He looked at his watch as the lights of the church began slowly to go up and the sanctuary became more brightly illumined. There were perhaps a dozen people scattered among the pews, but the significance of those bells had not changed. The midday Mass was about to begin.

Flee? Slip away? Did he dare remain and watch the commemoration of Christ's death on Calvary, the deed that had won us a victory over death, watch as someone spoke over bread and wine and then displayed the sacred species to the faithful? He could not have moved if he wanted to. Almost he believed that it was in order to be here, to visit the old haunts that he had refused to let haunt him, to neutralize them once and for all, that he had come. Phyllis. Dear God. He could see her reading the Scripture of the day from that pulpit as he sat in the celebrant's chair, fighting the memories her voice evoked.

The all too familiar banging of kneelers and the rustling of clothing filled the church when a little bell in the sacristy sounded and a vested priest emerged, walked swiftly to the center, and stopping at the steps leading up to the sanctuary bowed deeply. He then went rapidly up the stairs, kissed the altar, went to the celebrant's chair, and smiled out at the sparse congregation. Who was he? Raymond felt he should know him, but he was young, after his time. And then another vested priest in a wheelchair came into view, his motorized vehicle taking him silently and swiftly to a place beside the celebrant. Father Bourke! A dread he had not known since adolescent confessions filled Raymond. Could the old man fail to be aware of the presence in the church of his faithless protégé?

"Good morning," the priest said brightly, flashing a toothy smile as he boxed the compass, for all the world as if he were surrounded by hundreds of worshipers. "And good afternoon as well."

Indistinct murmurs from the scattered few. The celebrant blessed himself expansively and began. "As we prepare to celebrate these sacred mysteries . . ."

Raymond's lips formed the words with him. After all these years, he could have taken his place and carried it off without a hitch, the liturgy was so ingrained in him. Was it possible that he had not even thought of those words in years? ". . . let us call to mind our sins."

Father Bourke seemed hunched over in his wheelchair. His stole lay across his bent body and seemed to weigh him down. Raymond had not known of the wheelchair, how could he, and the crumpled man in the wheelchair whom he had recognized immediately seemed a parody of the Father Bourke he had kept at the edges of his mind.

"They'll do anything to stop us," Phyllis had said, her warm hand in his, when they were making their plans to go, and he had wondered if he shouldn't tell Father Bourke at least.

He had agreed not to see Bourke, agreed with relief, as if the decision were hers not his. He did not tell Phyllis of the letter he had left for Father Bourke, telling him what he meant to do and why. He had not mentioned Phyllis in his exculpating account.

The Mass went on. The reader was an elderly woman in slacks who had difficulties with the passage from Sirac, mispronouncing with amplified vigor, her head bobbing up and down as she sought eye contact with an imaginary church full of people. When she was done and said "The word of the Lord!", she turned and missed her step and nearly fell from the pulpit. But she steadied herself and made it back to her pew. And then the celebrant took her place, reading the gospel as if it were an account from the *Fox River Tribune*, matter-of-fact, no awed and altered tone to acknowledge that this was the good news. He preached his homily from the steps of the sanctuary, breezy, autobiographical, uninspiring.

Raymond felt a deep need to criticize the liturgical performance. He took dark pleasure in the fact that there was only a handful of worshipers, most of them old, none of them faculty, he was sure, and no students. Yet this was the traditional midday Mass for students and doubtless had been going on in all the intervening years. How much worse things were than he would have imagined, a parody rather than a continuation of the past. The Order had left him; he hadn't left the Order. It wasn't for this skeletal performance that he had in that very sanctuary dedicated his life to God. Already he was imagining how he would tell Phyllis of this. They were vindicated! It was as if they had foreseen this decline. The chatty manner of the celebrant had been one of those innovations meant to renew, to pack the church rather than empty it. My God, what if he had stayed on into these dark days.

At the altar, with Bourke in his wheelchair all but out of sight behind him, the celebrant offered the gifts, washed his hand — *O Lord wash away my iniquity and cleanse me from my sins* — and then the heart of the matter was reached. The priest took first the bread, then the wine, and said the ancient words in an altered and reverent voice: *This is my body. This is my blood.* The church had grown even more silent. From his wheelchair, concelebrating, Father Bourke lifted his hand and said the words with the priest. Like Dr. Strangelove, Raymond gripped his right wrist lest he too raise his hand. The words formed in his mind, but he pursed his lips lest he pronounce them. Immediately after the consecration, he got up and hurried to the door, pushing into the gray November day and the indifferent bustle of the campus. A passing figure stopped and stared at him.

"Raymond?"

There were jokes about husbands caught in flagrante delicto by their wives: "It's not me, Tessie. I swear to God it's not me." Or "What are you going to believe, the evidence of your senses or your husband?"

The man came toward him as Raymond froze on the church steps. The face was familiar, and then the name came to him.

"Hello, John."

"You're back."

The bald head might never have worn

hair, but Raymond remembered the thinning red hair that had once covered it. John had been several classes below him, a convert, an enthusiast, good as gold.

"My father's ill."

"Come to lunch."

He meant in the community refectory. Would no one else accuse him as his father had?

"John, I can't. I have to get back to the hospital."

"That serious?"

"He is dying."

The moonlike face clouded. "I will remember him in my Mass."

"Thank you."

"Come back later. Father Bourke would love to see you. Or have you already talked with him?"

"He is concelebrating inside."

"Of course. It's all he can do anymore, poor devil."

"What's wrong?"

"A heart attack. It's left him very weak."

Raymond shook his head at the slings and arrows of outrageous fortune.

"Well." He thrust out his hand and John took it.

"I'll tell him you're back."

If he had felt furtive coming onto campus

he had the sense of fleeing when he left. He should not have come here. He should not have entered the church. Now they would all know that he was in town and that he had been seen in church. John would assume he was there praying for his father. He stopped. It had never once occurred to him to do that. Didn't that prove it was all dead to him?

He half-noticed the approach of the cyclist, and then the man had swung in and braked. Great sneakered feet flat on the ground, the bike between his legs, he said, "You're Raymond Bernardo."

"And who are you?"

"Horst Cassirer. I teach here."

"And ride a bicycle."

"Your brother, Andrew, is in my department."

"English."

"He is opposing my promotion to tenure." He said this as one might mention a manifest outrage. There didn't seem anything to say. "I don't intend to sit still for this. I have a lawyer. This is war."

Academic quarrels continued by other means?

"I don't know anything about it."

"I'm telling you. I mean to discredit him. And his own family. I have informed myself

211

on the way you left the priesthood."

His beard twitched, and his intense eyes flashed. He drummed his fingers on the handles of his bike.

"You think that will get you tenure?"

"It may not stop your brother, but the college dreads bad publicity. Do you know Andrew is living with a woman?"

"Look . . ."

"I am going to blow the lid off the entire Bernardo family. Or threaten to. The college has to realize the kind of man who is opposing my promotion. You got him his job, didn't you?"

Raymond turned and headed toward his car, but his arm was gripped as the bearded nut tried awkwardly to follow him with the bike between his legs. Raymond shook his arm free. The bearded professor lost his balance and crashed to the ground. Passing students paused to stare.

Sprawled on the ground, the bearded Cassirer cried after him, "Good-bye, Father!"

22

"Where in God's name have you been?" Hazel demanded when Tuttle called his office. "Don't you have your cell phone with you?"

"I didn't turn it on, I guess."

"You idiot."

The cell phone had been Hazel's decision, so he could never be out of reach. That is why he never turned it on.

"What's up?"

"A professor named Cassirer has been here looking for you. He says he hired you."

"He did."

"Well, you might have told me."

Tuttle's relationship with Hazel was hard to explain. Technically she was his employee, but she acted as if he was hers. Her designs on him seemed to go beyond the office. The woman was a predator, not to be denied, and he was forever ducking out of the way of her attempts at affection, usually accompanied by a softening insult.

Hazel told him that she had interviewed

Cassirer and taken down pages of information.

"I am going to put Barbara on it. What do we know of academic law?"

Barbara was a paralegal whose knowledge of the law was undoubtedly impressive, however embarrassing it was to have to depend on it. But Hazel was right. He understood Cassirer's complaint even less after having talked with the bearded young man with the intense stare and nervous twitch of the shoulders — Atlas trying to relieve himself of his burden.

Tuttle had had lunch with Peanuts Pianone, whose status on the Fox River Police force was analogous to Tuttle's in the Fox River bar. Peanuts was a stolid, almost autistic man in his late thirties whose one emotion was resentment at the treatment he received as a cop. He owed his job to the influence of his family, family in the Sicilian as well as in the biological sense, and his superiors kept him out of harm's way and out from underfoot. He spent hours lazing away his workday in the pressroom of the courthouse, seething at the ascendancy of Agnes Lamb, a young African-American who had been hired for reasons of political correctness but who had proved to be a natural cop. Before Hazel, it had been their practice to have Chinese food delivered to Tuttle's office, where they could pig out at leisure and then drop into a nap. In the era of Hazel, Peanuts would not come near the office — one visit had sufficed to establish their mutual contempt — and today they'd had lunch at the Great Wall, lolling over a second pot of tea. Tuttle's fortune cookie had contained an enigmatic message: *Your Fears Are Not Unfounded.*

"I made a three o'clock appointment for you with Cassirer."

"There?"

"In his office. He said you would know how to find it."

"Right."

"Maybe I ought to be there."

Tuttle hung up as if he had not heard the question. Hazel's urgency confirmed his sense that he had stumbled into a good thing with Cassirer. And to think he nearly had not answered the phone when the professor called again after Tuttle's visit to campus. He usually ignored its ringing when Hazel was not in the office, and on the occasion she had been down the hall to the Ladies. But before the caller received instructions to leave a message after the beep, Tuttle had picked up the phone. He came to believe that once again he had been inspired to do so by his father in the beyond.

"How did it go with Andrew Bernardo?"

"He understands the situation."

"He voted against me again!"

"Hmmm."

"Tuttle, this is war."

And now he had called the office, wanting to consult his lawyer.

His first face-to-face with Cassirer had been in the cafeteria in the student center. Where would the man's office be? Tuttle parked across from the main entrance and stopped at the guard shack.

"Where would I find someone who teaches English?"

"You want to become a student?" The guard was in uniform, and his evil smile revealed a golden eyetooth.

"I figure with an education I could get a job like yours."

"You're Tuttle, aren't you?" An arthritic hand extended. "Woodward. I remember you around the courthouse. Who you looking for?"

"Horst Cassirer."

Woodward consulted a dog-eared campus directory, his lips moving as he ran a crooked finger down the page.

"English is in Arts & Letters. Know where that is?"

"Refresh my memory."

Tuttle followed the fulsome instructions through the maze of campus walks. Finally he stopped a passing group of students and asked where Arts & Letters was. A slack-jawed coed with snarled hair pointed it out. Tuttle thanked her.

"What are you looking for?"

"The English Department."

"Come on, I'll show you."

She left the others, took Tuttle's elbow, and steered him along as if she were placing him under arrest. Inside, the janitor had just swabbed the hallway, and there were signs in English and Spanish warning the less than sure-footed. It was the girl not Tuttle who lost her footing and whose grip on his elbow became functional. He steadied her.

"I would have sued," she said.

Tuttle took off his tweed hat and extracted a business card which he handed her. "In case you ever do fall."

"Usually it's the sidewalks in winter. This place is a hazard." She looked at the card, then at Tuttle. "You're Professor Cassirer's lawyer, aren't you?"

"Do you know him?"

"He's the worst teacher I've ever had."

"Well, you're still young." Tuttle thought of the lousy teachers he had in law school, many several times. Again she lost her footing and he steadied her.

"Keep me in mind."

"How can you represent someone like Cassirer?" She peered at him. "You're cute."

He was reminded of Hazel, as she must have been before she had become a harridan. The girl seemed more flustered by her remark than he was. She pointed to a door. "That's it."

Inside a little woman sat staring at a computer screen, hard at work. She seemed to be playing a game. When she became aware of Tuttle's presence, she turned the monitor so he could not see the screen.

"I am looking for Professor Cassirer."

A toothy woman popped out of a room that contained the mailboxes of the professors.

"You're looking for Horst Cassirer?" She inspected Tuttle and was unimpressed.

"I'm his lawyer."

She was transformed by this information. Now she took his elbow. "I'll take you to his office."

Cassirer's office was in another building, and on the way Professor St. Clair identified herself and pumped Tuttle, wanting to know why he wanted to see Cassirer.

"Lawyer-client privilege," Tuttle said importantly.

"I already know why. He's going to take them to court, isn't he? Look, I will help in any way I can. This is the worst injustice since the Galileo case."

"That bad?" Who was Galileo? Perhaps a client he might have had.

"In this day and age, worse."

When they arrived at Cassirer's door, she knocked, and there was an animal sound from within.

"Good. He's back from class."

The office was a mess, papers strewn everywhere, a wild-eyed Cassirer standing in their midst. He looked at his colleague.

"Those goddamn papers give illiteracy a bad name."

"I've brought your lawyer."

Cassirer subsided, taking note of Tuttle. He looked at his watch. "You're late."

"He went by the departmental office."

"Did you talk to Gogarty?"

"I got him out of there before she knew he was there," Professor St. Clair simpered. "I told him I am at his disposal." She turned to Tuttle. "What is your name?"

In answer he extracted another card from his hat and handed it to her. Suddenly the campus seemed a lush field of possible clients.

"I can stay if you want, Horst."

He shook his head. "No."

"I meant it about wanting to help. You have my total support, Horst."

He nodded as at the self-evident. "Not now."

With great reluctance she took her leave. Before closing the door, she flourished Tuttle's card. He smiled, but he was glad to see her go.

"Well, they've done it. They voted me down."

"Tell me in your own words."

He got out the little tape recorder that Hazel had equipped him with, along with the cell phone, turned it on, and placed it on Cassirer's desk. The slowly turning cassette tape galvanized Cassirer. He placed Tuttle in a chair across his desk, but it was to the tape recorder that he addressed his grievances. Hazel would type it out and follow up on it with Barbara. Tuttle nodded through the unintelligible narrative. Whoever Galileo was he didn't hold a candle to Cassirer in the matter of injustice.

"Did they tell you the result of the vote?"

"Ha! Lily did."

Employing his powerful deductive powers Tuttle surmised that Lily was Professor St. Clair.

"They will say that she violated the confidentiality of the committee. I assume you read the faculty manual."

Tuttle had tried. On the whole, he preferred *Mad* magazine.

"The question is how best to proceed."

"That's obvious. I want to sue the college."

"For refusing you tenure?"

"That is the cause, but I intend to bring this place to its knees. They are attempting to damage a reputation recognized far and wide. There are schools who will be influenced by a denial of tenure, even by such a wasteland as this. That will be our approach: the assassination of my professional character."

"Sounds good."

The thing about Cassirer, Tuttle would prefer being on the opposite side.

"Who is the college's lawyer?"

"I don't know."

"I'll find out."

Tuttle wondered if he might strike a deal with the college lawyer, man to man, to hell with Cassirer. In return, he could offer to testify to Cassirer's bad-mouthing of the college.

"I'll get on it."

"We have to work together on this, hand in hand."

"Exactly how I want it."

Tuttle left and maneuvered down the unslippery hallway of the faculty office building. From the guard shack, Woodward waved. Tuttle responded distractedly, came to a stop and got out his cell phone, and made a great drama of putting through a call to Hazel. He got the answering machine. After the beep, he said, "This is going to be a piece of cake."

23

Margaret seemed surprised when Eleanor told her the children thought it would be wise for her to look over things, to make sure everything was in order.

"What things?"

"Margaret, I know you don't want to think about this now, and you don't have to. I'll do it for you. Remember, I have had this experience twice myself."

Margaret was angered by the suggestion that Fulvio was dying, despite her campaign to have him see a priest.

"There is the soul, Margaret, and then there is the body. Where does Fulvio keep his papers?"

"Eleanor, I don't know what you're talking about. You act as if I'm a widow!"

"We don't know what might happen. How often we read of women left alone who have no idea what practical arrangements their husbands have made for them."

"I won't talk about it."

"Of course you won't. And you don't have

to do anything either. That is why the children suggested I take a look."

This exchange went on and on, Margaret refusing to acknowledge the seriousness of Fulvio's condition. Eleanor felt sympathy with her one-time sister-in-law, but her affair with Fulvio had lessened her opinion of Margaret. She could not imagine that Joe or Alfred could have acted as Fulvio had with her without her suspecting. Almost, she felt that Margaret was responsible for her succumbing to Fulvio. What had she thought they were up to at the lake when they sailed away around that island? For that matter, what had the children thought? Other than Raymond, that is. Raymond had known. She did not want to remember the awful day when he had walked in on them. Thank God, he hadn't pretended any loftiness with her when they met in the hospital after all those years. Of course Raymond had lost any moral authority he might have had.

Margaret had been at some parish affair, the children were in school, there seemed to be no risk in coming when Fulvio called. It was tasteless of course to deceive Margaret in her own home, but the whole affair was tasteless. That, she had come to see in retrospect, was one of its great attractions. She had been a prim and proper wife to two men, but with Fulvio she was a tramp.

When she arrived, Fulvio closed the door, took her in his arms, and all but forced her onto the couch.

"Let me catch my breath, for heaven's sake."

"I like you breathless."

"You haven't shaved."

In response, he gave her a whisker rub. He put his tongue in her ear. She writhed and struggled, in mock resistance. He liked to triumph and dominate. She hadn't been in the house ten minutes when the door opened and Raymond walked in.

Fulvio was on his feet and wringing his son's hand, blocking his view while Eleanor adjusted her dress, patted her hair, and wondered what in the name of God Raymond would think.

"This is a surprise," Fulvio said in a booming voice. He was pounding his clerical son on the back. "Got the day off?"

"No, not exactly." Eleanor was on her feet now too, and took her cue from Fulvio. She turned back to the couch and began to lift its cushions, as if she were looking for something.

"Aunt Eleanor," Raymond said, as if he had finally managed to identify her.

"Mom's at some church bazaar or other. Eleanor is going to join her there. Have you found it yet?"

Eleanor continued to look under the cushions.

"Her rosary," Fulvio said. "The Fatima one. She was showing it to me and I tried to steal it from her and . . ."

Eleanor opened her purse, back to the two men, and took out a rosary. She turned. "Here it is."

"Go along then," Fulvio said. "I want to visit with my son."

"I can't really stay long, Dad."

"All the more reason to use what time we have."

He gave Eleanor a peck on the cheek. "Off you go. And keep your darned rosary."

"He must have known," she said to Fulvio later, when he told her not to worry about Raymond.

"He is innocent as a lamb. He's a priest."

"Priests hear confessions."

"Eleanor, stop worrying about it."

But that had been their last time together, which meant that Fulvio was not as certain as he seemed that Raymond had not understood that they had not been looking for a rosary when he walked in. It seemed sacrilegious to use such an excuse. Perhaps Fulvio

226

thought it would appeal to the priest in Raymond.

"Didn't he say anything?"

"He said lots of things."

"I mean about us."

"Do you think he'd think I was groping his aunt?"

"I don't know what he thought."

"That's right. And even if he figured it out he isn't going to say anything."

She took consolation in his confidence. But as the weeks and then months passed and there were no calls from Fulvio, no suggestions that they meet here or there, she understood it was over. That is when she began to write those idiotic letters, letters she had to find if Fulvio had kept them, as he said he had.

Now she took advantage of Margaret's confusion and moved toward the room where Fulvio had a desk and a file cabinet. The sight of the four shut drawers in that metal cabinet made her want to push Margaret aside and pull them open.

"Andrew will look after the financial side, checkbook, that sort of thing. Where would he keep things like insurance policies?"

"I don't know. I don't care."

"Margaret, go to him. That is far more important than this." She was seated at the desk now and laid her hands upon it as if it were an Ouija board that would tell her what she wanted to know. Her letters could have been lying about in the open, and Margaret would never have seen them. The suggestion that she be with Fulvio was an inspiration, but there was a catch.

"You'll have to drive me."

She wanted to suggest a cab, get her out of the house. But she checked the impulse.

"Of course, I'll drive you. Margaret, I just want to help."

So she had driven Margaret to the hospital, let her off at the main entrance, watched her hurry inside, and then gone back to the house.

For two hours she searched the desk and file cabinets, having found the key in the center drawer of the desk. She had no idea what half the papers Fulvio kept were. The identifying tabs on the dividers in the drawer might have been written in a foreign language. In fact they were. Italian. The language he had not cared to speak but had learned in childhood was used as a kind of code.

She did find letters, letters from women, and read them with shocked avidity. Had she imagined that she represented Fulvio's single excursion into infidelity? She had been one of a series. There were letters before and after the years of their affair and during it. *Poor Margaret,* she thought. But she meant poor Eleanor. How cheap it made her feel that she was just one of half a dozen women who had been stupid enough to let Fulvio have his way with her and then to write him about it. Some of the letters were embarrassingly graphic, but Eleanor understood their meaning from her own experience. The signatures were all nicknames. Fulvio had called her Mona Lisa, but she had not had the good sense to write under that name. She had signed hers Eleanor. But she could not find them.

She sat back and tried to feel relief. She was different from the others. Fulvio had respected her enough to get rid of her letters. But why on earth had he kept these? Trophies? Any relief she might have felt at not finding those damnable letters evaporated when she realized he could have kept them somewhere else. But if he had kept them, why not here with these others? Because she was different; it hadn't been the same thing at all.

It had been worse. Whoever these other silly women were they were not related to him. She thought of Margaret. Good Lord, she would have to bring her back from the hospital. The inconvenience seemed a kind of expiation.

24

The trustees' board room at St. Edmund's contained the portraits of past presidents, all but the current one a priest of the order. Alloy had served previously as vice president of one of the lesser campuses of the University of Wisconsin, and he brought to the position experience in everything but how to run a Catholic college. Amos had been in the minority when the vote was taken to hire him. Did Alloy hope to use St. Edmund's as a springboard to a better job, back into secular higher education, where the politics were fierce but there were no theological complications?

Alloy took his place at the head of the table and wished them all good morning.

"Good morning," they answered, like a grade school class.

Alloy's mindless smile gave way to a frown. "I want to begin the meeting with an item not on the agenda, and I will ask Box to explain."

Box was the onboard legal counsel to the

college, a fellow alumnus of the Notre Dame Law School, a good man.

"One of our junior faculty came to my office and informed me that he intended to sue the college."

Everyone sat straighter. Box went on, telling them of Horst Cassirer, a young professor of English who had applied for early tenure.

"He was turned down by the departmental committee."

"I would have vetoed it if he hadn't been," Holder said. "He is one of the most obnoxious young men I have ever met, seething with contempt for the college, convinced that he far outclasses his seniors."

"He has hired a lawyer," Box said.

Amos asked who the lawyer was.

"A man named Tuttle."

Despite himself, Amos laughed. All but Box looked at him with surprise.

"Tuttle is the buffoon of the local bar," Amos explained. "This young fellow could not have made a worse choice."

"It still spells trouble."

"I doubt that Eugene Box thinks so."

It was a sign of the times that St. Edmund's felt threatened by the likes of Tuttle. In his own mind, Amos formed an image of Horst Cassirer along the lines of

231

Tuttle. That someone described as a brilliant scholar, however defective in the other qualities expected of a permanent member of the faculty, should have regarded Tuttle as an effective instrument of his revenge on the school called into question the meaning of brilliance and scholarship. *Revenge* had been the provost's word, in response to a remark that Cassirer must like his job to be fighting to keep it like this.

"He hates his job, he hates the school, he hates his students."

"Then why is he here at all?"

"He doesn't hate Horst Cassirer. The universe exists to advance the cause of Cassirer. To the degree that it fails to do that, or fails to do that intensely enough for his liking, he hates the universe too."

Alloy smiled wryly at his provost. "Obviously this has weighed on you."

Amos asked Box just exactly what sort of legal move Cassirer or his counsel could make.

"It is not unheard of, after someone has been denied tenure, for that person to demand a review. There are procedures provided in the faculty manual for such a review. The provost appoints a committee, they go over the procedure that was followed, and report to the provost."

"Second guessing the departmental committee?"

"The review emphasizes procedure. Obviously you wouldn't want people in history deciding who is and who is not a good chemist, or vice versa, but any member of the faculty can determine whether the correct procedures were followed in a field quite different from his own."

"Holder has to make such decisions every day," Alloy said. "Not tenure decisions, of course, but it falls to him to direct the work of all the divisions and departments within the college. And he is an economist."

"As I understand it," Amos said, having consulted the faculty manual that was part of the packet placed before each trustee's place at the table, "he has not yet actually been denied tenure."

"The decision is in its early stages. The departmental committee has met."

"Have they reported to you?"

"Oh no. Nor yet to the dean."

"But they informed Cassirer of their vote?"

"The proceedings of such committees are governed by complete confidentiality."

"Then," Amos said, "from a procedural point of view, Cassirer cannot yet know that a vote has been taken or that it has been unfavorable to him."

The provost conceded that this was a delicate point. "Obviously he knows the outcome of the vote. It was all over campus within an hour, to those interested, in any case."

"So someone broke confidentiality."

The provost nodded. "Not, I should add, an unusual occurrence."

"Perhaps Box should bring a case against the English department's committee."

"I will issue a directive, reminding the faculty of the confidentiality rule."

"If he has not been turned down, at least as yet, his suit against the college is still speculative. I mean, he could scarcely file it in any court."

"I don't think he intends to wait. Actually this dispute has been public for some time. I probably should have prepared a dossier on this, but the idea was simply to forewarn the board of a dark cloud on the horizon. Cassirer has already carried his campaign to the pages of the student newspaper."

A stir around the table. A recurrent item of their meetings was complaints against the student newspaper, which struck a liberal stance somewhat to the left of the *Village Voice*, featuring items that seemed aimed at outraging the more sedate of its readers and running Personals that reminded one knowledgeable trustee of notices pinned up in doorways near Piccadilly in London. The president's allusion to the paper turned the meeting in that direction and when, after some fifteen minutes of needed venting, the president got them onto the prepared agenda, matters settled into their customary dullness.

Amos was passive for the rest of the meeting, although matters more serious than the fate of young Cassirer came up, matters on which in earlier days he would have spoken with eloquence. Just as the official administrative reaction to the assaults on faith and morals in the student paper was the very stuff of the academic world, so the proposed production of some monstrosity called the *Vagina Monologues* was regarded as arguably within the bounds of the college mission.

"It's been produced on campuses all over the country."

Amos sat in frozen embarrassment. Missy Phillips, the newest member of the board, CEO of Dot Dash, supplier of essential computer components, shuffled her papers without apparent unease at the discussion. Father Fish, the lone Edmundite on the board, recounted the divided opinion of

235

theologians on the matter of such productions. Was he himself for the production or against it? In response he listed the reasons for allowing the production and went on to list those against. That seemed to be his view, that there were conflicting views on everything. Dear God, if Father Bourke were still on the board, this item would have been stricken beforehand or decided in a trice. What on earth was there to discuss in such a matter?

"I saw it in New York," Missy Phillips said.

"Ah. And what did you think?"

"Nasty talk at girls camp."

God is merciful, and they went on to other items, which meant that the students could produce the propaganda play for perversity. Had the time come for him to resign? Amos felt that he was colluding in the destruction of the Church and of Western civilization, two entities he considered essentially connected. Item followed item, but Amos did not follow the discussion closely. Afterward, there was coffee, but Amos was inclined to slip away. He had reached the door, unobtrusively he thought, when Eugene Box hailed him.

"Amos, could we talk?"

He meant in his office, which was down

the hall. They went through the outer office, where Box dropped his trustee packet on his secretary's desk, and led the way into his office.

"As I mentioned, Tuttle has been to see me," he said when they were seated.

Amos just shook his head.

"If I understood him, Cassirer is considering a wholesale assault on the college, aimed at showing our hypocrisy. Specific faculty members will be named. Do you remember Raymond Bernardo?"

"The Edmundite? Of course."

"And of how he left?"

Box was still in law school when that had occurred, whereas Amos then as now was a member of the board.

"I remember it well."

"He has a brother on the faculty."

"Andrew?"

"You know him?"

"I know the family, have for years."

"Do you know anything of Andrew's living arrangements?"

"Living arrangements!"

"Tuttle seemed to be insinuating that Cassirer's foe lived in flagrant violation of the requirements of the faculty manual for personal morality."

"Dear God."

Amos thought immediately of Margaret Bernardo, a dear woman of the long-suffering variety.

"Technically, it's grounds for dismissal, but Alloy has no desire to invoke the requirement for moral rectitude on the part of the faculty. He considers it archaic."

After the discussions in the meeting, Amos was not surprised.

"Whatever Holder says, I think the president wants to placate Cassirer."

"No matter what his department thinks of him?"

Box brought his hands down his cheeks. "He will do anything to forestall bad publicity."

Box was letting him know that, whatever happened, it was Alloy's decision. What did his fellow lawyer think, in his heart of hearts? He was afraid to ask.

When he rose to go he thanked Box for confiding in him.

"I wanted to give you a heads-up."

"Holding our heads up is becoming increasingly difficult."

Box came with him to the door of his office. "What changes you must have seen, Mr. Cadbury."

Amos sighed. "Change and decay in all around I see. Do you know Waugh?"

Box did not. Amos did not explain.

"Of course she's a saint," Eleanor had said to him two days ago. She crossed her hands on her lap. "Are you Fulvio's lawyer?"

"I have done legal work for him, yes."

"When he dies . . ."

"Is it that certain?"

"There is said to be little chance that he will ever go home from the hospital. Have you visited him?"

Amos looked at Eleanor. The suggestion seemed to have more to do with her question about whether he was Fulvio's lawyer than any friendship that existed between him and the Bernardo patriarch.

"No."

"I wish you would."

Amos nodded noncommitally. It might have been a generic invocation of the corporal works of mercy. Visit the sick.

"His papers will be put under lock and key, won't they? I am thinking of the probate of Alfred's estate."

"That depends." Mention of Alfred renewed Amos's uneasiness about the unsecured money Alfred had turned over to Fulvio, a matter on which Eleanor exhibited something approaching insouciance. Or was this concern about papers related to that?

"You're thinking of the money Alfred invested with Fulvio?"

"Yes. Yes, that's it."

"Do you have any records of that transaction?"

"It must be in his papers. As my lawyer too, you will want to protect me."

Amos assured her that she would receive the full benefit of his legal representation. He found Eleanor a difficult person to like, yet two men had been sufficiently taken with her to marry her. Despite her undeniable beauty Amos found her cold. What attracts a particular man to a particular woman was one of those mysteries he had sometimes discussed with Father Dowling.

Eleanor said, "I've made a preliminary survey of the papers he has at home."

"And you found nothing."

She looked over his head and shook hers. "There were lots of letters."

"But none to Alfred?"

"I could have overlooked them."

"How did you come to look over his papers?"

"It was the children's suggestion."

A call from Father Dowling brightened his day.

"Marie is eager to prepare a lunch for you, Amos. I don't make sufficient demands on her culinary talents."

"If I were ruthless, I would hire her away from you."

"After my noon Mass tomorrow?"

"I'll be at the Mass."

"Good, just come into the sacristy afterward, and we'll go over to the rectory together."

25

There is a tide in the affairs of men, and in their deaths, as well, at least the violent ones that occupied Phil Keegan and the detective bureau of the Fox River Police Department. Since losing his wife, Phil had immersed himself more and more in his work, scarcely having any life outside it, save of course for his visits to Father Dowling at St. Hilary's. Roger didn't remember him from Quigley, of course — Phil had been several years his junior — but the view up differs from the view down, and little Philip Keegan had been very aware of the older boys in the preparatory seminary. Roger Dowling had impressed him then, and since Roger's appointment at St. Hilary's the two men had formed a close friendship. Latin had been Phil's downfall as far as a vocation to the priesthood went, a blow at the time, which as the years passed struck him more and more as providential. It was bad enough to witness what was happening to the Church from the outside, so to speak, but he would have been undone by all the changes if he had become a priest. Of course, Latin his old nemesis was no longer a factor. Roger Dowling's equanimity was a solace to Phil. But now he fretted because the workload of his department had dwindled to a few routine matters. Even Cy Horvath, his impassive Hungarian lieutenant, seemed a little edgy. Then Phil remembered something Marie Murkin had said and was able to put Cy on it, wild goose chase though it doubtless was.

"Does the name Alfred Wygant mean anything to you?"

"The insurance man?"

"The dead insurance man."

Cy's expression never changed, but Phil had the impression he was consulting his phenomenal memory bank.

"Some kind of accident, wasn't it?"

"Marie Murkin wonders about that."

"How so?"

"Why don't you see what you can find out about it?"

"We didn't investigate it at the time."

"I know."

Cy rose. He was a huge man whose athletic career had been thwarted when he was injured as a freshman at Illinois. He came out of the service, where he had served as an MP, and Phil had been instrumental in getting him on the force. From the outset he had seen Cy as his good right arm, and so it had turned out. Whatever Cy found out, likely nothing important, at least it would serve to placate Marie Murkin.

When Cy passed the pressroom he heard Tuttle pontificating and went in.

"Lieutenant Horvath," Tuttle cried. The little lawyer seemed uncharacteristically jaunty.

"Why aren't you out chasing ambulances?"

"I am moving in a new sphere, Horvath. Academic law."

The reporter Tetzel made an obscene noise and turned away to contemplate the monitor of his computer. Tuttle was unfazed.

"I have a professor at St. Edmund's for a client. Tetzel is peeved because he knows I will make headlines."

"You always do, Tuttle."

On the way to picking up a car, Cy stopped in the cafeteria, having seen the lovely Dr. Pippen pushing a tray along the line. He got into the line, wanting just a cup of coffee. If Pippen were alone, he would join her. If she weren't, he wouldn't. Cy was made uneasy by his attraction to the beautiful assistant coroner and tried to think of her as a sister, not an easy thing to do. But now she too was married, so his infatuation seemed doubly innocent or at least half as dangerous.

When he turned with his cup of coffee, Pippen was settling in at a table, alone. Cy went to join her.

"Where are all the bodies?" she asked. "We have nothing to do."

"We're supposed to be glad at a drop in crime."

"The least you could do is go out and shoot someone for me."

"Who would you like it to be?"

Her lips moved but no sound emerged. Lubins. Her boss. Reading Pippen's lips had its rewards.

"It would take a silver bullet. I'll go back with you when we're done here. I want to look up some old records."

"And I thought you just wanted my company."

He let it go. His ability for banter was limited in any case, but he could not risk even joking about her. He tried to think of her as an occasion of sin, but that was ridiculous. Even if he . . . He shook the thought away. He loved his wife. He wished they had kids, but they didn't. Keegan had kids, two daughters, whom he seldom saw; they lived so far away. He had grandchildren too, something Cy would never have. It seemed sad. It was sad.

"Are you going to have children?"

She actually blushed, the unflappable Pippen blushed. "Why you nosy old thing, you."

"You don't plan to grow old performing autopsies, do you?"

"I don't know." She was still flustered. She leaned toward him, looking at the table. "We're trying."

Good God, this was not a confidence he had expected. Fortunately there was not much to say except that it was his great regret that he and his wife had never had children.

"I always think of you as a father."

"Try brother."

"Okay." She was herself again. "So what are you looking into?"

He told her. There was no way to make it sound important. "Keegan just wants me out of his hair."

In the morgue office, he looked up the W's on the computer where the records were stored. No Alfred Wygant. But Phil had sounded sure that there had been an autopsy. Meanwhile, Pippen had gotten a customer, and Cy left her to her grisly work. How could a woman conceive when she spent all day with cadavers?

The so-called morgue of the *Tribune* had been computerized as well, and Cy was soon reading the obituary of Alfred Wygant. There was the standard account but another as well, prepared by the family, florid and a little embarrassing. But the newspaper account of his death, which had appeared several days before, gave him the information he sought. A report on the death of Wygant had been performed by Sorensen Labs.

"He was married to my aunt," the girl at Sorensen's said when he told her why he had come. "I'm Jessica Bernardo."

"That explains the name tag."

She wore a lab coat and her thick blonde hair was pulled back on her head. He must be getting old. All young women looked beautiful to him now.

Bernardo. There was a chain of garden stores in the greater Chicago area called Bernardo's.

"That's my father, Fulvio. Alfred Wygant was my uncle, sort of. My Aunt Eleanor was married to my father's brother, and when he died she married Alfred."

"Your dad still alive?"

A look of pain altered her expression.

"He's in the hospital. He's quite ill."

"I'm sorry."

"Why are you interested in Alfred Wygant's test?"

Suddenly his task acquired delicate dimensions. He did not want to tell this lovely young woman that he was filling out a slack period in homicides by checking out how her sort of uncle had died.

"I'm not sure."

She tipped her head to one side. Her lower lip puffed moistly out. "Secrets?"

"I'm not sure of that."

"All right, all right. I'll leave you alone." And she went brightly off. At the Last Judgment Cy hoped to get credit for the fact that he watched her only halfway out of the room. Then he turned and began to plink away on the computer keys.

26

Marie outdid herself, providing a feast incommensurate with the noonday meal, at least at the rectory of St. Hilary; risotto, veal, and a spinach salad. Not even Amos Cadbury could find superlatives enough as he dabbed at his mustached mouth with his napkin, rolled his eyes, and settled for the inarticulate sigh of the satiated diner.

"Marie . . ." he began, but words failed him again.

"This is an audition, Marie. I can tell you now. Mr. Cadbury wants to hire you."

"Oh, I would never leave here," she cried with the tones of a maiden moving closer to her tempter rather than farther away.

"And I would never go to heaven if I did. Where does Dante put gluttons, Father Dowling?"

"In the sixth cornice of purgatory. But I think the temptation would be to *luxuria*. It is not that you would eat too much but that you would enjoy it too much."

Marie did not like this theoretical turn to

the conversation. She preferred paeans of praise to be straightforward and kept to the matter at hand.

"It is a pleasure to cook for someone whose taste buds are still alive."

Father Dowling let the two of them go on for a time, versicle and response, like a choir. Finally, even Marie wearied of praise and tossing her apron disappeared through the swinging door into her kitchen.

"I have no news on Earl Hospers, Father. But I have a good young lawyer looking into it. As soon as I learn anything, I will pass it on to you."

"That is very good of you."

Father Dowling had not asked Amos to lunch to find out about Earl, though of course he was interested. Something had happened that made him want to know more about the Bernardos, and he was certain that Amos Cadbury would know what he wanted to know. The whole matter was quite delicate of course. It would have been imprudent to tap Marie's somewhat biased view of the family.

"Ah, the Bernardos," Amos said, sitting back.

"Before you get too comfortable, why don't we move into the study?"

"I would like a cigar."

"And I shall smoke my pipe."

The significant silence in the kitchen ceased, indicating that he had been right to suspect that Marie was on duty, as she conceived her duty. Anything short of a confession she could eavesdrop on was simply part of her job description as housekeeper.

Amos lit his cigar with devoted attention, drawing it to an even and aromatic glow. The pastor filled and lighted his pipe, and once more Amos said, "The Bernardos. Father, I will tell you things I would tell no one else in the sure and certain knowledge that it will go no farther."

"Things you know professionally."

"Yes."

In this Father Dowling could not of course reciprocate, but he was grateful for Amos's confidence.

"Of course much of what I say is in the public domain."

Amos had a gift for narrative, and Father Dowling had the impression that he was benefiting from much meditation on the subject at hand, perhaps fresh and recent meditation, as the sequel suggested. But he listened to the account of Fulvio's success, the modest little nursery on a dirt road to which the discerning gardeners of Fox River found their way in increasing numbers. The original nursery had been left intact though it was supplemented by a newer building, a building that was the model for the Bernardo Nurseries that soon were to be found in most of the suburbs of Chicago, as even the still-autonomous communities were called.

There was no need to hurry the account, though it was not for this economic saga and entrepreneurial coup that he was consulting Amos.

"And now the family: a saintly wife, one daughter, two sons, one of them, the oldest child, a priest."

"Raymond?"

"Raymond."

Amos had first become closely acquainted with Raymond through his role as trustee at the college.

"He was the golden boy, Father Dowling. If the Edmundites had a future it would depend in large part on Raymond Bernardo. He held responsible positions in the Order at an early age. He was assistant superior when he left."

Amos sighed forth smoke. There was no trace of morose delectation in his reaction to Raymond's defection, all the more impressive because in the purest heart there is a tendency to take however muted pleasure in another's fall. It is one of the baser emotions whose virtuous remedy is "There but for the grace of God go I."

"No one had any inkling that he would do such a thing. By all accounts, it was precipitous."

"There was a woman."

"Of course. Nonetheless, he professed to have profound theological difficulties as well as distaste for the discipline of the Church. Do you know Father Bourke?"

"No."

"He was Raymond's mentor. The defection of his protégé broke his heart. We talked of it only once, and when I asked why, he said after a prolonged silence, 'Amos, he lost his faith. It is as simple as that.' "

"Who was the woman?" Father Dowling asked.

"I believe they are still together, whether married or not I can't say. She was a nun, sent by her Order to the college. They met . . ."

"And he lost his faith?"

"Perhaps he is just a logically consistent man. What he wanted to do was incompatible with his faith, his vows, his whole way of life. It was an either-or. He chose or and drove off to California with the young woman." Amos puffed for a moment. "He

253

had with him a credit card of the Order's. They financed their expedition with it, most lavishly, I understand. I believe that once I compared them to Bonnie and Clyde."

"You did. And what of Fulvio?"

"This broke his heart too. He has not been in a church since. I have this on the authority of his sister-in-law, Eleanor Wygant."

"I have met her."

"*Formidable,*" Amos said, trilling the R. "She was married to Fulvio's brother. When he died she married Alfred."

"You knew them both."

"I knew Alfred better."

A pause. And then Amos confided in Father Dowling the story of Alfred's near-million-dollar investment in Bernardo's. No, he corrected himself. "It was personal, between Fulvio and Alfred. A very astute man turned over to another very astute man nearly one million dollars, and to this day I have been unable to find any written commitment to pay the money back."

"You have an explanation?"

"*Cherchez la femme, M. l'abbe. Toujours chercher la femme.* In this case, *femme* in the sense of wife."

"Eleanor?"

Amos nodded. "She was putty in Fulvio's hands."

"Odd."

"Yes."

"When you suggested a woman was the explanation, I thought . . ."

Here Amos fell silent, but his silence spoke. Father Dowling dared a further probe.

"Fulvio was a womanizer?"

"There were stories, but there are always stories."

Father Dowling smiled. He doubted that such stories circulated about Amos Cadbury.

They returned to the subject of the college and of what might have been if Raymond Bernardo had not done what he had done. Amos's account of the recent board meeting was told in the sepulchral tones of Job's servant come to tell the bad news.

"The low point of that day, Father, came after the meeting. I was speaking with Eugene Box, counsel of the college, and he suggested that this oaf Cassirer intends to accuse Andrew Bernardo of sexual irregularity."

"Oh no."

"Not the best phrase, perhaps. The accusation is that Andrew shares bed and board

255

with a woman not his wife. However commonplace that has become, it is cause for dismissal in the faculty manual."

"I hope there is no bad news about Jessica."

"I pray not. She is the best of the lot."

If Amos had any intimation of the cause of Father Dowling's curiosity about the Bernardos he did not show it. He would not have shown it if he had. Surely he would not think the pastor of St. Hilary's was hungry for mere gossip. And he would have been right.

When the call from Jessica had come yesterday Marie was over at the school, and he was able to go off to the hospital without fanfare.

"Would you come see my father?"

"The question is, will he see me?"

"He has asked for you."

Jessica and her mother left him at the door of the room and returned to the waiting room down the hall. Fulvio's eye was on him from the moment he entered the room. He waited until Father Dowling was beside the bed.

"Did you bring the oils?"

"They're in the hospital chapel."

"I'm an old sinner, Father Dowling."

"We all are."

He shook his head. "I'm in a class by my-self."

Father Dowling slipped on the little stole he had brought, purple side out. "You want to confess?"

"I don't know where to begin."

With the capital sins. Fulvio confessed to breaking them all. But lust predominated.

"I don't know how many women I've had."

When did Father Dowling first suspect that Fulvio was engaged in a performance, that there was more than a macho memory involved in these claims to a dozen adulterous affairs?

"And I've been a thief. I took nearly a million dollars from a man and gave him nothing in return."

Amos's account of the transaction between Alfred Wygant and Fulvio bore that out. And that gave credence to the final revelations.

"I am responsible for that man's death, Father. I might as well have murdered him."

27

"Father Bourke called," his mother said.

"I saw him the other day. Not to talk to."

"Where?"

"He was concelebrating the eleven-thirty on campus."

"You were there?"

He did not discourage her reaction, although perhaps he had sought it. Since his father had seen Father Dowling she clearly believed anything was possible. Was it? As the days multiplied since his arrival in Chicago the distance from Thousand Oaks increased exponentially. His present surroundings, his parents' home, the grim gray urban sprawl that was, in the phrase, the greater Chicago metropolitan area, exerted their familiarity, and the setting of the past decade seemed unreal, almost imaginary. He told himself that he should call Phyllis. He had not told her of his visit to campus, although as he walked through its altered landscape he had been rehearsing his account to her.

He called her on his cell phone from the parking lot of the hospital after he had dropped his mother off.

"Do you realize what time it is here?"

"Whoops. I forgot." There was a two-hour difference in time between Chicago and Thousand Oaks. He had an image of a sleepy Phyllis reaching for the phone beside the bed. "I miss you."

"How is he?"

"He seems to have stabilized." Since seeing Father Dowling? That was his mother's explanation. The burden of all those missed Masses had been lifted from his soul, giving the body a new lease on life.

Phyllis hummed.

"If I should leave I would very likely be called back here."

She continued to hum. This familial piety had not been much on display in recent years. He explained to her that he was caught now, whatever he might have done. The length of his visit depended on his father's health.

"My mother has become dependent on me. I'm calling from the parking lot of the hospital."

"You're trying to make it up to them."

Of course she would be engaged in long-distance analysis, half awake but on the job, looking for the real reason he was in Chicago still and she was alone in Thousand Oaks.

"Well, shortly I will be making it up to you."

"That sounds nice."

"Sound has nothing to do with it."

"I have been seeing Julia."

"Professionally?"

"Of course. Raymond, she is infatuated with you."

"Then the two of you have something in common."

"Oh ha."

On something of a light note he brought the conversation to an end, glad to have called her, glad to have it over. He crossed the lot to the entrance and went upstairs to be with his mother. He might try to make the eleven-thirty on campus if his father was okay.

He joined his mother at his father's bedside, but Fulvio did not acknowledge his presence. He did look different, more serene. The head turned, and their eyes met.

"Good morning, Father."

He squeezed his father's hand, the one without the IV needle stuck in its back. That was all, one dart to remind him. Fulvio was content to lie there silent with a silent Margaret at his side. Raymond went down the hall, avoided the waiting room where television went on night and day, and continued to the cafeteria. In its anteroom was a cigarette machine. He stopped and looked at the familiar brands. There were Camels still, his old brand. Everyone had smoked, it seemed, all the members of the order. He and Phyllis had quit on their way to California. They ran out, and did not want to leave their bed to buy more.

Raymond got out his wallet and began to feed dollar bills into the machine. A package now cost what a carton once had. "Thou shalt not smoke" was the only commandment left, the decalogue become a monologue. He took the package from the machine and realized he had no matches. Outside, smokers were gathered, shoulders hunched against the wind, stamping their feet, puffing, puffing. He decided to wait. He could use the lighter in the car to taste his first cigarette in years.

And he did light up, on the way to campus, neither liking nor disliking it, but imagining Phyllis wondering why he was doing this. He and Father Bourke used to walk in the evening after supper, smoking, talking, from time to time sitting on a bench. How many cigarettes had been smoked on those evening walks? The number that occurred to him seemed scarcely credible.

It was shortly after eleven when he settled into a back pew in the campus church. The prodigal returned? That was ridiculous. As he sat there he told himself that, yes, he did miss this place that evoked memories at every turn; he did miss the camaraderie of other priests, his status among them, the routine of their day. But the one thing needful was gone. He looked at the distant altar, at the original altar beyond with its elaborate tabernacle. The lamp glowing in the sanctuary signified that the Blessed Sacrament was in repose in that tabernacle. A ciborium full of hosts, with a golden cap from which embroidered linen strips fell. The body and blood of Our Lord Jesus Christ under the appearance of bread. As he had said to Jessica, the sacrament was central to the Church because it was central to the faith. And everything else radiated from it. Priests must be ordained to confect the Eucharist, and bishops were needed for the task of ordaining them, bishops who were in a direct line from the apostles, an unbroken chain linking the present Church to its historical past. But the Eucharist was now, here, in that tabernacle, about to be reencted at that altar. Raymond knew all this, but now there were only words.

Why stay? Because he hoped Father Bourke would concelebrate and he could get another glimpse of his old mentor. Because he hoped that in some unplanned way, some accident, he would find himself again talking with Father Bourke. What the topic would be, what he would say to the old priest, what Father Bourke would say to him — Raymond stopped himself from imagining any of that. But he did wonder whether the old priest's reception would be like his mother's or like his father's. Would he condemn or forgive?

A few people, about the same number as before, began to arrive, distributing themselves through the church at random intervals, banging kneelers, looking around, getting settled. Raymond checked the desire to criticize these people. They seemed the same ones as before; perhaps like his mother they came every day. What better practice if one believed? Still, they were an unimpressive bunch, the halt and the lame, the old and arthritic, many ostentatiously pious. Were they the elite of the race?

Mass began with the tinkling of the sacristy bell and the appearance of the celebrant, not the same priest as before. But after a minute, Father Bourke once more rolled into the sanctuary in his wheelchair and came to a stop to the right of the celebrant. The Mass began.

How many Masses had Raymond himself said? It would be possible to calculate, but the number of Masses said each day around the world was incalculable, the commemoration of the Last Supper and of Calvary, repeated endlessly through the time zones of the world, the words spoken over bread and wine that made Christ sacramentally present on the altar. On this altar and all the others. When he had studied the Eucharist in theology they had talked of the seeming impossibility of this. How could Christ be present in so many places simultaneously? Sacramental presence was different, that was the answer. Raymond had seen the difficulties but had no personal doubts. If God could become man what could he not do? The creator of the universe was not limited by his own laws. As he remembered it, his faith had been untroubled and serene, the air he breathed. Almost with dread he recalled the day when standing at the altar, holding the bread, he could not at first even say the words. How could sound coming from his mouth effect such a miracle?

In class such a difficulty would have been

handled easily. It was not a personal power the priest possessed but one that had been conferred on him by ordination in order to fulfill the command of Christ. Do this in memory of me. But it had been more than doubt that had gripped him. Doubt engaged the mind more than the heart, but his heart had failed him then. Finally he managed to utter the words of consecration. He ascribed it to a sense of unworthiness, but of course that wasn't it. Or he had not acknowledged the source of his unworthiness.

He had been in a state of mortal sin as he stood at the altar. He was a fornicator, one who had broken his vows and with a woman who had taken the vow of chastity herself. What was happening with Phyllis had little of mind about it; a condition of its happening was that he not think of what they were doing. And then they were caught in the web of their desires, in their little conspiracy against the commandments and rules and duties of their state of life. Ah, the sweet secrecy of those weeks during which his faith had seeped away, as had hers. He stopped saying the office. He no longer prayed. He avoided saying Mass. He was assailed by a remembered passage in the autobiography of St. Teresa of Avila who had seen devils writhing around a priest saying

Mass in a state of sin. So much of what he had read and learned had to be put into escrow, kept from his conscious mind. But the time came when conflict had ceased.

Daydreaming through the Mass. Once he would have called it distraction at prayer. He had sat through the readings oblivious to the words, but then the acoustics in this church had always been bad. Now Father Bourke had wheeled to the altar, and the heart of the rite began. The old arm lifted when the celebrant consecrated in a gesture of me too. He remembered that Father Bourke had been a foe of concelebration.

"A priest should say his own Mass. There's only one Mass when priests concelebrate; many when they don't."

The angels danced during the subsequent quarrel in the common room, where drinks in hand, cigars, pipes, cigarettes, the members of the order discussed the ins and outs and pros and cons of concelebration. But whatever Bourke's misgivings, concelebration was approved and accepted by the Church, and that was the end of it.

"*Roma locuta est* . . ." Father Bourke conceded, but his voice was reluctant.

Once in class that phrase had been mentioned — *Roma locuta est, causa finita est* — and Barwell was asked to translate. "*Rome* is

266

a word," he had replied uncertainly, "and causes are finite." It had seemed another argument for the vernacular.

The pews emptied as the people went up to receive communion. Raymond sat. The familiar had become as strange as some alien rite, but he was becoming used to it. Someone tapped his shoulder. It was John.

"I told Father Bourke I saw you the other day. He'd like to see you."

The earnest expression, the whisper on which rode the smell of tobacco. Raymond was filled with terror.

"Not today!"

John looked sad. "He's going in for an operation tomorrow."

Raymond found himself nodding. "All right."

John slid in beside him. "I'll take you over."

Raymond felt he was under arrest when John led him under the great oaks to the community dining room.

"I don't want to have lunch."

"Oh, you and Father Bourke will eat alone. He doesn't come to the refectory often. He's in Purgatory."

Purgatory was the name given to the building in which the old and infirm priests lived, nurses on duty, medicines administered, doctors dropping in at intervals.

They turned off the path leading to the community residence building and headed for Purgatory. A faint voice called them, and they turned to see Father Bourke slowly approaching in his wheelchair. John hurried to get behind him and push. Raymond, frozen where he stood, met the gaze of Father Bourke.

"He's going to have lunch with you," John said over the old priest's shoulder.

A hand stretched, and Raymond took it. "I heard you were back." His slurred voice was intelligible enough.

"My father is ill."

"I'm sorry to hear it. You can tell me everything over gruel."

Raymond took over from Purgatory, wheeling Father Bourke up the ramp to the door, over which in Latin was engraved *Domus Sanctae Marthae*, recalling the semicloistered nuns whose convent it once had been, the cooks and maids and launderers for the community. John scooted off for lunch at the residence.

His earlier question was answered when they settled in at a table in the refectory of Purgatory. Father Bourke's reception was like his mother's. You might have thought

Raymond had been on priestly assignment elsewhere for a time and now was back. Around them, in various stages of senility and dementia, other old warriors toyed with their food and looked vacantly about. Some had obviously had strokes. Young uniformed girls helped those who could not help themselves. What a job.

"How changed you must find everything, Raymond."

"Yes."

"How ill is your father?"

"Very."

"I will pray for him."

"What's this about an operation?"

He dismissed it. "I had an operation a year ago. They did a biopsy and had to cut out my prostate."

Old Father Bourke's reproductive organs had been as superfluous as his appendix during his long life so he could bid adieu to his prostate without regret. Raymond could not help but think of himself in the condition Father Bourke now found himself. The sight of his father on his apparent deathbed had not brought such thoughts, but now he thought of himself grown old, helpless, in need of care. That would happen to him, if he were lucky, as it would happen to Phyllis. It happened to everyone.

"What is it this time?"

"Open-heart."

"Good Lord," he said, but Father Bourke dismissed it with a wave of his hand.

"How good it is to see you," the old priest said suddenly. "This is an answer to a prayer. I have missed you very much."

"I disappointed you."

"Yes. How have you been?"

"Fine. Fine."

"And what do you do?"

Describing the practice he and Phyllis had developed in this setting was unreal. He could hear himself with Father Bourke's ears, and he realized how weird it must seem that a man who had deserted his priesthood should be making a comfortable living advising California neurotics. He did not want to go into details of the advice he gave.

"Have you married?"

"Civilly."

Father Bourke nodded. Suddenly Raymond found himself telling the old priest about the meeting with his parents, of his father's taunting demand that he give him absolution.

"You could have."

Raymond shook his head. "He was just being theatrical. He has seen a priest."

"Thank God."

270

His own reaction when he heard of Father Dowling's visit had been relief that now his father would leave him alone on that matter. Now he could almost share Father Bourke's reaction. After all, if it were all true . . . But life is not lived on the basis of hypotheticals.

"When you left things had not gotten too bad, Raymond, but dear God, today. Sometimes I think you were wise to go."

He wanted to protest. It was one thing not to be condemned, but he did not want approval, not from Father Bourke. The old priest would die with his boots on, at his post to the end, and that is how it should be. But the old priest went on, a lamentation about these dark days, the state of the Church, of the Order, of the college.

"You wouldn't believe the stories. It's a mockery of one's whole life."

How could he not sympathize with the old priest's sadness at the changes he had lived to see? But this was not what he wanted to hear from him. He wanted the vibrant confidence of old, the enormous solidity with which he had lived his vocation. He wanted to hear that all the changes could not touch the essential thing, that in any case one must be true to the vocation to which he had been called. And Father Bourke had been faithful. For over fifty years he had kept his vows, done his work, said his prayers. Raymond felt that these complaints were an excursion out of character. Were they meant to ease his own sense of guilt?

Guilt. Not even the imagined witness of Phyllis could make him disguise what he felt.

"I have caused so many people pain."

"Your parents?"

"Yes. And you."

"God bless you, my boy."

Tuna salad on a lettuce leaf. Father Bourke ate little. Raymond had no appetite at all, but he cleaned his plate. In the community, one did not waste.

"Come see me again," Father Bourke said. "I'm off for my nap."

"I will come see you in the hospital."

The old hand squeezed his.

It was with a riot of conflicting emotions that Raymond walked to his car. He saw nothing. His eyes were swimming with tears. He stopped, lit a cigarette, and blinked his eyes dry.

With his father in intensive care and Father Bourke just down the hall awaiting his operation, Raymond felt that he had come home just in time to bid good-bye to the two most important men in his life. Father

272

Bourke had pretended the other day to understand why Raymond had left, exculpating him, as if the prospect of the coming dissolution was more than a loyal Edmundite could bear. It made his defection seem a blow for integrity. But it was Father Bourke, the person, he heard rather than these supposedly consoling words. Hunched in his wheelchair, living with men in the advanced stages of senility, at the door of eternity as they all believed, Father Bourke somehow seemed to stand tall in the courage with which he bore the unpalatable changes in the college and order. The simple fact was that he had given the lifetime to God that he had promised.

Young Rocco explained open-heart surgery to Raymond with clinical relish. How could the old priest survive such a massive shock to his system?

"He could go at any time if he doesn't have the operation."

Father Bourke would doubtless have been prepared if death suddenly came upon him, but Father John had accompanied him to the hospital, Cronin had supplied the oils, and John had given the old priest the last rites, with Raymond in attendance. As he anointed Father Bourke, John acted with dispatch, an artisan at work. Had the young priest ever wondered if the life he lived was worth it? Probably not. It did not seem a failing. Raymond spoke to his old mentor briefly before he was wheeled away.

"God bless you, Raymond."

He choked at the old man's goodness, leaned over, and touched his lips to his forehead.

"I'm so glad you came back. I had thought I would never see you again."

The taste of oil came with the kiss. Raymond mentioned it.

"The Four Last Things," the old priest murmured.

"You'll make it."

"Is that a promise?"

"A prayer."

And it was. He realized that he was more moved by the fact that Father Bourke was at death's door than by his father's condition, arguably worse. Father Bourke was taken away, doors swung shut, and Raymond turned with tears in his eyes to face John. John patted his arm as if he were the chief mourner. Perhaps he was.

"He managed to say Mass before being brought here."

Father Bourke had once told him that he had never missed saying daily Mass since his ordination. Raymond remembered that, in his final days before leaving, he had avoided the altar, unable to confront his own lack of faith in what he would do there.

The Four Last Things, the old priest had said. Jessica had mentioned them as well. *Death, judgment, heaven, hell.* For millennia those words had summed up the facts of life, inspired art and literature, Dante notably. What do we know that has rendered them obsolete?

The following day, Father Bourke was apparently doing well despite the seriousness of the operation. "They'll open him like a clam," Rocco had said. "Saw through his breastbone . . ." Raymond had stopped him. But Father Bourke was so heavily sedated there was no chance of talking. Again Raymond pressed his lips to the old priest's forehead.

His father seemed suspended in a stable condition, hovering near death but holding on. His mother alternated vigils at the bedside with prayers in the waiting room. What would become of her after his father died? Of course, there were Andrew and Jessica. Would she live on alone in the old house, among the bric-a-brac and memories? The thought of himself in far-off California seemed a kind of desertion.

Andrew seemed distracted when Raymond saw him and he asked why.

"I'm okay. So you went to see Father Bourke?"

"It just happened."

Andrew nodded. "What does he think of the modern world?"

"What you'd expect."

"He may have a point."

"Is something the matter?"

"Just because Dad's in intensive care and Mom's a frazzle?" Andrew smiled wryly. "I don't feel I've been much of a son to them."

It might have been an accusation, but it wasn't. Eleanor came. She seemed to come and go throughout the day. It had taken a while, but finally Raymond had admitted to himself what he had seen the afternoon he came by the house unannounced and his father scrambled off the couch and got between him and a flustered Eleanor. At the time, he would have imagined his father was well beyond the temptations of the flesh. Did such a time ever come? Had he been shocked? When he quit trying to kid himself about what he had seen, he found he really wasn't surprised. Eleanor did seem to cling to his father on all occasions. How long had it gone on? Looking at Eleanor now, the well-groomed older woman, economically comfortable, not much to do, just busy

276

being a busybody, he wondered what his father had seen in her. He decided that Eleanor must have been the aggressor. Not that his father would have put up much opposition.

"Has Jessica spoken to you of her new novel?"

"Do writers talk about what they're writing?"

"It's about all of us." She looked at Raymond meaningfully.

"They'll never publish it." He laughed. What did he seem to Jessica, really or in imagination? His going and the manner of it could occupy a large place in her musings about things. But he did not feel threatened.

28

Hazel plunked a pile of pages on Tuttle's desk and folded her arms, awaiting praise. Tuttle glanced at the top sheet and nodded. "Good."

"Good! Take a look, for heaven's sake. Get a legal education. This could be your big chance."

The only tolerable thing about Hazel's office behavior was that there were no witnesses, by and large. He looked at her formidable presence and what he saw was a buxom obstacle to his friendship with Peanuts Pianone. He had just come from lunch with Peanuts: great platters of fried rice, cold Mexican beer, and the joys of wordless fellowship. He briefed Hazel on his visit to the campus, in the course of which she sat down.

"You might have told me."

"I just did."

"Lily St. Clair sounds as if she can be a real ally."

"She's nuts about Cassirer, that's all."

"All? That's plenty. Now read that stuff, and we'll talk about the next step."

She rose and sailed from the room on a cloud of perfume. It was a time to brood about the dark day when he had hired her from a service providing temporary help. Temporary! Now he couldn't blast her out of the office. She took care of the books and paid her own salary, such as it was, so there was no way for him to cut her off without a major battle. Sighing, Tuttle pulled the papers she had brought to him and began listlessly to leaf through them. But Hazel came back.

"Who's Mabel Gorman?"

Tuttle shrugged.

"She has called several times." Hazel waited. "She says she's a student at St. Edmund's."

"Ah yes."

"Ah yes, what?"

Tuttle adjusted his tweed hat. "I befriended her."

Hazel observed a moment of silence, as if for the future departed. "Keep it up, and you'll need a lawyer yourself."

She huffed out, and Tuttle turned to the paralegal's papers.

Barbara was good; there was no doubt of that. She had gathered all the legal prece-

279

dents. There were photocopies of newspaper accounts of local cases, written by Tetzel. He would have to talk with the reporter. So well organized were the materials Barbara had prepared that something like a strategy began to form in Tuttle's mind. The essence of the law is to avoid going to law. What he needed was to intimidate the college into buying off his client before he was turned down for tenure. The basic complaint was that Andrew Bernardo's presence on the committee made it impossible for Cassirer to get a square shake. And that Andrew himself lived in flagrant violation of the college's requirements for the lifestyle of its faculty.

On another visit with his client, Cassirer had all but salivated as he discussed Andrew Bernardo's living arrangement. Professor St. Clair had looked in, and Cassirer waved her to a chair.

"My only regret is that this will involve Gloria," Lily St. Clair said.

"The friend of my enemy is my enemy," Cassirer announced.

Cassirer's notion was that Tuttle should sit down with Box and let him know the kind of rotten publicity the college faced if it didn't come through with a tenured appointment for Horst Cassirer. The prospect of meeting with Box again did not exhilarate Tuttle. Box was a clone of Amos Cadbury, a man who regarded Tuttle as he might the squirming creatures discovered by turning over a rock. At least Cadbury had earned his righteous air of superiority. But Box?

Resentment is a powerful incentive. Tuttle began to write on a yellow legal pad, outlining what he would lay before Box. With that objective in mind, he finally read systematically through Barbara's materials. He could cite precedents, although the cases Barbara had found were after-the-fact suits, brought when the plaintiff had been formally turned down. At the moment, all Cassirer had was hearsay of what a supposedly confidential committee meeting had voted.

"Everyone knows," Lily St. Clair had assured him.

In the course of the little confab a man named Zalinksi came in, adding his own two cents. It was difficult for Tuttle to tell which of them held the college in greater contempt, making it a puzzle why they were there and why Cassirer was willing to declare World War III in order to be there permanently.

The intercom crackled, and Hazel's voice

asked if he had read the stuff.

"Very interesting."

"I'll call and make an appointment for you with Box."

Before he could delay her, she had switched off and he saw the light on his phone go on. Two minutes later Hazel was once again heard electronically.

"Tomorrow morning, ten o'clock."

"Did you tell him the purpose of the visit?"

"He already knew."

She switched off. Box's expecting the call seemed ominous to Tuttle. He was going up against a local institution, one highly respected, with a history that claimed the loyalty of many. Of course he could expect Box to exude confidence with all that goodwill behind him. The crux of the whole argument came down to the fact that Andrew Bernardo was shacking up with a colleague. That was almost as bad as being caught lighting up in one of the smoke-free buildings on campus.

Hazel left at four. Tonight was her night to play duplicate bridge, and her competitive juices were flowing. She was a black belt or something in bridge and had tried to interest him in a hand or two of honeymoon bridge. The thought terrified Tuttle. He had no doubt that Hazel had designs on him. Where else could she find someone that looked like so much malleable putty? If she could shape him to her wishes at the office what might she not do in the privacy of their own home? Tuttle was a celibate by inadvertence and because by and large women frightened him. He sat alone in the inner office, tweed hat pulled low over his eyes, communing with his late father. The other Tuttle in Tuttle & Tuttle was his constant point of reference. He prayed that his father had not heard of Hazel in the next world. Since he was sure his paternal parent was in heaven, that seemed unlikely. He sought advice from his father, and the advice came, almost audible. He picked up the phone and called Peanuts.

"Come on over."

"No way."

"She's gone."

"For good?"

"For the day."

Peanuts grunted and hung up. Twenty minutes later Tuttle heard the huffing sounds of Peanuts, who had mounted the four flights from the street floor. He looked in warily, fearful that he had been lured here under a pretext. But he was satisfied that Hazel was not there.

"You come by car?"

"I was in my car when you called."

"Good." Tuttle got to his feet. "We'll load up with take-out food first."

"First."

"We're going to do a stakeout."

"I want a hamburger."

With Peanuts you never knew. Had he thought Tuttle meant Steak 'n' Shake? In any case, Peanuts changed his mind when Tuttle mentioned Luigi's, adding that this was his treat. After all, Peanuts was providing a tax-payer-owned car; the least he could do was feed him.

An hour later, with Styrofoam cartons of lasagna, house salad, and a bottle of zinfandel, they set up shop across the street from the condo where Andrew Bernardo allegedly lived with Gloria Monday.

"What we looking for?"

"That depends."

But Peanuts had exhausted his curiosity and returned to his lasagna. He had expressed reluctance to drink wine out of plastic cups, so Tuttle had snatched some glasses from a table on the way out of Luigi's. He poured; they toasted. This was living. As for what they were parked there to see, Tuttle could not have said, but he had the sense that he was following paternal orders. Something would turn up, as his father had often said. Against that possibility, Tuttle was equipped with a fancy camera Hazel had insisted must be part of his standard equipment.

"I don't handle divorces."

"You couldn't handle a marriage." She tried to chuck him under the chin, and he danced away. She insisted that a camera with lenses like this had multiple uses. It was digital, and one could scan the memory to see what he had taken. Hazel had spent a day taking candid shots of Tuttle in the office. Later, when he looked through them, he was glad he had been wearing his tweed hat. For a time, Hazel had tried to snatch it from his head every chance she got until she decided it was his persona.

Twilight came, but there was still light when Andrew pulled up in a rust bucket and handed a gorgeous girl out of the car. Tuttle had the camera up and took some lovey-dovey shots of the couple on the way to the door. Andrew fished in his pocket and came out with a key but the woman had already taken one from her purse. She let them in.

"Who are they?" Peanuts asked.

"My ticket to fame and fortune."

"Take a look at that car."

"Yeah." Tuttle's own wasn't much better,

which is why he preferred riding at city expense with Peanuts at the wheel. Amos Cadbury had a driver. So in a way did he.

They could have left then, but it was not unpleasant sitting there with Peanuts, belly full of Italian food, night coming on. He had got what he came for, but Peanuts did not realize it. Besides, he seemed as content as Tuttle.

For such accidental reasons they were there when a young woman came briskly down the walk, her purse swinging from her skinny shoulder like a pendulum. Mabel Gorman, the girl who had guided him about the campus. She turned in and went to the door through which Andrew and the woman had gone. She did not let herself in but rang the bell. She cupped her hands around the intercom when she spoke, but Tuttle could not have heard her anyway. What the hell was she doing here? He recalled her lament about his representing Cassirer. The woman he had seen with Andrew had to be Gloria. Mabel pulled open the door and went inside.

A man appeared from behind a hedge, pushing a bicycle. Hand on the seat, head thrust forward, he turned into the same building and studied the list of occupants. Had he too been a witness to the little parade into the building? Tuttle willed himself, Peanuts, and the car into invisibility when the man turned from the door and pushed his bicycle to the sidewalk and prepared to set off. But first he looked up and down the street. His gaze went over the car and on down the street. He soon followed it, flinging his leg over the bicycle and pedaling away into the night.

"Who's he?" Peanuts asked. So he was awake.

"A client."

"Can't he afford a car?"

29

They had just gotten out of their coats when
the bell rang and Gloria went to the intercom. Andrew stopped as the nervous voice
of Mabel Gorman crackled into the room.
Gloria turned to him, her brows arched.

"One of my students."

Gloria pressed the button that opened the
front door and then went down the hall to
her study. Professional courtesy.

Mabel came shivering into the room some
minutes later when Andrew opened the
door. She stood hugging herself and looked
around.

"He's been following you."

"Who?"

"Cassirer."

Andrew wished she would stop shivering.
On the other hand, it gave him an excuse for
not asking her to take off her coat. He was
very conscious of Gloria down the hallway,
within earshot. He knew that Cassirer had
been making a pest of himself with Raymond and Jessica. Andrew had tried to dis-

miss this, telling himself that even if worse came to worst and Cassirer decided to inform the world that Andrew Bernardo and Gloria Monday shared an apartment, no one would care. Except himself, of course. He did not want his parents to face more trouble than they already had. He had already lost any moral superiority over Raymond. Jessica didn't really know Gloria, but she knew who she was from her student days. Mabel made a face, wrinkling her nose. What would Jessica make of Mabel Gorman?

Mabel had stopped shivering, but she still stood there hugging herself. She looked past Andrew and whispered, "Is she here?"

"Professor Monday answered your ring."

"I could hardly hear her."

Outside, voices over the intercom had to compete with all the street noises, the wind, whatever.

"How do you know Cassirer is following me?"

"I've been following him. The man's mad. He's capable of anything."

"Andrew?"

It was Gloria, an admonitory call as she came down the hallway from her study. Her face lit up with a professorial smile when she saw Mabel. She strode toward her, hand

289

outstretched. For a moment, it seemed that Mabel would go on hugging herself, but she warily put out a hand.

"What class are you in?"

"I am a junior."

"I meant what class of Andrew's? Professor Bernardo's."

"I came to warn him that Cassirer is following him around."

Gloria's manner changed abruptly. "That's nonsense."

"It may be, but it's true. He's crazy."

Mabel looked a little crazy herself. A strand of hair emerged from her woolen cap and lay across the bony expanse of her forehead. Gloria became patronizing.

"Please sit down."

A shake of the head, and the strand of hair moved like a windshield wiper over her glasses.

"I don't know what you know about academic procedures," Gloria said soothingly. "Horst Cassirer is being considered for tenure, and these are tense moments for us all."

"He should be fired. He's a disgrace."

Gloria hesitated. Was this an abused woman crying out to an older woman for help? That would have changed her whole attitude toward Cassirer. "Has he been bothering you?" she asked delicately.

Mabel's laugh could have been her fortune on the soundtrack of animated cartoons. "Yes, he's been bothering me!"

"In what way?" Gloria moved toward the girl.

"He is quite simply the worst professor I have ever had. He shouldn't be allowed in the classroom. He mocks his students as well as the authors he teaches."

Gloria moved back. "That's quite an accusation."

"It's the truth."

Gloria sat on the arm of the sofa, crossed her arms and looked wise. "These are judgments that will be made by his peers. There are procedures . . ."

"They don't have to sit in his classes."

Gloria might have been remembering the irate letters that had appeared in the student paper. Light came. "What did you say your name was?"

"This is Mabel Gorman," Andrew said. He had been content to let the two women deal with this. He had no idea what Mabel expected of him, now that she had delivered her warning.

As if in answer to this thought, she said, "You have to notify the police."

"The police!" Gloria cried.

Mabel ignored her. She came to Andrew and put her hand on his arm. She might have been making a claim on him. My God, was that it? Students got crushes on professors and harmless platonic exchanges went on in faculty offices with no harm done. But Andrew had never suspected this of Mabel. Her hand on his arm was warm and insistent.

"He would kill you if he could."

"Oh, nonsense," Gloria said, standing. Her eyes were riveted on that clinging hand on Andrew's arm. Andrew put his hand over Mabel's, then patted it.

"I am very grateful for your concern, Mabel. But perhaps you are making too much of this. Academic quarrels are mainly smoke and noise."

"We're both grateful," Gloria said icily and moved toward the door. Andrew escorted Mabel as if he were about to give her away. Gloria opened the door. Mabel looked at the door, at Andrew, at Gloria, then at Andrew again. She could not keep the pathetic affection from her eyes.

"Be careful," she whispered. And then she was gone.

Gloria shut the door and turned. "Be careful indeed."

"Oh for heaven's sake."

"Do all your female students have a crush on you?"

He dropped a chin. "Gloria, please. We are not going to quarrel about that pathetic girl."

And so they got over it. But in his heart of hearts Andrew was grateful to Mabel. Her heated imagination and absurd devotion had a kind of nobility. Gloria's hand came to rest on the arm where Mabel's had lately lain.

30

"Is everything all right in there?" Margaret asked, glancing toward Fulvio's home office.

"He was very neat about everything."

"That's what Jessica said."

"Jessica?"

"She had a look around too."

"When?"

Margaret wasn't sure.

"Before I looked?"

"Perhaps. Yes, I think so."

My God. Eleanor was flooded with the certainty that her niece had found those letters. Worse, Jessica's manner convinced her that she had removed the ones signed Eleanor. Anger rather than embarrassment came. She could hardly wait for late afternoon when Jessica would return to her apartment from work. After taking Margaret to the hospital, just dropping her off, she drove around, distractedly, just wasting time, and finally parked across the street. Eleanor waited in a fever of excitement, scenarios of the coming confrontation rocketing about in her mind. But Jessica did not come. Eleanor took a phone from her purse and called the hospital. She asked for Fulvio Bernardo's room.

A half minute went by. "He's in intensive care."

"I know."

"We don't put through calls to intensive care."

"I am a relative. I know others are with him."

"I'm sorry."

"Is there a phone in the waiting room there?"

"You want the waiting room?"

"Please."

A phone began to ring. Eleanor thought of the ugly little room where Margaret sat praying when she wasn't at Fulvio's bedside. Would no one ever answer? But someone did.

"This is the waiting room."

"Is that you, Raymond? This is Eleanor. Is Jessica there?"

"She just left."

Eleanor remembered to ask how Fulvio was and fidgeted through Raymond's report.

"I drove Margaret there," she said.

"I appreciate that. I'll take her home."

"You have the car?"

"I had some errands to run."

He sounded as if she had wanted an explanation. "How odd everything must seem to you after all these years." At the moment, she felt an extra kinship with Raymond, those letters establishing her own position as a family renegade.

"It gets more familiar all the time."

"Have you gone out to . . ."

"St. Edmund's? Yes."

"Now, that place has changed almost beyond recognition."

"You'd be surprised."

But Eleanor had all the surprise she could handle in her conviction that Jessica had found and removed her godawful letters to Fulvio. Of course she would have found them. Anyone making the most cursory inspection of that file cabinet would have found them. Her cheeks burned in memory of the identifying label for the folder that held the letters of Fulvio's conquests. *Gatte.* She had looked it up. Female cats.

Would Jessica never come? She should have asked Raymond if his sister were going home, but would he have known? She had no idea of how Jessica lived her life, other than writing silly novels. She banged her gloved hands impatiently on the steering wheel and accidentally hit the horn. Just then, Jessica drove up and waved. Eleanor beeped the horn again on purpose and got out of the car.

"I've been waiting for you."

"Come on in."

Eleanor followed Jessica to the door of the building, where her niece opened the door and then held it for Eleanor to precede her.

The apartment was small, simply furnished, books everywhere, and a computer very much in evidence, almost in the center of the room. Photographs of the Bernardo family stood on every available surface. Eleanor was touched to see herself well represented.

"What a lovely place."

"I like it."

"The bachelor girl."

On the mantel of the little fireplace, occupying pride of place, was a Lladró porcelain of the Blessed Virgin. Eleanor went to it and moved an ungloved finger over the smooth surface.

"Your mother said you looked through your father's things." She kept her back to Jessica as she spoke. There was no answer. She turned.

Jessica, coat off, shoes kicked free, said, "I

am going to have a beer. Would you like one?"

"No, thank you. Yes, I will."

Jessica pattered off to the kitchen and returned with the beer, handing one to Eleanor, no glass. She tipped her own and drank thirstily.

"Ah."

"Is it true?"

Jessica did not pretend she had forgotten her remark. She collapsed into a chair, leather with matching leather footstool to which she lifted her stockinged feet.

"I wondered why you were so eager to see Dad's papers."

"And you found out why."

"Your letters? Yes."

"What have you done with them?" There was a desk against the wall served by the same chair on which Jessica must sit when she used her computer, and just revolved from one to the other. The desk was littered with papers.

"They were quite a revelation."

"Jessica, you must know about your father. There were other letters."

"I couldn't figure out who they were from."

"I suppose one could guess, with a little thought and hard remembering."

"What's the point?"

"Exactly. I was going to suggest that they all be removed and destroyed. To spare your mother."

"And the women?"

"Jessica, this is extremely embarrassing for me. I was a fool. It was all a long time ago."

"Not all the letters are dated."

"Are they here?"

"Yes."

"I want them."

"Not yet."

"Not yet? Jessica, you can't mean to use those letters in the novel you're writing."

"If I did, only you and I would know the basis."

"You are going to use them?" Eleanor tried to imitate the way Jessica drank out of the bottle and beer dribbled down her chin. She wiped it off with the back of her hand.

"I haven't decided."

"You're toying with me."

And she was. Jessica pretended to resent the advice Eleanor had given when she had prattled about entering the convent. Was she taking her revenge?

"I suppose you want to destroy them."

"Of course. It was awful of your father to keep them, but so like him."

"Didn't you ever ask for them back?"

"Your father wouldn't even tell me if he had kept them."

"So you wanted to search."

"Not soon enough, obviously."

"They are technically his property, of course."

"Oh, Jessica, stop! Give me those letters. If you have read them I suppose I can't stop you from somehow using them in your story, but I won't rest until I know they've been destroyed."

Jessica took another thirsty drink, then looked thoughtfully at Eleanor. "I have been trying to remember the times when that was going on, between you and Dad."

"You were only a girl."

"Was it going on when you advised me against the convent?"

"You were never serious about that."

"You seemed to think so at the time."

"Jessica, are you trying to get back at me or something?"

Jessica finished her beer and set the bottle on the floor beside her chair. "No."

"Are you going to put me in your novel?"

Jessica laughed. "Real people can't be put into novels, Eleanor."

"Just their letters?"

Eleanor would have given anything to be able to rummage through the papers on

Jessica's desk, as she had gone through Fulvio's. It was insufferable to have to sit here bargaining about those letters. She imagined breaking in, while Jessica was at work. Oh, dear God, what a fool she had been.

When at last she left, mission unaccomplished, Eleanor did not start her car at once. She laid her forehead against the steering wheel and wept, thinking of Jessica reading what she had written to Fulvio. Eventually, she drove away, headed home, heartsick.

31

"You can't seriously mean to use them."

Would she in the end portray the character based on her father as a womanizer, unfaithful with her aunt and others? It was not her father's actions that shocked her. Had her mother ever suspected? The letters made Eleanor intelligible now in a way she had never been before. All that fussing concerned-aunt manner made clear that Eleanor could not imagine herself except as a Bernardo, an honorary Bernardo or Bernardo emerita; it was her identity. Of course Uncle Joe would have been second best to Fulvio, so she had to worm her way into the affections of the paterfamilias too. Half-forgotten memories from years ago came to Jessica. The lake, the little sailboat, her mother wondering where her father had gone. "I can't see the boat. Can you see the boat?"

"Were you ever discovered?"
"I want those letters."

"I could have copies made for you."

Her aunt's open hand swept through the air and clapped against the side of her head, causing her ear to ring, her cheek to burn. Almost immediately she was sorry for what she had done but turned away. She would never have the satisfaction of getting even copies of those letters now.

"I'm sorry."

"For what? Writing those letters? Seducing my father?"

"Seducing!"

If there is laughter in hell it would sound like her aunt's.

It had been Eleanor's pushy insistence that had prompted Jessica to go to her father's study and snoop around. When she found the file of letters written to her father by his abject conquests, she was bemused, saddened, fascinated. And then she had come on those signed "Eleanor." Dear God. She took all of them from the folder and put them in her briefcase. She told herself that she would destroy them, but she hadn't. They suggested an interesting twist in her novel.

The bearded man on a bicycle had been waiting for her in the parking lot some days before when she came out of the lab.

"Jessica Bernardo? I am a colleague of your brother's."

"Raymond?"

"Not likely. Andrew. I want to talk to you."

"That's what you're doing." There was menace in his manner, his stance awkward, the eyes narrowed but with strange feline flecks in them.

"Right here? All right."

"Who are you?"

"Cassirer. Horst Cassirer. Your brother has launched a campaign to prevent my receiving tenure at the college and I want you to stop him."

"You're not serious."

"I am deadly serious. Perhaps I seem young to you, but my scholarly achievements are well known. Throughout the land. Apparently your brother feels threatened by the comparison between my career and his own."

"Threatened? Andrew has tenure. What could you do to him?"

"I am here to discuss what he is doing to me. I do not intend to take this lying down. I will mount an attack of my own. But first I am trying indirection."

"Coming to me?"

"Are you aware that your brother shares an apartment with Gloria Monday?"

"What on earth has that to do with you?"

"His lifestyle is in violation of the faculty manual. If known, it would be cause for dismissal, tenure or not."

"You want to blackmail him?"

"I want him to understand the consequences of his effort to thwart my career. If he wants to destroy me, I will destroy him."

"Aren't tenure decisions made by a committee? How could Andrew's vote threaten you?"

"His vote could save me, that is the point. Will you talk to him?"

"You mean will I warn him?"

"If you like."

"What was your name again?"

"Cassirer." He spelled it for her. "Horst. I am deadly serious," he repeated.

He turned and went away among the parked cars to the street. Jessica watched him go, the angel of destruction. Of course she knew about Gloria, and of course Andrew knew that she knew. A sign of this was that they never referred to it. Jessica had put two and two together, or rather one and one, and seen how it was. Why did the realization make her despise Gloria, whom she scarcely knew, and think of Andrew as being snared in her web?

Her father, Raymond, Andrew, all of them succumbing to the temptations of the flesh. Of course they were men, and men are different.

"He came to you!" Andrew half-lifted from his chair in the cafeteria.

"And threatened to reveal that you are living in sin with Gloria."

The old phrase altered his manner. He smiled. "That makes it sound quaint."

"No, just dumb. Did you ever think of marrying her?"

"And making an honest woman of her?"

"Well, a wife anyway."

Andrew moved his coffee mug as if it were a chess piece, then moved it back again. On his face was written the truth that he would not want to commit himself for life to Gloria. Perhaps the reverse was also true. Meanwhile they had an apartment at half-rent apiece, companionship, and she supposed endless sex. No, familiarity breeds temperance. Regular fornication would pall. How did she know this? I'm a novelist. And Andrew wasn't. That creep Cassirer was right that Andrew's career was not stellar. His suffered by comparison with

Gloria's, forget about Cassirer. How did he see his life?

"Even if I moved out he could still make the accusation."

"Sins of your past life."

"What's all this about sin?"

"It's what what you're doing is called. Remember?"

"Who are you, Mom?"

"I wish."

"Are you a virgin?"

"Would you think less of me if I were?"

She would be damned if she would talk about herself when he was the problem. She had little doubt that Cassirer meant what he said. Perhaps even if Andrew crumbled and voted for him he would play the morality card.

Andrew said, "I doubt the administration would care to make a fuss about how I live."

But the media would. A permissive age was prurient about the behavior it ostensibly approved. Vice and virtue were simply instruments of accusation. Jessica was certain that Cassirer himself did not condemn the way Andrew lived. As she did.

"Well, I've delivered his message."

"I could kill him for going to you."

"If 'twere done 'twere well 'twere done quickly."

307

All the way home she wondered if she had gotten the quotation right.

There was a message on her phone. She half-hoped it was Walter. But it was Raymond.

"Jessica, I'll just say it. Dad died at five ten this afternoon. Could you go home and be with Mom?"

She was so stunned that she could not even cry. She turned and went back out to her car and drove off to be with her mother.

32

Eleanor had taken Margaret to the hospital and went with her into Fulvio's room. He now had a plastic mask over his face and was being given oxygen. Margaret gave a little cry at the sight of him. Well, he did look awful, complexion gray, his chest rising and falling in the effort to breathe. His eyes went back and forth between Margaret and Eleanor. He lifted the bottom of the plastic mask and said, "Boo."

Margaret put the mask back in place and leaned over him. She wanted desperately to do something, but there was nothing to do.

Eleanor whispered to Margaret, "I'll check with the nurses."

Margaret said nothing. Eleanor went out to the nurses' station, where she stood at the counter and was ignored. Doctors scribbled their notes, nurses came and went, busy, busy. There was no one she could ask how Fulvio was. What answer did she expect? After a time she went back to the room.

"My turn, Margaret. Go to the waiting

room. Did you sleep at all last night?"

On the drive down Margaret had lamented missing Mass that morning. Apparently she had tossed and turned until dawn and then fallen into a deep sleep. Eleanor found her in early afternoon, a bewildered woman sitting on a couch, unable to drive herself to the hospital.

"Of course I'll come with you," Margaret said when Eleanor suggested she stay home and rest. But she responded to the suggestion that she sit in the waiting room. "I'll say a rosary."

Eleanor went to the restroom, and when she passed the waiting room, Margaret was already asleep in her chair. She went on to Fulvio's room. His eyes were closed. He continued to breathe in a way that involved his whole upper body. Had she ever really thought she loved this man? What Eleanor saw was the man who had made a fool of her, driven a wedge between Alfred and herself, and kept her silly letters where they could be found by Jessica. What a hateful man he was, sick or not.

The oxygen mask was connected to an outlet in the wall by a clear plastic tube like that which led from the needle in Fulvio's wrist to the wrinkled plastic bag from which, drop by drop, fluid was released. Just below the bag, there was a little handle, like a faucet. Eleanor imagined her hand going to it, her fingers gripping it, slowly turning it. The flow to his arm would stop. There was a silver handle over the oxygen on the wall. Eleanor imagined turning that off too. But her hands were gripping the frame of the bed. She stood there and looked down at the man who had ruined her life. How else could she describe it? Her two marriages had been farces, because of him. And Alfred . . .

"Is there something between you and Fulvio?" he had asked out of the blue.

"Don't be silly."

"Yes or no!"

"No!"

But her half-hysterical tone negated the word. Alfred stared at her and seemed to age as she looked at him.

Perhaps if she had been honest, he would have forgiven her. As it was, he decided to confront Fulvio, accusing him of . . .

"He didn't know how to put it." Fulvio grinned as he told Eleanor.

"Oh my God."

"He wants to take his money out of Bernardo's."

"What did you tell him?"

Another grin. "Maybe later."

But there wasn't to be much later. If Alfred had aged visibly in the minutes after he put the dreaded question, he went rapidly downhill in the weeks that followed. The first time that, waking in the wee hours, she went downstairs and found him in the study, a glass in his hand, his eyes red with drink and tears, she drove pity from herself with anger.

"Alfred! What are you doing?"

"I always wondered what it was like to get drunk. Now I know."

How long had that gone on? Like a fool, she told Fulvio, and one night he showed up unannounced to have a talk with Alfred. He wanted Eleanor to leave them alone but she refused. Alfred offered Fulvio a drink.

"I only drink wine."

"Eleanor, is there wine in the house?"

"I don't want any wine. I've come to talk to you about your money."

"To hell with the money." And then a drunken inspiration. "You can keep the goddamn money. Keep the money but leave Eleanor alone."

Fulvio snickered. "Don't you realize what that would make her?"

Alfred rose from his chair and charged at Fulvio, but he was unsteady on his feet and when Fulvio pushed him he stumbled backward and fell. From the floor, he stared ignominiously at Fulvio. He spoke in a low and broken voice. "Keep the money. What do I care?"

After Fulvio left, Eleanor got him to his feet and tried to get him to come upstairs.

"I suppose I should, now that you're bought and paid for."

She slapped him. Hard. "You drunken ass."

She lay in her bed sleepless for hours, hearing him banging around downstairs. It was nearly three when he came upstairs, laboriously, talking to himself. Then he stood in the door of the room. Eleanor lay still, pretending sleep. When she felt his hand on her breast, she screamed, threw back the covers, and leapt from the bed. Her fury cowed him. She pushed him out of the room, sending him reeling into the hallway and slammed the door. A moment later she heard a crashing sound. She came outside and looked over the bannister at the crumpled body of her husband.

In his hospital bed, Fulvio's chest continued to rise and fall. He seemed to be sleeping. Digital displays on the console over his bed blinked in ways she could not understand, like moving figures in a broker's office. Suddenly they seemed to be blinking out of control. Eleanor stepped back, wondering if she should do something. Surely if there were danger, the nurses would come on the run. That was the point of intensive care. But she thought of the overworked crew, distracted, scampering about. It was ten minutes before the nurse ran into the room.

The nurse pushed her aside and busied herself with her patient. She leaned across the bed and shook the plastic bag. Fulvio awoke, wild-eyed. He began to gasp. The nurse pressed the oxygen mask more tightly to his face. He began to struggle, as if she were trying to harm him. His arm jerked up and the needle in his wrist came loose under the bandages that held it in place. Blood began to ooze from the edges of the bandages. The nurse sounded the alarm.

Fulvio was surrounded by nurses and doctors when the fatal stroke came. Eleanor had moved to a corner of the room, ignored as she had been earlier at the nurses' station. They were thumping on Fulvio's chest, trying to revive him. A machine was hurried into the room and great jolts shook Fulvio's body. Finally, they gave up. It was over. A nurse turned and glared angrily at Eleanor.

"I'll tell his wife," Eleanor said. "She's in the waiting room."

Margaret still dozed in her chair. Eleanor sat beside her. The muted television flickered with inanities. Fulvio was dead. She felt that she had killed him. There are sins of thought, after all. Eleanor had lost two husbands, and now Fulvio was dead. It seemed a shame to wake Margaret. Let her rest. Bad news can always wait.

33

Thunder, her agent, called every day now, sometimes with news, but mainly to find out how it was going.

"I'm on schedule," Jessica assured him.

"Did you mean that about three months?"

"Did I say that?"

"Do you want me to look at what you have done?"

"I don't think so. Not yet."

She had not written her previous books like this. Those she had begun at the beginning and written through to the end. Now she was putting down vignettes, not even chapters, disconnected, moments in the eventual narrative. Jessica had just started and what she did had not followed chronology or anything like a narrative line, but there were things she wanted to try out, sketch, to get down in some form to see what they looked like, beads on an unchained rosary. She had imagined the scene between Raymond and her father. How could she not adopt her father's view of what his son the priest had done? The fact that her father had agreed to see Father Dowling, thereby quelling all her mother's fears, had not been welcome to Jessica the novelist, however it pleased her as a daughter. She had her mother's visceral identification with the faith. Sometimes, thinking of Eleanor and the vocation Jessica had once imagined, she felt like the girl in *Persuasion* whose love had been sidetracked by a busybody older woman.

"It's a phase every Catholic girl goes through," Eleanor had said.

"Did you?"

Aunt Eleanor ignored the question. "What Order did you think of?"

"The Carmelites."

"The Carmelites! They sound like candy. I have never liked the Little Flower."

Jessica had pulled the Carmelites out of a hat. But Eleanor would have reacted the same if she had said the Dominicans or Ursulines or whatever. The truth is that she counted on a negative reaction and did not find it wholly unwelcome. She had not discussed it with her mother because she could imagine a reaction quite the opposite of her aunt's. Her surprising success as a writer had suggested to her that she was meant to do that all along. It was her vocation, and besides there was her work at the lab, a work that was prosaic and routine yet important, the perfect foil to sitting at her computer and entering the world of imaginary characters. But what she was now engaged in seemed more a documentary than a novel, and getting it right had a very different valence. Her brother's defection no longer seemed the aberration her parents considered it but somehow emblematic of the times. They thought of him as unique. For Jessica, fidelity was unique, the kind of unquestioning adherence to a promise made that characterized her parents' marriage, the foundation that sustained all their lives. Did any of them, her brothers or herself, have the character to provide that kind of support for a new generation? She looked at her computer screen and its imagined version of a real-life confrontation.

"Judas," the dying father said, his eyes fixed on his errant son.

"Perhaps I should hang myself."

"You wouldn't have the guts for that either."

"What I did took guts."

"Is that what you call lust?"

"Dad, you've never even met her."

"I've met her a dozen times. I know the type."

"She's not a type. She's my wife."

Was the Phyllis Raymond mentioned his wife? He had never said so. Jessica knew about Andrew and Gloria, not because he had told her, but because such things always did become known. That at least was a secret to her parents. Andrew was much more discreet than Raymond. And what did her parents make of her?

In her father's case, that was not a compelling question. All he expected of her was that she should find a husband and have children. She knew that this was the object of her mother's prayers. All prayers are answered, but sometimes, perhaps usually, the answer is no. Walter had suggested dinner and then immediately added that he knew she could not be in the mood for it now. He was so diffident he even refused for her. She was almost disappointed. The truth is that her father's illness, by ruling out all else, had left her with more time on her hands than usual. Time for her promised novel. She scrolled back to the scene between the runaway priest and his younger sister.

"I would like to meet her."
"I think you'd like her."

"Tell me about her."

But he seemed oddly reluctant to do so, as if he expected her to disapprove. Did he think she imagined a Jezebel, a femme fatale who had lured him from the altar?

"She was a nun?"

"It sounds like a cliché, doesn't it?"

"Oh, I don't know. I suppose you have a lot in common."

(What if I'd become a nun and had fallen in love with a priest and done what Raymond and Phyllis did?)

"What do her parents think?"

"She is technically an orphan."

"Technically?"

"Her father is dead, and she is estranged from her mother."

"Yet she had a vocation?"

"She thought so."

"Don't you?"

"It's not easy to explain."

What view of him did her omniscient narrator have? It was easier to put her parents' judgment of Raymond into the mouths of characters than adopt it as unequivocally her own.

"I thought I had a vocation," she said to Raymond. He was almost shocked. "Eleanor talked me out of it."

320

"If someone could talk you out of it, you didn't have one."

"Did they try to talk you out of it?"

"Quite the opposite."

She knew the pride her parents had taken in their son the priest.

But as she continued to work in this fragmentary way on her novel, scenes based on her confrontation with Eleanor came forth.

34

Cy Horvath had been struck by the lab report on the amount of alcohol found in the bloodstream of Alfred Wygant, a level seldom reached by the most dedicated alcoholic. In the quantity the late insurance tycoon must have consumed it, alcohol could be a poison. His widow had been indignant when he questioned her about this.

"All that happened years ago. This is harassment."

"Was your husband a secret drinker?"

"If he was I wouldn't know, would I?"

"From what you did know, what would you say?"

"Alfred was a notorious teetotaler. He made a point of announcing it. He made it sound like a religious obligation. I sometimes wonder if that wasn't a cover."

"For his drinking?"

"Well, apparently you saw the lab report. Presuming that it is accurate . . ."

"Do you deny that?"

"I am incapable of judging."

"It was Sorensen's Lab that did the testing. Isn't that where your niece works?"

"Did you talk with her?"

"As a matter of fact I did."

"Did she put you up to this?"

"Up to what?"

"Digging up dirt on Alfred."

"A lab report isn't dirt, Mrs. Wygant."

"Well, what do you want from me?"

"I have been trying to understand how your husband died. The police report was routine, and the newspaper stories just called it a tragic domestic accident."

"That is just what it was."

"He fell?"

"Over the upper hall railing onto the floor below." She said this angrily, but having done so emitted a little cry. "It was so horrible."

"You were there?"

"The sound wakened me. This happened in the dead of night."

"The police report said three in the morning."

"That sounds right."

"There was some conjecture that he was sleepwalking. Was he a sleepwalker?"

"I might have said that. I was desperate for an explanation."

"What was the explanation?"

"A tragic domestic accident."

"And he was drunk."

"That is what I was told. I found it unbelievable then, and I find it unbelievable now."

"The amount of alcohol in his blood was astronomically high."

"I can't explain it."

"He was your second husband, I understand."

"Yes."

"And before that you were married to Giuseppe Bernardo."

"Joseph."

"Sad news about Fulvio Bernardo."

She burst into tears.

"He seems to have died suddenly."

"Nonsense, Lieutenant. I was at the hospital when he died, in the room. He had a final heart attack. You could say this was the result of medical treatment. There some kind of emergency, and doctors and nurses flew into the room and frightened him to death. Quite literally."

"You were there at the time?"

"I drove Margaret Bernardo to the hospital. Fulvio was my brother-in-law. I've stayed close to the family."

So what did he have for his pains? The

mysterious death of Alfred Wygant, but doubtless what it had been called, a tragic domestic accident. A man married to Eleanor could be excused for drinking into the wee hours — if he were a drinking man. Cy hadn't liked Eleanor Wygant. And the sobbing seemed phony as could be. Well, they couldn't charge the departed Alfred Wygant for being drunk in the privacy of his own home, and they were even less likely to hale Dr. Rocco into court for malpractice.

That was the trouble with a slack period. You wasted time wasting time. But when he got back downtown, he was told to call Phil Keegan right away.

"We've got a murder," Phil said almost gleefully. He was in his car on the way to the scene.

"Who?"

"A professor at St. Edmund's. Horst Cassirer."

"He's the murderer?"

Phil paused. "He's the victim. Meet me there, Cy."

35

The radio went on when Peanuts started the car and Tuttle, about to turn it off, stopped and listened to the account of the body that had been dumped in the middle of Pulaski Street from a passing car.

"Let's go."

Peanuts grunted. He was understandably reluctant to show up unasked at the scene of a crime. Even Peanuts understood that he was more an honorary cop than anything, tolerated because of the influence of his family, allowed to while away his day pretty much as he saw fit. Keegan told Peanuts that he was on a roving assignment. Tuttle reminded him of this.

"So let's rove."

Tuttle himself was still licking his wounds from his meeting that afternoon with Eugene Box, college counsel. His intention in going had been to put the fear of God into Box, convince him that the college had far more to gain by bending a few rules and granting Cassirer tenure than by being guided by his jealous colleagues in the English Department.

"The decision is still pending," Box said. "I wouldn't presume to predict what it will be."

"The departmental committee has voted him down."

"How could you possibly know that? Such meetings are completely confidential."

"I know the result."

"Well, I don't. Certainly not officially. There is nothing to discuss." As a concession, Box added, "Yet."

"Let's discuss it as a hypothetical then. The department committee turns him down. Why? The man is a genius, nationally recognized, an adornment to the faculty." How easily the words came after his interviews with his client. Tuttle had encountered self-confidence before. He had known an inflated ego or two, but usually such people were deluding themselves. The annoying thing about Cassirer's boasting was that it seemed well grounded.

"I never discuss hypotheticals."

Tuttle, always slow to anger, felt his resentment alter to a desire to disturb the smugness of Eugene Box. He ticked off the points on the fingers of his left hand, spreading the fingers as he did so, giving the process the look of a series of obscene gestures.

"Numero uno. Andrew Bernardo is not exactly a poster boy for this college. The mission statement in the bulletin is very explicit, and the faculty manual more so. Andrew Bernardo, for reasons of his own, had decided to torpedo my client's chances."

"Individual professors do not act for the college."

"A committee meeting of the department is just the collective act of individual professors. Second," Tuttle said, closing point one, "on the basis of the shift toward business and the like, the college can be charged with false advertising. You bill this place as a college of liberal arts. I am informed that you could shoot a cannon through the Arts & Letters Building and never hit a liberal art. This is the atmosphere in which my client has to achieve tenure."

"Tuttle, this is all bushwa. If they turn him down, he is turned down. That's it. It's not a high crime or misdemeanor. It would be simply ordinary academic procedure."

Box stood. He looked at the clock on his desk. He punched a button on his phone and his secretary swept in.

"See you in court," Box said.

"If you're lucky."

His exit would have been more satisfying if it had not been accompanied by derisive laughter, Box's and that of his secretary. Probably something going on there too. Sometimes it depressed Tuttle to find that everywhere he looked the world seemed to be falling apart. Where were the men of integrity, men like his father? In a better world Tuttle himself would have been a better man, he was sure of it.

A uniformed officer tried to stop Peanuts from entering the street. It had been blocked off temporarily by a glow-in-the-dark sawhorse and the cop. Peanuts nearly knocked the sawhorse over trying to drive and show his I.D. at the same time. But the cop finally recognized Peanuts and danced out of the way, waving him through.

Tuttle was out of the car immediately and mixing with the group at the curb. The body bag had just been zipped up. Tuttle took Horvath by the arm.

"Who was he?"

Horvath lost a debate with himself and answered. "A prof from St. Edmund's."

Good Lord. Tuttle's first thought was that Cassirer had cracked and done in Andrew Bernardo.

"Got a name yet?"

"Cashew. Cassel. Carrier."

"Cassirer!"

"You know him?"

"Know him. Horvath, he's my client."

His client in a rubber bag was being carried out to the M.E. vehicle for transportation to the coroner. Tuttle ran into the street and stopped those carrying the gurney. Pippen recognized him.

"What is it, Tuttle?"

"I want to identify the body."

"We know who he is."

"I have to see."

She shrugged and pulled on the zipper of the body bag. Tuttle stepped back. The beard, the Cro-Magnon hairline, sufficed, but the nose and eyes, well, Tuttle was glad he had already eaten.

"Know him?"

"Horst Cassirer."

"That's right."

"Was he a client?" Pippen's voice was gentle.

Tuttle nodded and turned away. The opportunity of the half century seemed zipped into that body bag. Pippen patted his shoulder. He could have wept.

Horvath gave him what they knew, and Tuttle listened. But what difference did any of it make now? His ticket to fame and fortune, his entry into academic law, was gone. Game canceled, no refunds. What did he have to show for his pains? The dollar he had taken from Cassirer to seal their bargain.

He had Peanuts drop him off at the office. He didn't ask Peanuts up; the way he was yawning he might fall asleep while driving home. Tuttle slowly mounted the steps to his office, let himself in, settled behind his desk, and pulled his tweed hat over his face. He would get drunk, but he didn't really like alcohol. And vice versa. He tried to doze and perhaps he did, but in that sleep what dreams did come as images of the smashed-in face of Cassirer rattled around under his tweed hat.

Maybe the college had hired a hit man to rid themselves of this pesky professor.

But his thoughts kept coming back to Andrew Bernardo. From the first time Tuttle had talked with Cassirer, Andrew had been identified as his sworn enemy. Talking with Andrew, it was hard to believe this. Cassirer had almost as many enemies as he had acquaintances. Zalinksi and Lily St. Clair were exceptions, but they were about as lovable as Cassirer himself. Lily probably had amorous designs on her bearded colleague. Half asleep, half-awake, Tuttle was chuckling over this when the ringing of the phone brought him to with a start and he nearly fell out of his chair. This was no time of the night to answer a business phone. If he had been alert he would have realized that.

"Tuttle? I figured you were hiding there."

It was Hazel. He eased the receiver back onto the phone and sat tensely for half a minute until it began to ring again.

"I know it's you," she cried.

"I was just checking to see if it was a crank call."

"Have you heard about Cassirer?"

"I was there."

"What do you mean you were there?"

"Why in God's name are you calling at this hour?"

"Why in God's name are you snoozing in your office when any fool can see what has to be done?"

"What do you see?"

"Tell the police what you know. No one at that college will give them a clue."

"Snitch?"

If Hazel were docked for insulting her employer she would owe him a fortune. Tuttle hung up and then took the phone off the hook. Was marriage like this? He refused the thought, thinking of his sainted parents. Both his mother and father had assumed mythic status with the passage of years. But Tuttle could not regain even the half sleep that had been his before Hazel's intrusion.

She was right. He had lost a client, but he was still a lawyer with obligations. Someone had done in Horst Cassirer, and by God Tuttle would make sure justice was done. Surely the bumptious lad had a family who in their grief would assume the financial obligations of their son. He began to compose in his mind the bill he would present, and on this consoling note drifted into dreamless sleep.

A thump on his door brought him awake. Sun shone in the windows, a pale accusing wintry sun. In the doorway stood Cy Horvath.

"Good morning."

Tuttle got to his feet, adjusted his clothes, sailed his tweed hat toward the rack, and missed.

"Cassirer was your client?"

"Have you had breakfast?"

Horvath looked around. "Someone clean up this place?"

"I'd rather not talk about it. Come on, I'll buy you a McMuffin."

"No you won't. Let's have a real breakfast."

Fifteen minutes later they were ensconced in a corner booth of Rafferty's, with platters of bacon and eggs being readied, hot coffee easing away the pains and aches of sleeping in his office chair.

"Tell me about Cassirer."

"I speak as an officer of the court. Privileged communications lay on that cold street with my client."

Horvath was patient. Tuttle told him all he knew about Cassirer, his grievances, his desire to make a preemptive strike to forestall the bad news that seemed inevitable unless he headed it off. With some hesitation, he mentioned Andrew Bernardo and his live-in girlfriend, Gloria Monday.

"No one cares about that kind of thing anymore."

But it was clear that Horvath cared. Western civilization was crumbling around them, and the representative of law and order must feel like a relic.

"It was murder, wasn't it?"

They had found Cassirer's bicycle, which had careened to a stop where he must have been assaulted. His smashed glasses were located. A theory had been devised.

"He's riding along on his bike and someone caught him in the face with a baseball bat, which was dumped in the street along with the body."

"The murder weapon."

Horvath nodded.

"Why would a murderer provide you with that along with the body?"

"Good question."

It was clear that Horvath had considered that the wielder of the bat and the disposer of the body might be different parties.

"It takes two to dump a body. The car hardly slowed when he was pushed out."

"Where was the bicycle found?"

Tuttle did not react to the answer. The street on which Andrew Bernardo lived. He thought of the ten-year-old car Andrew drove. At the moment there seemed no need to tell Horvath everything. He had already mentioned Andrew. The connection Tuttle had made would eventually be made by the police. If they hadn't already made it. Horvath could be holding back too. They made odd allies; Horvath must be thinking that too. Meanwhile, Tuttle enjoyed the breakfast that Cy had insisted on paying for. Had eggs and bacon ever been more succulent?

36

Jessica took a break from the writing she had begun at seven with a glass of orange juice serving as her breakfast, anxious to get to her computer. She aimed the remote at the television and pressed the Power button, but as soon as it began to hum she hit Mute. She did not really want diversion from her story. Her promise to Thunder no longer seemed unrealistic. She continued to write bits and pieces, scenes, dialogue, in the order that they occurred to her. Unity could wait. She did not foresee that as a problem. What she was writing were pieces of a mosaic that would emerge.

An image on the screen caught her attention. She fumbled for the remote, but by the time she got sound the image of Cassirer had faded. The wide-eyed female reporter with a mindless smile had gone on to the next story. The phone rang.

"Have you heard?" Eleanor. "Someone has killed that dreadful man who has been harassing us all."

"I just saw a picture of Cassirer on the screen. Killed?"

Even as Eleanor spoke, Jessica switched to the web and brought up the page of the *Fox River Tribune*. Their account of Cassirer's death was as enigmatic as Eleanor's. The body dumped in the street, a color photo of the night scene with police and paramedics and reporters milling about. Quotes from Sipes and Fussell, no speculation on who had killed the hapless professor. A spokesman for the college spoke unctuously of the loss of a promising young faculty member. But all Jessica could remember was the menace the bearded Cassirer had posed.

"And on the day of the funeral!"

Jessica glanced at the clock. Just after nine. She had less than an hour to get to McDivitt's and join the others as they took her father's body to St. Hilary's, where Father Dowling would say the funeral Mass.

"Eleanor, I'll see you at the funeral home."

"Of course."

The phone went dead, Jessica turned off the television. Automatically, she stored what she had written. Words on the screen, how inconsequential they seemed. Knowing that Cassirer had indeed been harassing her family, she was filled with foreboding.

Where did all the people come from who filled the church for her father's funeral? Jessica was pleasantly surprised even though some of the older ones looked like professional mourners. Didn't her mother show up for funerals of anyone and everyone? She sat beside her mother in the front pew, Raymond next to her, then Eleanor, elegant in black. She looked a question. Where is Andrew? Jessica guessed he was unobtrusively in back, with Gloria, not wanting to make her part of the family, even in these circumstances, particularly in these circumstances.

The ritual was not the funereal one Jessica vaguely remembered. All the prayers seemed to assume that her father was safe in heaven. Her mother sat stoically through it all, Eleanor wept continuously, Raymond seemed awkward. Jessica tried to realize that it was her father's body in the casket now covered with a liturgical cloth. At the wake, kneeling at the open casket, she had cried for her father, surprising herself in a way. His illness, the days in intensive care, had inured her to the sense of loss. It was the thought of her mother all alone now that released the tears. How sweet grief can be, she realized, and how self-centered. She remembered citing Hopkins's line from the poem that begins "Margaret, are you grieving / Over goldengrove unleaving . . ." Not at all typical of Hopkins but her favorite. Untypical too the chiding final lines: "It is the fate man is born for. / It is Margaret you mourn for." Was it indeed her mother for whom she wept? Suddenly she felt like a little orphan girl whose daddy was gone. That simple truth was sufficient reason to cry.

She had thought of her father as simply gone, not elsewhere, but the funeral underscored the continuing existence of his soul, off somewhere with billions of others awaiting the General Resurrection. Her mother's rosary slipped through her fingers, bead by bead, even during the little homily in which Father Dowling avoided canonizing the deceased, reminding them that his was the fate that awaits us all. However true, it seemed as remote as a report on the chemicals her body contained.

Most of the mourners got into the long cortége of cars going to the cemetery. Snow lay banked along the road and blurred the monuments and markers. Another rite, a sprinkling of the body. Would they now lower it into the camouflaged ground? The answer was no. McDivitt came and took her mother's arm and led her away. Several times Margaret stopped to look back at the grave. Eleanor went weeping with her. And Raymond.

Jessica decided to stop by her apartment and change out of black before going to the house to be with her mother. The phone was ringing when she came in. It was Andrew.

"Are you alone?"

"What a question."

"You've heard about Cassirer?"

"Yes."

"Can I get in a back way there?"

"A back way? Sure, what's going on?"

"That's why I want to talk with you."

She told him she would be downstairs at the back door and let him in.

"I'll be on foot."

It was a curious Jessica who awaited her brother downstairs, looking out at the slushy parking lot, trying not to think the thoughts that came. Then she saw Andrew peering through the hedge that bordered the parking lot. He looked right and left. Jessica pulled open the door, and when he saw it open he scurried across the lot and pressed past her inside. If *distraught* were an adjective awaiting its bearer, it had found him in Andrew. For all that, he stopped and wiped his shoes before they went up in the elevator in silence. As she opened her door, she said over her shoulder, "Eleanor called."

"Good God."

Inside, he walked up and down the room several times, looking around. He had never before been in her apartment, but then she had never been in his, the one he shared with Gloria Monday. His curiosity about how she lived and worked was under control, though he did take note of the computer stand and the desk behind it.

"How's it going?"

"It?"

"Aren't you writing that novel?"

"More or less."

Suddenly he collapsed in her favorite chair. "I have done something extremely stupid."

"Who hasn't?"

"My fate is in Gloria's hands."

Jessica sat in her writing chair and waited. She felt that she could have written the narrative that followed. He and Gloria had dumped Cassirer's body into the street where it was found.

"My God."

"She drove. At first she didn't even know

he was in the backseat. She was nearly hysterical when I told her. I dumped him out before she could head for the police. Him and the bat."

"Andrew, did you . . ."

"No! But don't you see, that's the point. Everyone would have thought so. I went out to my car and nearly tripped over the body. It was just lying on the walk. I turned him over, and when I saw it was Cassirer I just did it. I opened the back door and lifted him in. And the bat."

"The bat."

"It has to have been the weapon. His bike was there too. Dear God, I should have put that in the trunk."

He had gone in, pled a headache, and begged Gloria to drive him to a pharmacy for some Advil. "She knows my migraines, or she would have thought I was nuts. Once we got going, I told her what was in the back."

"Andrew, you can't keep this a secret. You're right. It was about the stupidest thing you could have done. Whatever anyone thought before, this puts you in a far worse light. But you have to be the one who tells them what happened. Going to them is the only way to make your innocence plausible."

"Do you think I killed him?"

She thought about it, then shook her head. "No. I believe what you're telling me."

He came rapidly across the room and took her in his arms and began to weep. His words just tumbled out. She gathered that Gloria had proved less credulous.

"Would she do anything?"

He stepped back. "Go to the police?" He tried unsuccessfully to dismiss the thought.

"Andrew, you have to tell them first, before she does."

"They won't believe me."

"What happened to the bicycle?"

"When we got back I wanted to do what I should have done before, put it in the trunk, but Gloria just pushed me away and went inside. I had to go with her and explain what had happened. That is when the bike was discovered."

"In front of your building?"

He nodded. She picked up the phone and handed it to him.

"Call Lieutenant Horvath. I've talked with him. He came to the lab. He's okay."

"Meaning he might believe me?"

"I didn't say that."

"Would you call him?"

"I have a better idea. Father Dowling

seems to know Horvath. Let's go see him."

"Father Dowling!"

"The man who said Dad's funeral Mass."

"I wasn't there. Jessica, I couldn't go."

"Come on."

37

There is a superstition that deaths come in threes, and, as will sometimes happen, subsequent events lent credence to this. The death of Fulvio Bernardo was followed, within hours as it seemed, by that of the Edmundite Father Bourke, two deaths that might be said to have occurred in the fullness of time. Natural deaths, insofar as those who have suffered much under many physicians, in the gospel phrase, may be said to have died naturally. But the death of Horst Cassirer, professor at St. Edmund's, was unequivocally not natural. Any thought that the lethal injuries had been caused by an ordinary bicycle accident had been quickly dismissed.

"Imagine someone riding a bicycle in winter conditions," Phil Keegan said. "Ice, snow, dry patches, drifts. But that isn't what did him in. Someone hit him full in the face with a baseball bat as he was zooming along the walk. At least, that is the best construction of events."

"And then carted off the body to dump it

in the street a mile away?"

"That assumes that it was the same person. Or persons. The way the body was pitched into the street, and the bat, there had to be more than one."

There was no note of lamentation in Phil's voice. After weeks of inactivity, his department was at last confronted with a violent death to be explained.

There was no opportunity for the two men to discuss it in their usual manner, at leisure in Father Dowling's study. There was the wake and funeral for Fulvio to occupy the pastor of St. Hilary's. And a collegial visit to the chapel at St. Edmund's out of respect for a priest Father Dowling regretted not having known. Raymond Bernardo was more devastated by the death of the old priest than he had been by that of his father.

"He was the reason I joined the Order."

Father Dowling had encountered Raymond several times at the hospital but could not say that he knew the man whose abandonment of the priesthood had had such a profound effect on his family.

"My mother especially," Jessica had confided as he sat with her in the waiting room down the hall from her father's room in intensive care. "He is ten years older than I am. In a sense, I never knew him."

But her expression belied this. How can an older brother fail to loom large in the mind of a younger sister? Father Dowling felt that, next to her mother, Jessica had been most struck by her brother's defection. Fulvio's reaction had been harder to assess. He seemed to think that it was he who had been betrayed, not the priesthood, and he had made a fated effort to blackmail his son into recanting his recanting. And of course Father Dowling had heard the dying man's confession, thus becoming privy to things not even his family could know. The bravura with which Fulvio had ticked off his sins of the flesh might have been a kind of valedictory chest thumping, a macho adieu, but his enigmatic remark about Alfred Wygant, after he confessed bilking the man out of a large sum of money, had been difficult to discount.

"I killed that man, father. I might as well have murdered him."

Nothing that Father Dowling had learned of the death of Wygant lent credence to this, but there is a literal as well as a deeper version of events, and morally speaking Fulvio could well regard himself as a murderer even though he had not been there in those early morning hours when Alfred Wygant, legendary teetotaler, but for the occasion asea in alcohol, had pitched over the railing on the second floor of his house and fallen to his death below. It was clear that one of Fulvio's adventures had involved Eleanor.

A priest does well not to dwell on what is told him as confessor. It is not an occasion when one person is speaking to another but when a sinner is speaking to God and the priest is there to represent the divine mercy. But Fulvio had been vivid in his account of his misdeed and ignored Father Dowling's caution that there was no need to name names.

"She talked him into it against his better judgment."

"Did you quarrel about it?" They were on the topic of the vast injustice of Fulvio's taking Wygant's money under the pretense that it was an investment. To some degree, it seemed to be revenge on the man who had claimed his erstwhile mistress. Except that Fulvio took credit for having urged her to marry Wygant.

How could Father Dowling not think of Eleanor's visit to the rectory in which she had expressed her concern about the novel Jessica was writing, one based on her family? Fulvio's confession had provided a good basis for the alarm this caused in Eleanor. Raymond, on the other hand, seemed unconcerned about any role his actions might play in this fictional drama.

"No one could judge me more severely than I judge myself."

Was this a change since his arrival home? Raymond had told him of his visit to St. Edmund's and his talk with Father Bourke, what had been a dreaded confrontation turning out to be anything but, the old priest more forgiving than Raymond expected, or than he knew he deserved.

"The quality of mercy is not strained," Father Dowling said.

Raymond smiled. "There are phrases one has known all one's life and never really understood, until . . ."

Until he had reconciled with his mother, until he had spoken with Father Bourke.

"I suppose you will return to California now," Father Dowling said.

This was at the cemetery. They had moved away from the gravesite, and Raymond came to Father Dowling and tried to slip an envelope into his pocket.

"No, no. That's not necessary."

"You've been a great support to my mother."

"A priest sometimes derives as much support as he gives."

349

Raymond looked away, his expression pained.

"I'm sorry. I didn't mean to . . ."

Raymond smiled. "Remind me that I am a priest? It has been very difficult to overlook that since I came home."

"Jessica said you had a good reunion with Father Bourke."

"The funny thing is, no one has ever suggested I come back."

"Would you like me to?"

Raymond looked at him, unsure what to say.

"Not that I have any status in the matter."

"Can I come visit you at the rectory, Father? Before I leave."

Of course he could. Father Dowling thought of warning him about Marie Murkin. God only knew what reception a flown priest would get from her if he showed up on her doorstep. But Raymond had the charm of his father, and Father Dowling did not think Marie could long resist it.

But it was Jessica who came to the rectory that afternoon. Marie brought a very distracted young lady to the study. Of course, Jessica had just lost her father. "I could make tea," Marie said.

But Jessica did not want tea, and Father

Dowling never drank it. Nor did she want a cup of the lethally strong coffee that simmered in the study. Marie closed the door on them. Jessica's expression became more tragic, as if she had been restraining herself in the presence of the housekeeper.

"Oh, Father."

"What is it?"

"Everything!"

Well, not quite. He knew that it would be best just to let her say whatever it was in whatever way she chose. But it was surprising when she began talking of the death of the young English professor from St. Edmund.

"He was threatening us all."

"Threatening?"

"Because of Andrew. Andrew is on the committee that voted against giving Cassirer tenure, and he blamed Andrew. He declared war on the college and on our whole family. He seemed to think that I would convince Andrew to change his vote."

"On what basis?"

"This is embarrassing."

"Jessica, I'm a priest."

"Andrew is living with a woman. A colleague. It's not all that unusual anymore, but it is against the rules for the faculty of St. Edmund's."

"They explicitly forbid cohabitation?"

She laughed. Her spirit seemed to rise with the opportunity to talk. "Oh, it's generic. They are expected to live in accordance with Christian morals as taught by the Church. Cassirer thought he could blackmail Andrew on that basis."

"And he came to you with this story. Had you known about Andrew?"

"Yes."

"I didn't see him at your father's funeral."

"He wasn't there." Her spirits visibly sank. "Have you read the details of the death of Cassirer?"

The conjunction of Cassirer's blackmail attempt and his death prepared Father Dowling for what followed. Jessica told the tale Andrew had told her in flat tones, as if she were prepared not to be believed. Did she believe it herself?

"Oh, yes. He wouldn't make up something like this. His imagination is not very lively."

"Jessica, he has to tell the police what happened."

"I know. He agrees, but he hasn't been able to do it."

"Where is he now?"

"At my apartment. What he expects is that Gloria Monday will call the police and tell them everything."

"It would be far better if he did."

"What I was hoping, Father, is that you could arrange a meeting with someone like Horvath. I met him, and he doesn't look as if anything would surprise him."

"Call Andrew and have him come here."

"I better go get him. He came to my place on foot."

"Meanwhile, I'll call Lieutenant Horvath. Have you met Phil Keegan? Either one would do. Maybe both."

Jessica slipped away, but before Father Dowling could make a call he heard the voice of Phil Keegan jollying Marie Murkin. She followed him into the study, carrying a glass of beer, which she put down next to his chair. Phil drank half the glass, smacked his lips, and generally looked satisfied.

"Where we found Cassirer's bicycle was definitely the scene of the crime. His glasses. Student theme papers blowing about. The bike wasn't damaged all that much. It actually came to a stop leaning against a fence."

"The blow knocked him off?"

"He was clotheslined, more or less."

Cy had found footprints in the snow he was pretty sure were the assailant's. "Tennis shoes, size seven, one of a zillion pairs. Maybe no two snowflakes are alike, but every tennis shoe of this make is."

"Male or female."

"Male presumably."

"So whom do you suspect?"

"Do you know who lives in the building in front of which the assault took place?"

"Andrew Bernardo."

"How did you know that!"

"Jessica told me."

"It turns out that Andrew and Cassirer were blood enemies. Cassirer claimed Andrew was ruining his career. He was threatening him, trying to get him to change his vote."

It would have been much better if Phil had learned all this from Andrew himself.

"Cy is out there now with a court order to look at Andrew's car."

Half an hour later, Jessica returned with an unshaven Andrew. Father Dowling had needed no excuse to keep Phil Keegan at the rectory, and the arrival of the Bernardos came as a bit of a surprise, given what Phil had just said.

As soon as Andrew was introduced to Phil he said, "Captain, I have done something very stupid."

That seemed a mild description of what Andrew had done. Listening to him, watching him as he spoke, Father Dowling wondered if this were the whole story. Certainly Phil would find it difficult to believe that Andrew had simply removed a pesky body from his doorstep, dumping it in the street a mile away.

"You knew the man who was killed?"

"Horst Cassirer." Andrew took a breath. "He hated me. He had vowed to destroy my reputation."

"Why?"

Phil listened patiently to the tale of academic politics. But the question that had been forming in Father Dowling's mind was put by Phil, dismissing the account of campus vendettas.

"You couldn't have dumped the body in the street all by yourself."

"I don't want to involve anyone else."

"Whoever was with you is already involved."

Jessica said, "For heaven's sake, tell him. She is no more guilty, or innocent, than you are."

"Gloria Monday," Andrew said in a small voice.

"And who is she?"

Andrew glanced at Father Dowling and then at Jessica who said, "If you're worried about shocking Father Dowling, forget it."

"We live together."

"And she helped you move the body."

"She didn't know what we were doing. I had put it in the back, and she was driving. Why would she look in the backseat?"

Gallantry is not dead. Of course there was more. "Has she called you?"

"Gloria Monday?"

"She was furious when she realized what I had involved her in. I don't blame her."

"This all comes as news to me," Phil said. "Which is good for you. If you're telling the truth."

"Captain, I swear to God."

Let your speech be yes yes or no no. Do not swear by God . . .

Marie, her curiosity too much for her, tapped on the door and looked in. "Would anyone want tea?"

"Bring me a beer," Phil said. "I never drink tea on duty."

38

Eleanor went from the Bernardo house, where Margaret was in good hands with Raymond, to Jessica's apartment. When she knocked on the door it began to move. It was unlocked. Eleanor pushed it open.

"Yoo hoo. Jessica. It's Aunt Eleanor."

The apartment had an empty feel. Eleanor closed the door behind her, and her eyes fell on the desk. In a moment, she was turning over the papers on it, opening and shutting its drawers, in a flurry of excitement. Where were those damnable letters? Consoling the grieving Margaret had made her more ashamed of her affair with Fulvio than she had ever been at the time. What a terrible thing to have done to that good woman. This thought lent intensity to her effort to find the letters. Once she had them in her hands, she felt she would destroy them on the spot. Similarly motivated women have lifted automobiles off children, moved rocks three times their own weight. Eleanor felt that at the moment she could tear the metropolitan phone book in half.

The letters were not on the desk, not in the desk, nor were they among the papers stacked beside the computer. Had Jessica herself destroyed them? She didn't believe it. Her niece had taken too evident pleasure in annoying her when they discussed them. Eleanor dropped into Jessica's reading chair, which moved back and forth. What a wonderful chair. If she had earlier thought of how Margaret would regard what she and Fulvio had done, it belatedly occurred to her how she must have seemed to her niece, talking about her candid love letters to the girl's father.

A newspaper lay on the floor beside the chair, and Eleanor glanced at it. The photograph of Horst Cassirer glowered up at her. She picked up the paper and read the story avidly. My God. This was the man she herself could cheerfully have throttled. Thrown into the street from a passing car!

The remote control lay on the floor where the paper had been. Eleanor turned on the television, but it was nothing but daytime blather. She pushed the radio button and WBBM came on. It was thus, seasoned with commercials, a man's and a woman's voice mindlessly alternating, that Eleanor got the details of what had happened to Horst

Cassirer. On the morning of the funeral she had had no interest in paper or news reports as she decided on a black dress that fell almost to her ankles. It had a matching black mantilla. As she had had occasion to think before, Eleanor realized that she made a most attractive widow. Would she steal the show from Margaret?

Recalled now, the pusillanimous thought shamed her. But her mind was on that awful Cassirer. Where was Jessica? Where had Andrew been? Eleanor had not seen him at the church — he had not sat with his family — and he was not at the cemetery either. So much for the thought that he was unobtrusively present with his friend. Whatever inconsistency there was in Eleanor's contempt for the woman who lived without benefit of wedlock with Andrew did not occur to her. But then she would have thought the same of herself if she were not the self who had acted so shamelessly with Fulvio.

Moral hauteur gave way to thoughts of her nephew. Why would a man not attend his own father's funeral? All too vividly Eleanor remembered her absurd encounter with Horst Cassirer, the bearded madman demanding that she put pressure on Andrew to vote for him in some silly committee at the college.

"This is war," he had cried. "I will destroy the whole Bernardo family if I have to."

Her fears about Jessica's novel paled before this threat. What would she have done if she thought he might learn of herself and Fulvio? But it was Andrew who was vulnerable to Cassirer's counterattack. Eleanor stopped rocking in Jessica's wonderful chair. Andrew. Cassirer. Could her nephew be responsible for the death of his nemesis?

A sound in the hall, and then Jessica came in. She stopped and stared at Eleanor. She glanced at her desk.

"Did you find them?"

"Jessica, the door was open. Where have you been?"

"Oh Eleanor," Jessica cried, and then she was in her aunt's arms, weeping uncontrollably. Patting her niece's back as she embraced her, Eleanor felt more like an aunt than she had in years.

"What is it, dear?"

"Andrew!"

Listening to the incredible tale, Eleanor felt like weeping herself. Dead he might be, but Horst Cassirer was getting his revenge on the Bernardo family. Jessica, under control now, described the meeting with Captain Keegan at St. Hilary's.

"Where is Andrew now?"

"They took him downtown to put it all in writing."

What Andrew had done was scarcely credible. Was his the action of a man guilty of more than desecrating a body? She did not have to express the question; it filled Jessica's mind as well.

"I believe him, Eleanor. I want to believe him. The wonder is that Gloria Monday hadn't turned him in before he went to the police himself."

Jessica made coffee, and they sat drinking it. This was more somber than Fulvio's wake. They might have been mourning the death of the Bernardo good name.

"Who's with my mother?"

"Raymond."

"Oh, thank God he is here."

Jessica had been looking across the room, unseeing, but then her eyes took in her desk.

"You didn't find them?"

The letters. How inconsequential they now seemed. Her affair with Fulvio was a long-ago peccadillo compared with the plight Andrew was in.

"No."

Jessica got up and went to a bookshelf. The letters were there, behind some books. She brought them to Eleanor and handed them to her. Eleanor hesitated, then took them. How the long sought loses value when it is in one's hand.

"Did you read them?" she asked in a small voice.

"Destroy them, Eleanor."

She nodded. The main thing was that they cease to exist so that there would never be the chance that Margaret might see them. The letters were stapled to the envelopes in which they had arrived. Had there been so many? She looked at Jessica.

"What you must think of me."

39

Attending to his mother, Raymond felt that he was beginning to make up for all the years when his absence had broken her heart. He felt like an orphan, fatherless anyway, and twice over; first his father and then Father Bourke. Tomorrow would be the funeral for his old mentor, in the campus church. Raymond felt almost as much obligation to be there as he had to attend his father's funeral.

"Did your father talk to you about practical matters?" his mother asked.

"No."

"Eleanor looked over his papers here."

"Eleanor!"

"She said you children asked her to."

Raymond said nothing, and his mother added, "Jessica looked things over too."

Were they worried about whether Margaret was well provided for? Raymond had never doubted this and did not now, but he found it somewhat distasteful that Jessica and Eleanor had been rummaging through his father's effects. Looking into the home office, which in recent years had been his father's only office, Bernardo's Nurseries having been sold when neither son could carry it on, he felt no desire to sit at that desk and see what might be there. But if any of them was practical enough to appraise their mother's situation, it was Jessica. And Eleanor too. She had had experience of losing a husband and probably had learned a thing or two.

Occupying a front pew with his family at the funeral — all but Andrew — Raymond had followed the liturgy as if it were something wholly new to him. Roger Dowling said Mass with great concentration and devotion, and his homily had been just right. How completely pastoral the priest was. And he could not have been nicer to Raymond. Had former priests become so commonplace that they raised no questions in others? Dowling, like Father Bourke, was so immersed in his vocation that it was impossible to imagine him having doubts or hankering after the fleshpots of Egypt.

He smiled. What a way to think of Thousand Oaks, California. It had been days since he had talked with Phyllis. What did she make of his silence? He did go into his father's office then and called her.

"We buried him today," he said.

"When will you return?"

"Soon." But it sounded like a question. "I'm with my mother."

"Oh good."

"She's taking it quite well."

"And your brother and sister?"

There was an edge to her voice, the question a statement that there were others to look after his mother, that he should be on his way home to her.

The conversation was inconsequential, echoing with things unsaid. It was a relief to put down the phone. It rang almost immediately and he answered it.

Jessica said, "Has Mom heard the news?"

"What news?"

"Didn't you say that Cassirer came to see you?"

"Well, I ran into him on campus. Quite a jerk."

"Raymond, he's dead."

Her voice had dropped to a whisper as if she thought their mother might overhear.

"Tell me about it."

But of course it was what Andrew had done that explained why she worried that their mother might turn on the television and find that her son was making a statement to the police about the strange death of Horst Cassirer.

"I felt like pushing him in the face when he accosted me, I can tell you. What an abrasive man he was."

"I know, I know. He called on me too. And on Eleanor."

"Eleanor!"

"Raymond, I'm coming over to spell you, and we can talk some more."

"I would like to get away for a while."

The wake for Father Bourke would be held in the little chapel in Purgatory. Raymond no longer felt ill at ease with the thought of revisiting his old haunts. No one other than himself seemed to see his situation as he himself did. Of course he waited until Jessica got there, by which time his mother had lain down for a nap, the strain of the past week taking its toll.

"Did you tell her?"

He shook his head. "I wish she didn't have to be told. What will they do with Andrew?"

"Father Dowling has asked Amos Cadbury if someone in his firm could represent Andrew."

"And?"

"I got the impression he would do anything for Father Dowling."

"That's a break."

"Just so it isn't the kind of clown Cassirer hired. A man named Tuttle."

Raymond had not even considered telling his mother what Jessica had called to tell him. Did she even know that Andrew shared an apartment with a woman? He was suddenly overwhelmed by a sense of the dissolution of the house of Bernardo. His father had apparently made a good end, but seeing Eleanor had reminded Raymond of the flaws in his father's character. He and Jessica were sitting in the very room, that was the couch, where he had surprised his father and Eleanor in all but flagrante delicto. How coolly his father had taken it, doubtless practiced in deception.

"You should go downtown to be with Andrew," Jessica said.

He wanted to protest. In hours the wake for Father Bourke would be held, and he had been looking forward to walking the campus and inviting thoughts of self-recrimination. How ridiculous his life seemed, broken in two with the first part one of rectitude and fidelity, the second one of self-indulgence. Why had he proved so vulnerable to Phyllis's blandishments?

It was easy in her absence to imagine that she had been the aggressor. It was she who had begun talk of leaving, taking a perverse glee in the thought that their westward trek to freedom would be financed by the Order of St. Edmund. She had resented her own vocation, felt that she had been entrapped by a romantic dream, a dream that had turned into a hallucination if not a nightmare.

"It isn't at all what we expected, is it?"

He had agreed, comparing the fuzzy promise of their flight with the ordered and disciplined life that was his. At his father's funeral Mass, at the consecration of bread and wine, he had difficulty recalling his disbelief. He bowed his head and closed his eyes and might have been the idealistic, credulous young man he had been in the novitiate. The thought of not returning to California formed in his mind and had all the allure the thought of flight had once held for him. He wanted freedom from the freedom he enjoyed with Phyllis, which now seemed a kind of enslavement. But he told Jessica he would go downtown to see what was happening with Andrew.

"I'm his brother," he told the sergeant at the desk.

"I'll call Captain Keegan."

The officer nodded as he listened on the phone, then said that Keegan would come get him.

Keegan was a distracted, busy man, lost in his function, or so it seemed to Raymond, until the captain expressed sorrow at the death of Fulvio.

"Your family is really taking it in the chops," he said. "Come on."

Andrew was in a consulting room with Ambrose Zwingli, a crew-cut young lawyer from Cadbury's firm. The name Cadbury had rung a bell, of course. So many bells were rung lately. He seemed to be recovering his past.

Andrew jumped to his feet when Raymond came in and, as he had at the airport some days before, embraced his brother.

"What a revolting development this is." Andrew seemed to be imitating someone.

Zwingli waited to be introduced, and Raymond could see the flicker of recognition at his name. Not that Zwingli knew him, but he clearly knew of him. The renegade priest.

"I stopped here on my way to Father Bourke's funeral."

"I am afraid your brother will be arraigned," Zwingli said.

"On what charge?"

"Tampering with the scene of a murder," he said. "For now."

Andrew looked abject. "I am finding it hard to convince anyone of my innocence."

Zwingli summarized the situation. Andrew had admitted to moving the body of Horst Cassirer and dumping it in the street. That of course aroused the curiosity of the police. Andrew's car had been impounded, and it was clear it had been used to transport the body of Cassirer.

"If Andrew wasn't innocent he would not have told the police what he did."

"Of course they think that was a preemptive strike."

"Would they have impounded the car if he hadn't gone to them?"

"Certainly not as soon as they did."

"If ever."

"There was a pretty public feud going on between Andrew and the deceased."

"Who was the most obnoxious man I've ever met."

"You met him?"

"He pursued me, harassed me. I all but knocked him down to get away from him. He was spouting libelous accusations, threatening to ruin our family."

"Yes."

Raymond felt that he had inadvertently added to the case against Andrew.

"Surely they won't hold him."

"At least tonight. I will try to arrange bail in the morning."

40

In his office Horvath was interviewing Gloria Monday, who was explaining her role in the movement of Cassirer's body.

"I had no idea Andrew had put him in the car. He asked me to drive him to a pharmacy to get medicine for his migraine. Only when we were underway did he clamber into the backseat. I had no idea why he would do that. He told me to just keep driving."

Her face would have been pretty but for the expression that tightened her mouth and narrowed her eyes. The memory of a male barking orders at her was not pleasant.

"I slowed the car, and that is when he opened the back door and pushed poor Cassirer into the street. And then he threw out the bat he had picked up near the body. I was furious."

Horvath nodded. Who could blame her? His problem was that her story was as self-serving as Andrew's.

"Why would he want to move the body?"

"Why? Apparently it was lying on our

371

doorstep. Horst had vowed to destroy Andrew. I suppose he thought . . ."

"Yes."

"You're going to have to put that question to him."

"I wondered if you had."

"I didn't have to."

"He thought he would be accused of attacking Cassirer?"

Reports were coming in from various interviews. Agnes Lamb had spoken with the chair of Andrew's department and with several colleagues, Lily St. Clair and Zalinski. It was pretty clear that they considered Andrew the guilty party, at least so far as Cassirer's fate at St. Edmund's was concerned. The reports provided a basis for further questions to Gloria Monday.

"Andrew voted to turn down Cassirer's application for promotion?"

"It was a committee vote."

"Why did Cassirer concentrate his wrath on Andrew?"

"It's a long story."

Cy settled more comfortably into his chair. "I'd like to hear it."

"I know this will sound odd to an outsider, but academic quarrels can be very bitter. St. Edmund's is on the threshold of becoming worthy of its aspirations. There is a division between the new blood that has been added to the faculty and those who represent the past."

"Like Andrew."

"Horst Cassirer thought so. Andrew does not have a Ph.D." She might have been reporting the lack of a limb. "That is a fundamental credential for a faculty member."

"So how did he get hired?"

The mouth tightened. "You are getting to the heart of Horst Cassirer's complaint. He felt that he was being judged by someone without the credentials to make that judgment."

"A Ph.D."

"Horst, whatever else might be said of him, was a productive scholar whose reputation was being established across the country. I myself told Andrew that he was wrong to oppose tenure for Cassirer."

This was the woman with whom Andrew lived, but she sounded like a witness for the prosecution. Cy turned her over to a stenographer and went down the hall to Keegan's office.

"Raymond Bernardo is with his brother and Zwingli."

Keegan called in Agnes Lamb, and they went over what they had.

Cassirer had been on his ten-speed hurtling along the walk in front of the building where Andrew and Gloria had their apartment when someone hit him full in the face with a bat, the force of the swing added to the speed of the bike. Given the fact that the bicycle had wobbled to a stop and propped itself against a fence, the blow must have lifted him right off the bike.

"Wobbled?" Phil said.

"Tire tracks," Agnes replied.

His smashed glasses had been found in the snow by the curb. Andrew's admission that he had carted away the body prompted the impoundment of his car. It corroborated his story. But what a story.

"He expected that anyone would think that he had killed Cassirer."

Agnes had tried to form an image of the aspiring tenured professor, but it depended on her sources. Lily St. Clair and Zalinski were agreed that Cassirer had been too good for St. Edmund's, a young whale in a fishbowl.

"So why did he want to stay so badly?"

"It was the only job he had, whatever his promise."

The chair of the department and Michael Pistoia gave a very different story. "They don't think he deserved tenure. He was a lousy teacher and a lousy colleague. That is two strikes. The third is a home run. That's his scholarship. They admit that. But that didn't make up for his deficiencies in the other two categories."

"They have any guesses who hit Cassirer with a baseball bat?"

"I got the impression they would have been happy to do it themselves."

Cassirer had been told of the committee vote, which was supposed to be secret, and decided not to wait to get the official news. He went on the offensive. He hired a lawyer.

"Who?"

"Tuttle."

It might have been a punch line. Agnes smiled when she said the name and Keegan guffawed. There was an imperceptible alteration in Cy's expression that was the Hungarian's equivalent of Keegan's derisive laughter.

"I thought the man was smart."

"Tuttle?"

More laughter from Keegan. Cy blinked his eyes. They settled down and Agnes went on.

"Pistoia said that Cassirer had been visiting members of the Bernardo family. We're going to have to talk with them."

"Visiting them?"

"Threatening them."

Keegan made a face. "Maybe one of them did it."

"Andrew says it wasn't him."

Horvath said, "They will have the same alibi."

"What?"

"Fulvio Bernardo's wake."

"Was Andrew there?"

Phil Keegan shook his head. "He didn't show up for his father's funeral either."

Cy said, "We should talk to Tuttle."

"Not me," Agnes said.

"I'll do it," said Cy.

41

From the street Cy saw the light on in Tuttle's office, but when he climbed the four flights he found Hazel Barnes. She seemed to be packing up.

"He is an idiot," she said when he asked where Tuttle was. The inner office door was closed.

"He in there?"

"Probably asleep at his desk."

"Was he representing Horst Cassirer?"

"Ask him. I'm out of here."

"I want to ask you a few questions."

"Me?"

Hazel looked like the woman who was Groucho's foil in the old Marx Brothers movies. She was built like a refrigerator, her arms out from her body, her hair done in a style Cy hadn't seen for years. A permanent. She sat and looked slack jawed at Cy.

"Tell me about Horst Cassirer."

A hooded half-length coat, waterproof, hung from a hook like a western villain; a pair of tennis shoes stood beneath them.

Hazel had on spike heels.

"Whatever I know Tuttle knows."

"Are you a runner?"

"What?"

"The tennis shoes."

She looked at them. "I wear them to and from work. I walk."

"Where do you live?"

"This is outrageous!"

"Would you like to have your lawyer with you?"

For answer, she leapt up and pounded on the door of the inner office. She rattled the knob. It seemed locked. She went to her desk and picked up the phone and punched a button.

"The police are here and want to talk to you." She looked angrily at Cy. "What's your name?"

"Horvath."

She listened, then held the phone toward Cy. He heard Tuttle's voice as from the bottom of a well.

"He is hiding from me," she said.

She took off her heels and put them in a plastic bag and began to tug the tennis shoes over her silk stockings. When she stood, she seemed to have shrunk. She got into the coat and pulled the hood over her permanent, put the plastic bag with her shoes in it under her arm, and picked up the shopping bag she had been filling.

"I am leaving." She hesitated as if he might not let her go.

"Better leave that." He nodded at the shopping bag. She let it drop. It tipped to its side, and its contents slid from it as from a cornucopia. It was tempting to detain her, but he wanted to talk to Tuttle. He stepped aside, and she swept from the office, her tennis shoes making rubbery sounds as she headed for the stairs. Keegan tapped on Tuttle's door.

"It's Cy Horvath, Tuttle."

Silence. And then a whisper. "Is she gone?"

"Yes."

A key turned, and the door opened on a darkened office; Tuttle in silhouette as he surveyed the outer office. Then he flicked the switch, lighting the room.

What a contrast with the outer office. Tuttle circled the desk and sat in the chair that tipped back when he did so. He grabbed the desk to prevent himself from rolling to the wall.

"That's quite a secretary, Tuttle."

"She's temporary."

"Everyone is. Tell me about Horst Cassirer."

Tuttle leaned forward and scrubbed his face with his hands, pushing back his tweed hat in the process. "I saw the body," he told his palms.

"I know. You left pretty quick."

"Peanuts wanted to go."

"Is that how you heard of it, police radio?"

Tuttle took away his hands and looked at Cy. He nodded. Cy cleared debris from a chair and sat.

"Doesn't the Amazon clean up in here?"

"She made this mess. She was tearing the place apart. She is demented. I threw her out and locked the door." He paused and remembered with fleeting pleasure this moment of courage.

"She looking for something?"

"She thinks I keep secrets from her. She's right."

"About clients?"

A tragic look disfigured Tuttle's face. "Beware of good luck, Horvath. I thought Cassirer was my ticket to . . ."

The preposition pointed to some vague possible world in which Tuttle would flourish and prosper.

"Tell me about him."

"A real son of a bitch. He hated everything but himself."

"He wanted to sue St. Edmund's?"

"He wanted to destroy it. And the Bernardos. He was out to get Andrew Bernardo for blackballing him."

"What were you supposed to do?"

"Good question. He rode around on his bicycle harassing the whole family. Even Eleanor Wygant." Tuttle paused. "Why aren't there more women like her? They broke the mold, that's why."

He made Eleanor sound like penicillin.

"How mad do you think he made them, the Bernardos?"

Tuttle caught the implication. "Cy, anyone who knew that guy would want to take a baseball bat to him. I could have done it myself."

"To a client?"

"How would you like to sit in the office of Eugene Box the college counsel and make a case for someone like Cassirer? It can't be done. I would have switched sides in a minute to see him get his."

"He got it. Were you and Peanuts together before you heard the radio report?"

"We had dinner at the Great Wall."

"Tuttle, who do you think did this?"

"It could have been anyone who knew him." He thought better of it. "No there were a couple of professors who took his side."

"Who?"

"A man named Zalinski. Lily St. Clair. They were in the same department."

"English."

"They were on the committee with Andrew Bernardo, but they voted for Cassirer's promotion."

"Two to one?"

"There were two others who voted with Andrew. Pistoia and the chair, Anne Gogarty."

"Did Cassirer threaten them?"

"His argument was that he was so goddamn better than the rest of them that he threatened them all. A real sweetheart."

"So they got rid of him."

"Well, they voted not to promote him."

So why hit him with a baseball bat if he wouldn't be around long anyway? Cy looked at the mess of Tuttle's office.

"What was she looking for?"

A sly look came over Tuttle. He took off his tweed hat and rummaged in it, and came out with a check. He showed it to Cy. Made out to Tuttle for five hundred dollars and signed Horst Cassirer.

"Better cash that before they close his account."

Tuttle sprang to his feet, wild-eyed. "I never thought of that."

He came around the desk, grabbed his coat from a stand, and looked at Cy.

"Thanks for telling me, Cy. I gotta run."

Out the door, through the outer office, then pounding down the stairs. Cy took one more look at the shambles and turned off the light. In the outer office he sat in Hazel's chair and looked through the shopping bag. Reports from a paralegal named Barbara and a file with Horst Cassirer on the tab. Cy took the shopping bag with him when he left.

42

Lily St. Clair had assumed the mien of a widow, and Zalinski conceded her the role of chief mourner for Horst Cassirer. Not that she felt Zalinski had ever liked Horst. He had simply been an ally in Horst's campaign to separate himself from the deadwood of the St. Edmund faculty. When Lily went to the morgue to see about the body, there was a young black officer there with the assistant coroner, both women and, she hoped, sisters in the feminist sense. The officer was Agnes Lamb, black, a double basis for solidarity, and the assistant coroner Dr. Pippen.

"I was a colleague of Horst Cassirer." She dropped her eyes. "And his friend."

"Do you want to see him?"

Lily shuddered and looked from one woman to the other.

"Can I?"

"If you want."

After a moment she nodded. The thoughts that filled her mind were not those of the feminist she claimed to be. When Aeneas sailed away, the abandoned Dido had climbed onto a pyre and gone up as burnt offering to her fleeing lover. *Agnosco veteris vestigia flammae.* Horst hated the classics, but he knew them thoroughly, cursing the retrograde education that had immersed him in the dead languages. For all that, they could discuss them, something he could not of course have done with Zalinski. English was Zalinski's notion of a dead language.

She followed Dr. Pippen's swaying ponytail into a very cold room that reminded her of the archives at Stanford. Drawers along the wall. Pippen leaned over, grabbed a handle, and pulled. The body of Horst Cassirer slid into view. With a little cry Lily blacked out.

Lily came to in the room where she had identified herself, with Pippen and Lamb hovering over her.

"Sorry," Pippen said. "That can be quite a shock."

"His face!" Lily cried in horror.

"You're his friend," Agnes said. "What about family?"

"He had none."

"None?"

"No. He was an only child of aged par-

385

ents, and they took their own lives two years ago. Rather than face further ravages of age. They were members of the Hemlock Society."

"No relatives at all."

"That is why I am here. I will make arrangements."

"Was he religious?"

The question seemed serious. She smiled at Agnes. "He was a man of reason."

"No funeral?"

"A ceremony, a few friends. Of course he will be cremated." Again she thought of Dido.

"Did you live together?"

A significant pause. "We kept our separate apartments." Who could gainsay her claim to have been more to Horst than an academic ally? What heated dreams she had entertained of a Horst Cassirer suddenly aware of her, of her femininity if not her beauty. But he was sullen and self-centered. "Comfort me with apples," she had murmured once at lunch, offering him fruit as Eve had offered the apple to Adam. He ignored her.

"The body can't be released immediately. Have you chosen a funeral director?"

Lily looked nonplussed. "Could you suggest one?"

"McDivitt's?" Agnes said, looking at Pippen.

"McDivitt's."

"Should I go there?"

"If you're in charge."

Lily went out to her car and felt one of a long line of heroines who'd had the sad task of burying their fallen lovers. Following Dr. Pippen's directions to McDivitt's she began to think of a ceremony in the presence of Horst's ashes. Catallus's farewell to his brother? After she recited it, she would translate it for the benefit of the others. What others? Of course the room would be crowded; people attended such affairs out of a sense of duty if nothing else. Perhaps Zalinski would summarize Horst's scholarly accomplishments. For a frightening moment all that seemed silly, articles in journals that ended up unread on library shelves, the interested praise of others, the whole choir doomed to eventual silence when death came.

"Was he religious?" Angela Lamb had asked.

Of course he wasn't. But Lily wondered if she had completely liberated herself from the Presbyterian girlhood she had known. Perhaps they could sing "Amazing Grace." No one thought of that hymn as religious anymore; it was like the national anthem.

Mr. McDivitt, with his rosy complexion and cotton white hair, could not have been nicer. He understood perfectly.

"We can have the ceremony right here. Come. I'll show you the room I have in mind."

"Not a religious ceremony."

He laid a hand on her arm. "Everything will be exactly as you wish."

The room would do. There was a stand on which the urn of Horst's ashes would sit, an arrangement of chairs, a podium. Lily could see herself standing here, a portrait of Stoic grief. *Ave atque vale.*

"Cremation is a wise decision, professor. Considering the way he died."

She took that thought with her out to her car. She had fainted at the sight of poor Horst in that drawer at the coroner's. How Andrew must have hated him to do such a thing. No, feared not hated. Horst had represented everything he was not. But would Andrew pay for what he had done? Lily had no experience of law or of the police, of course, but the fact was that the Bernardos were a quintessentially bourgeois family; the courts and the police would rally to Andrew's side. Lily found it intolerable that Andrew should return to the academic

388

round, no longer troubled by the accusing presence of Horst Cassirer, scot-free no matter what he had done.

She drove to campus and went to Andrew's office. Foster answered her knock, and she went in, stopping as his presence made itself known. The air freshener was not on.

"Lily," Foster cried, as if she had come to visit him.

"Andrew isn't here?"

A clouded expression. "I think he's under arrest. Sheer nonsense. He couldn't do such a thing."

On Andrew's desk lay his palm top, propped in a little tray that connected it to his computer. Lily sat at Andrew's desk, a handkerchief held discreetly to her nose. Did Foster never bathe? There had been a masculine aura around Horst, the result of the pace he kept, always rushing around, but Lily had always found it an aphrodisiac. With Foster she had the gagging sensation passing a gymnasium could bring.

"I am arranging for a commemorative ceremony."

"For Horst?"

"Yes."

Foster seemed about to say something, then decided against it.

"I will say a few things. Zalinski too perhaps."

"There should be some representative of the administration."

"Never! I would bar their way if they tried to force themselves in. How lovely your books look."

Foster turned to the shelf behind him, and Lily put the palm top in her purse. She rose.

"I will let you know the details later."

In the hallway, she breathed deeply. How had Andrew managed to sit in that terrible place with Foster? It would probably make prison less unpalatable to him.

In her car, she drove carefully to where poor Horst had been attacked. While she was there she would pay a call on Gloria Monday.

43

Phil Keegan had to sit in on the meeting between Pendle, the prosecutor, and Zwingli as they discussed the fate of Andrew Bernardo. Zwingli seemed to see himself more as an officer of the court than as Andrew's defender. Eugene Box, the college counsel, was there, hoping to keep the connection of all this with St. Edmund's to a minimum. Not that he put it that way. He was there to lend such support as he could to employees of the college.

"Both of them?" Phil asked.

"Both."

"Victim and accused?"

Zwingli said, "Let's not beg any questions."

Phil was never sure what that phrase meant, at least as it was often used. Did Zwingli doubt there was a victim and that they were here to talk about prosecuting Andrew Bernardo?

"Go through this with us, will you, Phil?" Pendle held the summary Keegan had hoped would make his presence here unnecessary. Well, at least he had a script. He went through the items that pointed to Andrew Bernardo as the one who had killed Horst Cassirer.

1. By his own admission, Andrew Bernardo was responsible for removing the body of Horst Cassirer from his front door and throwing it into the street a mile away.

2. Inspection of Andrew's car had confirmed that it was the vehicle in which Cassirer's body had been transferred.

3. Gloria Monday, his live-in girlfriend, denied any foreknowledge of what Andrew had tricked her into doing.

4. The rivalry between Cassirer and Bernardo was attested to by any number of colleagues. Cassirer had declared a state of war. One of his weapons was to expose the living arrangements of Andrew and Gloria, which was in clear violation of the code that faculty agreed to live by when they signed a contract with St. Edmund's.

5. Andrew could not account for his whereabouts at the time someone had smacked Cassirer in the face with a baseball bat and then clobbered him on the back of the head. Gloria Monday refused to corroborate his claim that he had been with her in their apartment at the time.

"No prints on the bat?"

"No."

"Any physical evidence linking Andrew to the scene of the crime?"

"Well, he lived in the building. And there are the tennis shoes."

"Tennis shoes."

"The assailant wore tennis shoes. Size nine."

"You found such a pair of tennis shoes in Andrew Bernardo's apartment?"

"The problem is I could find identical pairs all over town. They're not like fingerprints. Gloria Monday had a pair just like them."

"But the size."

"We're guessing size nine, but the prints don't enable us to say with exactness. Fairly big feet but not large." Keegan crossed his legs, as if to display his scuffed size eleven shoes.

"So it's all circumstantial?" Zwingli said.

Pendle said, "I wish he hadn't confessed to moving the body. If you had found that in the course of your investigation without his help . . ."

Phil went on to an item that was not on the list.

"There's something else. The officer assigned to the murder site found something

393

that had been overlooked before. Half-buried in the snow but even so we should have seen it earlier."

"What is it?"

"Andrew Bernardo's palm top. That's a little gizmo, a handheld computer . . ."

But they all knew what a palm top was.

"He could say he dropped it when he was picking up the body."

But Pendle seemed to be imagining a lie that Andrew might tell.

"Of course it's more likely to have come out of his pocket when . . ."

"Exactly."

Pendle had decided to prosecute even without the palm top, but learning of it had him beaming. "That will hang him."

Keegan returned to his office. How did Pendle keep his faith in the courts? Phil Keegan had lost his long ago as criminals were set free on technicalities, lawyers pled the cases on courthouse steps to gaggles of reporters, sentences were never fully served. Except for Earl Hospers. Phil hoped that Cadbury could get a parole for Edna's husband. The television repairman had not benefited from his crime, if that is what it had been. Impulsively hitting an old woman with a package of frozen meat did not put Earl among true criminals, not in Phil

Keegan's book. No, Roger Dowling was right. Hospers had paid his debt. The money? It had all been recovered.

He picked up Cy and headed across the street for a Guinness. In the booth he told Cy of Pendle's decision. "They check that palm top?"

"Wally says they went over that site with a fine tooth comb. He can't believe they missed the palm top."

"It's no bigger than your hand. A lot smaller than yours. Anything on it?"

"The usual stuff, addresses, phone numbers, Aristotle's *Poetics*."

"A book?"

"That little thing has an amazing capacity. And notes."

Only Keegan, from long experience, would have noticed the change in Cy's voice.

"Notes."

"A summary of the committee meeting and an account of a visit Cassirer paid him."

"Pretty bad."

"Pendle is going to love it."

Not even Guinness could lift the gloom Phil felt. Why did he think Andrew was innocent? From the sound of it, Cassirer had been asking for a smash in the mouth. But with a bat? Andrew Bernardo? This was heresy, of course. Anyone can do anything, if the circumstances are right. Or wrong. He and Roger Dowling were agreed on that. There is no criminal type.

"You might as well say sinners are a type, Phil, rather than all of us," he'd said.

"I'll leave that to you, Roger."

Besides, why did he think the Bernardos were so special? Fulvio had acted like an alley cat when he had the chance. Raymond had abandoned the priesthood and run off to California with a nun. Andrew was shacked up with a woman who sounded like she would testify against him at the trial.

"How's Jessica Bernardo taking this?" Phil asked Cy.

"She's the best of the lot, Phil. Pippen says she's read her novels."

"No kidding."

Once he had kidded Cy about Pippen, and the reaction had assured that it would be the only time. Anyone can do anything. Cy looked ready to deck him with that hamlike fist of his.

"Want another?"

Cy shook his head. "Maybe I'll check and see how she's doing?"

"Jessica?"

Careful, careful.

44

When he left Andrew to go on to the wake at St. Edmund's, Raymond felt that he was letting his brother down. He had come home to be with his dying father as the family pariah, and now Andrew had usurped the role, actually suspected of murdering a colleague — if such a civilized term could be applied to Horst Cassirer. The unreality of police headquarters, the improbability of the accusation, seemed a basis for optimism. Andrew would be dragged like a trophy through the media, but eventually they would find the one who had killed Cassirer and it would pass away like a bad dream. But hope came hard.

Snow was falling as he drove to the campus, soft, fluffy, descending like a benediction on the city, transforming it into unreal houses, their edges softened by the snow, and creating expanses of virginal purity. On advice from John, he rolled down the window and, with wet flakes swirling into the car, told the guard he was going to the wake at Domus Sanctae Marthae.

"The retirement home for priests," he added, when the guard looked puzzled.

"Purgatory?"

"That's the place."

A snarled smile, the barrier lifted, and he drove into the winter wonderland of the campus. It had been years since he had seen snow, not counting a trip to San Bernadino with Phyllis, but like so many other things it was not knowing winter that seemed strange to him now, all the years when the past had been deliberately forgotten. How easily he could imagine that this was a winter when he had driven along the campus roads as an insider, Father Raymond, the young man from whom so many things were expected. And he had betrayed them all.

The chapel in Purgatory was designed for the elderly, the halt, and the lame. There were half a dozen armchairs with comfortable-looking prie-dieux before them and ample space on either side for wheelchairs. When Raymond entered, there was an old fellow dozing in one of the chairs, another in a wheelchair staring fixedly ahead as if he were trying to get his bearings. And visible in the open coffin the profile of Father Bourke pointing toward heaven.

Raymond stood for a moment and, as he had not for his father, wept. His father had

not been able to restrain the anger he felt —
"Judas!" — but Father Bourke had been like
the father in the parable, welcoming home
the prodigal, finding excuses for his absence.
Raymond lowered himself onto the kneeler
and not thinking of what he was doing
prayed for the repose of the soul of Father
Bourke. The words came easily nor did his
words fly up and his thoughts remain below.
He lifted his mind and heart to God, who
had been there all along, and asked pardon
and peace for the old priest. And for himself.
Without drama he thought, *I have come
home*.

A sound came from behind him, and he
turned to see John settle into a chair. He
nodded at Raymond, who got up and took a
chair as well. He could relinquish it when
others came. But five minutes went by, and
there were no new arrivals. The man in the
wheelchair was snoring peacefully, and the
other old fellow still dozed. It might have
been the Garden of Olives. After a time,
Raymond slid back his sleeve and looked at
his watch. He leaned toward John.

"When do you begin?"

John smiled. "This is it."

"Aren't the others coming?"

"Others? Haven't you heard?"

Is this what had become of the Order of

St. Edmund? He stared at John. Of course Purgatory was for old and retired priests, but wasn't the other building — the name Paradiso had never caught on — full? John took his arm and led him outside.

"Raymond, there are only eight of us left. Not counting those here, of course."

"Eight!"

"It could be worse. Not that I counted on being the junior man for so long."

"No vocations?"

They wandered into the refectory and filled paper cups with coffee.

"They don't stay."

No wonder. Good Lord.

"Now you can see why Father Bourke was so happy you came back."

There seemed no *arrière pensée* in what John said. Did he think Raymond would seek reinstatement, move into Paradiso, get back to work as a priest? The thought filled him with odd excitement. Would it really be so easy? At the moment, no thought of Phyllis disturbed these oddly happy thoughts.

"The funeral is at ten."

"In the campus church."

"Of course. The cardinal will be here."

"I'll be here."

It sounded as if he wished to speak to the

400

cardinal archbishop of Chicago, the wanderer returned, seeking reinstatement.

The car was covered with snow, and when he got inside it was like an igloo. The wipers swept the snow off the windshield, and the breeze that came up sent snow swirling after him. As he drove, the other windows cleared.

When he got home Jessica was there, and it was clear that his mother had heard about Andrew.

"Raymond, what does it mean?"

"Amos Cadbury got him a lawyer, thanks to Father Dowling."

"Father Dowling! Oh, everybody knows."

Had that been her thought when he ran off with Phyllis? As far as he knew, there had been no media coverage of his defection, because the Order had not raised a fuss about it.

He sat beside her, but Jessica was her main consoler. He marveled at the little sister he knew and yet did not know. He had been impressed by her novels; even Phyllis was impressed and a little jealous. Why do women resent the success of other women? Inevitably, Eleanor came, just walking in with a tragic expression and standing before the couch and looking down at the three of them.

"How horrible to accuse Andrew of such a thing!"

Jessica said, "What he admits to doing is bad enough. I thought that if he told them . . ."

"You advised him to tell the police?"

"Father Dowling agreed."

"Father Dowling!"

"It was the right thing to do," Raymond said. "Imagine if they had discovered that by themselves."

"I'll make coffee."

"I want a drink," Jessica said.

A drink in the Bernardo house meant wine, and Raymond joined her in a glass. Eleanor made coffee, a huge pot, more than could possibly be wanted.

"I'll fix dinner," she said.

"I'm not hungry," Margaret said. "I think I'll have a glass of wine too."

Eleanor joined them. So much for the coffee. Eleanor had claimed Raymond's seat beside the grieving widow, and Jessica followed Raymond into the kitchen, rolling her eyes but saying nothing.

"Did you go downtown?"

"Yes."

"How does it look?"

"Bad. I heard on the radio that he will be arraigned."

"Good Lord."

"I went on to Father Bourke's wake. Such as it was."

"Everyone is dying."

"Not everyone." He took her in his arms. Some people are being killed. He didn't say that. Jessica cried quietly, without theatrics, brokenhearted.

"Do you think they would have found out what Andrew did with that man's body if he hadn't told them?"

"Yes."

"So do I."

"What a stupid, stupid thing to do."

"What will this do to your novel?"

She stepped back and looked at him. "You're the central character."

"Ouch. How will it end?"

"Of course it won't be you. I can't know enough about real people to write about them. They become characters."

"Thanks."

She punched his arm. "How long will you stay?"

"Trying to get rid of me?"

"I wish you'd never go back."

He looked at her. "Maybe I won't."

"Really!" Her face lit up. "Oh, Raymond, stay. Mom needs you so much now."

And what of Phyllis? She needed him too,

and he had given her every claim on himself. It was so easy to say that he would never go back, but it was not the sort of thing he could do over the phone. He would have to go back to Thousand Oaks and face Phyllis. The thought made him shiver.

Later, upstairs, in what his mother called his room, he lay awake and thought of the faith that had returned at his father's funeral Mass and his feelings in the chapel of Purgatory. What kind of faith was it that could go and come without warning? With Phyllis he would have to explain, and any explanation would be inadequate and open to obvious response. What would he have said if, in similar circumstances, Phyllis told him she wanted to go back to the convent? But there was no convent for her to go back to, as her Order had all but disintegrated. Well, so had the Order of St. Edmund. It occurred to him that if he did go back he would be boarding a sinking ship. But of course in his heart of hearts he thought he could save the Order.

John had ticked off the names of those residing in Paradiso, all but one of whom he had known, none of them, he thought wryly, among the best. It came as news to him that so many had left, sought and received laicization, or just left. As he had.

"You opened the door," John said, not accusingly but as a matter of fact.

My God, how responsible was he for the sad state of the Order? He thought of returning, perhaps attracting back others who had left, getting the Order back on its feet. Getting its feet more firmly set in the college.

Raymond seethed when he realized what an insignificant factor the Order now was in the college it had founded. Horst Cassirer was not an anomaly, just an exaggerated instance of the secular mind that dominated the faculty. Why hadn't Andrew kept him informed?

That was nonsense. He had not been kept informed of the Order or the college because he had not wanted to be. What did he care for Egypt now that he had entered the promised land? How differently things would have gone had he remained. Father Bourke's manner had brought home to him that once he had been regarded as the future of the Order, the man who would lead them through the choppy waters ahead. And he would have. He was sure he could have made the Order and college flourish.

There would have been no maniacs like Cassirer on the faculty, or if there had been, short work would have been made of their insolence. The faculty contractually accepted the mission of the college when they were hired, and actions contrary to it were reasons for dismissal. Father Bourke had insisted on that, had run it by the AAUP, checked with the lawyers; it was tight as a drum, legally. No claims to academic freedom could trump it because it was an agreement freely entered into from the outset. Since no one was owed employment, it could not be regarded as an infringement before one was hired. That meant the means to get the college on course and hold it there were available. What was missing was the will.

It had been Cassirer's inspiration to threaten to use that contractual agreement against Andrew. But that would have opened up a can of worms for such faculty members as Cassirer.

Raymond smiled. How the possibility of academic combat set the adrenalin flowing. But it was all a dream. No one could undo what had been done in the last decade and more. You could not fire half the faculty on the basis of principles that had been largely ignored for years. Cassirer's ploy had been cynical, a mindless counterattack.

Was Andrew really in danger? It was incredible that he should be accused of murdering Cassirer, but it was also incredible that he would find the body, put it into the backseat of his car, and trick his girlfriend into driving where he could dump the body and murder weapon. Now Gloria had turned on him, not only protesting her innocence of desecrating Cassirer's body but stating that she had supported the late professor's request for a promotion to tenure.

"We talk of excellence, but we seem to fear it when we find it."

Excellence. Cassirer. An excellent professor is not an egomaniac who despises his students and colleagues and writes jargon for the half dozen others in the world who share his desire to make the intelligible unintelligible. Andrew was a thousand times the teacher Cassirer was; Raymond was sure of it. Gloria Monday's notion of excellence would be the death of higher education.

It was two in the morning when the telephone brought him awake, and he hunted for the phone, not wanting his mother to be wakened.

"Raymond?"

"Phyllis. I was asleep."

"For days? Why haven't you called?"

He propped up his pillow and got into a seated position in the dark room. The snowy world outside provided a kind of lunar light. He felt that he was in some crawl space between the real and unreal.

"You wouldn't want to hear it all."

"Wouldn't I?"

"Two funerals, Phyllis. Not a barrel of laughs. My brother has been indicted for murder."

"Oh stop it!"

"I'm serious. A colleague who hated him was killed, and Andrew has been accused of doing it."

"Raymond, you poor thing. You have to get away from all that. Come home now."

"It will take some days to get my mother's things in order. The loneliness is beginning to sink in, the fact that she is all alone now . . ."

"I know the feeling."

"Phyllis, cheer me up. Tell me what you've been doing."

A prolonged sigh. "I have spent more time with Julia than I should have. Now she has a crush on me."

"Be careful."

"She is cute."

"So are you."

"That's what she tells me."

How Californian it all sounded. Life lived on the frothy surface: movement, diversion, fun, sex. The ribbons of highway seemed to symbolize a state whose population was always in transit, hurtling along, paying the price in road rage.

"I'm going to Catalina, Ray. I'd hoped you'd be here to come along."

He urged her to go. He did not want to think of her pining for him in Thousand Oaks.

"Who'll crew for you?"

"We'll go in Julia's boat."

After he hung up and lay fully awake he decided that all this talk about Julia was meant to do what it did, make him jealous. Jealous of that little neurotic?

45

Tuttle was a resilient man, but to have been seen by Horvath cowering in his office while Hazel raged without was worse than humbling. The silver lining was that, having changed the locks on the door, he seemed at last rid of the dragon who had occupied his outer office. He closed his account at the bank, delighted with the balance — Hazel had a business head on her shoulders, no doubt of that — and opened an account at another bank. He had feared that she would wipe him out with a single check, but if she tried that now she would get a surprise. Tuttle still had a card or two up his sleeve.

But he was ashamed to face Horvath, assuming he had regaled the department with stories of Tuttle huddled behind the locked door of his office. On the other hand, what might Hazel not have carted off if Cy hadn't surprised her filling that shopping bag?

Sitting at Hazel's desk, trying to figure out what she might have taken away, he fiddled with the phone, and old messages began to play. He let it go on. It was like having the radio on when you worked. Most of the calls were from Barbara the paralegal, reporting on her work. Hazel had gotten her money out of that girl, presuming she had been paid. He was startled to hear the distinctive snarl of Cassirer coming from the machine.

"I've decided I don't need a lawyer. Send me a bill."

Hazel burst into the message, answering the phone, and so she had been recorded too.

"Professor Cassirer?"

"You get that? I'm dropping Tuttle. I don't need a lawyer. What can he do I can't do anyway?"

"Now listen. We have done a great deal of work for you, engaged outside help, run up expenses."

"Send me a bill."

"It's not just the money! Your case represents a rich new field for Mr. Tuttle."

Tuttle was nodding and he liked that. How could Cassirer resist her honeyed tones? This was not the voice with which Hazel called him an idiot. But that voice came more and more into play as the conversation went on. Hazel was not going to let Cassirer go.

"Hey, that's it. It's over, okay? Send me

411

the bill. You want to sue me for dropping a lawyer, go ahead."

"You idiot!" Hazel finally said, but Cassirer had hung up.

There was another side to Hazel, no doubt of that. Insubordinate, pushy, a pain in the neck, but loyal in her way. She had been his champion with Cassirer. Mr. Tuttle. Tuttle would have dropped the guy in a minute, glad to get rid of him. He wondered if Hazel had gotten around to sending him a bill. It would never be paid now. Too bad. Hazel would have really socked it to him.

Eventually Tuttle's courage returned, and he was seen again in the haunts of men: the pressroom at the courthouse, across the street sipping a Diet Coke with Agnes Lamb, his eye on the door lest Peanuts find him consorting with the enemy. But it was because his self-esteem had not fully returned that he passed on the information to Agnes.

"You had a stakeout on Andrew Bernardo's apartment?"

"Right. Cassirer was my client. Andrew was his enemy. You never know what a stakeout will turn up."

"So what did it turn up? You weren't there

when it happened, were you?"

"Not at the time, no. Peanuts and I had gone to dinner. Before we went Mabel Gorman showed up and went inside."

"So?"

"She was wearing tennis shoes."

"Everybody wears tennis shoes."

"I don't. You don't. But didn't the one who clobbered Cassirer leave tennis shoe prints in the snow?"

"I've talked with Mabel Gorman. She tried to see Andrew Bernardo. She's just a little bitty thing."

"You don't have to be Sammy Sosa to swing a bat."

"She was on Andrew's side, wasn't she, in the big academic battle?"

"Have you talked with Lily St. Clair?"

"Tuttle, we have talked to them all, and we will talk with them some more."

"Check their tennis shoes."

"I'm not that kind of girl."

"You think because she was a woman she and Gloria Monday saw eye to eye? No way. Lily was after anything with shorts."

"In tennis shoes?"

"She even had it for Zalinksi."

"Meaning?"

"A woman scorned!"

Agnes finished her Coke. "Pretty far-fetched, Tuttle. How's Hazel?"

Oh no. Even Agnes knew. Had he become a figure of fun to everyone? He had half a mind to call Hazel and tell her to get to hell back to work. He needed a buffer against his enemies.

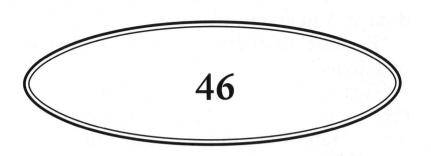

46

Father Dowling noticed that Raymond Bernardo came with his mother to the noon Mass but did not come forward to receive communion, as he hadn't at the funeral Mass for his father. The laicized priest is no longer an uncommon phenomenon, but still it was odd to have one in the pews of his own church. It used to be said that a nun could be recognized at a hundred yards no matter what she wore, a jab at the alleged poor taste in clothing on the part of those who doffed the habit. The habit did not make the nun, nor did the collar the priest. Whatever Raymond's status, laicized or not, he was a priest forever, in the words of ordination that would have been pronounced over him. What did he make of his brother Andrew?

"You think he killed that man?" Father Dowling had asked Phil Keegan.

"He admits to getting rid of the body."

"To divert suspicion from himself."

"And then he wanted to tell us he had

done it. You know that."

"Because he thought better of what he had done."

"Roger, it's out of my hands now. I'm neither judge nor jury; I just tell them what we've found out, and the trial can decide who did what."

Father Dowling looked at his old friend. "You're being disingenuous."

"I don't even know what it means."

"I can't believe you haven't formed an opinion of your own."

"Of course I have."

"What is it?"

"Andrew could have done it. Roger, we found his palm top at the scene of the crime."

"Outside his own front door."

"He says he didn't carry the palm top with him often. He thought it was on the desk of his campus office."

"Was it?"

"Roger, he could say it had been stolen, and I wouldn't know if he were telling the truth."

That afternoon Father Dowling drove to the campus. The guard halted him, saw the collar, and waved him through.

"I wonder where I would find faculty offices."

"All over the place. It depends on the department."

"English."

"You want Henley Hall, Father. Who you looking for?"

"There's something I want to check. Thanks."

"Anytime, Father."

There were lots of places not to park on campus, unless one were handicapped. We seem to have become a nation of the halt and lame, considering all the special places reserved for them. Of course *handicapped* has become an analogous term. After locating Henley Hall and circling it several times, Roger Dowling saw someone leaving a space and was able to claim it before anyone else did.

Henley Hall was not one of the new buildings. Built of roughly hewn granite blocks it rose to its green tile roof, which extended out over the walls, giving the three-story building a squat look. A ramp had been added to the wide old-fashioned entry — for the handicapped. Smokers huddled under the dripping eaves. The temperature had risen, and yesterday's snow had begun to melt. Great icicles had formed on the rain gutters of Henley. Inside he found a glass case with a list of who and what the building housed. Bernardo, Andrew, 203.

The stairway was wide with a smooth granite ledge on which the hands of millions had moved on the upward climb. Room 203 was in a corner of the building, and the frosted glass in its door was illumined from within. He had considered searching the list in the entryway to see if anyone else was in 203. The lighted door might be his answer. He tapped on it.

"Advance to be recognized," a voice boomed from within.

Father Dowling went in, stopping after three paces. The room was redolent of new and old body odors. Their source was obviously the smiling bearded man seated at one of the desks.

"You share this room with Andrew Bernardo?"

"Take a pew, Father. Yes, I do. Terrible what's happened. You a friend of the family?"

"I know them."

"You said the Mass for his father."

"So you were there."

"In the back." He identified himself as Foster, then pointed to the nameplate, as if to show they matched. He seemed to want to add more to his statement as to why he had been in St. Hilary's the morning of

Fulvio Bernardo's funeral. Father Dowling sat at Andrew's desk. There was a photograph of Jessica, of his parents, and of a lovely young woman he recognized as the Gloria Monday who had been vocal in separating herself from what Andrew had done.

"There were empty seats," he said.

"The usher said there weren't." Had this white lie been a corporal work of mercy for those already in the church? How had Andrew managed to share an office with this fellow?

"What's that?"

"A kind of air conditioner. Andrew always had it on. Asthma or something."

Father Dowling turned it on. There was a hum but not a noisy one. Breathing became less penitential.

"Do you think Andrew killed that man?"

"Cassirer? I don't think so. I will testify for him if he asks. Cassirer was slandering him, of course, but Andrew was not easily provoked. He is the only officemate I've had who lasted more than a semester. I must rub people the wrong way. But he never complained."

What would a jury make of such a testimonial?

"It's all circumstantial," Foster added. "A

419

good lawyer should be able to get the case thrown out."

"There is some evidence."

"What?"

"His palm top was found at the scene of the crime."

Foster laughed, then laughed some more. Father Dowling waited.

"She must have lost it then?"

"She?"

"Lily St. Clair. She's in English too. She was in here the other day and took the palm top."

"You saw her do it?"

"It was there in that little stand when I turned to this bookshelf, and when I turned back it was gone."

"Why would she take it?"

"You'll have to ask her that."

"Didn't you say anything?"

"No. She could just have denied it. I couldn't ask her to empty her pockets and purse. But I know she took it. Anyway, Andrew never used it much. The only time he mentioned it was to complain about it."

"Maybe I will ask her."

"I suppose you'll have to bring me into it."

"Maybe not. We'll see."

"She was kind of nuts about Cassirer, I

think. You'd have to be nuts to like that guy."

Having found far more than he expected, Father Dowling was overwhelmed by a desire for fresh air. He thanked Foster for taking the time to talk with him.

"No need to rush off, Father."

"Perhaps another time."

The corridor itself was a relief, but the outdoors, once he pushed through the entrance and stood on the front steps, was glorious. He stood and inhaled deeply, taking in a bit of secondhand smoke from the huddled smokers. Were they the same ones who had been there when he went in? Once restored, he went inside again and consulted the building directory. Dr. Lily St. Clair was in room 119.

He tapped on the unillumined door of 119 and received no answer. A card pinned to a cork board beside the door gave him the office hours of Dr. St. Clair. According to it she should be in. He tapped again. Still no answer. He left the building again, went to his car, lit his pipe, and looked around at the campus. It had been here all along, and yet it was a strange place to him.

As he sat there he turned on WBBM for the weather, to see if more snow was on the way. Commercials were interrupted by news items. Yet another faculty member at St. Edmund's had been attacked. They went to their reporter on the spot.

As he listened to the on-the-spot report of the attack on Professor Lily St. Clair, Father Dowling noted the antenna sprouting from a van not five spaces from his own. The television crew. He got out of the car and went over to it. The back doors were open, and a monitor carried the interview.

Lily stood supported by a sheepish officer from campus security. She had called security on her cell phone and stayed right where it had happened until they came.

"This is where it happened." Her arm swept out. "Someone came up behind me and threw something over my head. My resistance surprised him."

"Attempted rape?"

"A botched attempt!" Her chin lifted and her eyes shone.

The attacker had fled, and she had not seen him. She had to struggle to get the blanket off her head.

The real police arrived then, and Lily began her story again. Father Dowling went back to his car. When he arrived at the rectory, Marie had the television on in the kitchen.

"Well, they can't blame this on Andrew Bernardo," she said with some satisfaction.

Lily St. Clair had been taken to the student infirmary, where she was asked if her assailant had raped her. Her eyes rounded in disbelief.

She explained. She had spent months in an evening class at the Y learning how to disable rampant males. Her knee, she learned, was her most powerful weapon. If there was any defect in the class it was its similarity to training soldiers with broomsticks. The instructor was a woman, so practicing counterattacks was largely theoretical. Sometimes as she jogged about the campus on her daily run, her tennis shoes not quite absorbing the impact of the sidewalk, Lily had an impulse to carom off her path and flatten a passing male with what she knew of his vulnerability. Her confidence grew to the point that she blamed the victims rather than the perpetrators of rape. Any woman could defend herself!

"So how did it happen?"

They ringed her bed like an attentive seminar, a male student from the campus paper, a toothy woman from the *Trib*, Detective Agnes Lamb, and assorted medical personnel.

"A sneak attack. From behind. Just before he struck, I heard something, but it was too late to react."

The weapon had apparently been a baseball bat, an aluminum one. The bonging sound the blow made had been heard up and down the street, but no one had seen the assailant. The blanket thrown over her head had cushioned the blow. Agnes Lamb had been at the scene of the attack, had bagged up and sent downtown the aluminum bat. Of course the MO would be what everyone noticed. Maybe this would help Andrew.

"How long will they keep you here?" the *Trib* reporter asked.

"I feel ready to go now."

The infirmary was not a hospital. Lily had not been rolled into an emergency ward and examined; she had been driven to the infirmary by campus security, along with one of those who had heard the sound of the bat hitting her head and helped her inside, where she was put to bed. As a rape victim she might have commanded more attention. But then word spread, and the result was this rather pleasant interview. It was the student reporter who remarked on the similarity of the attack on Lily and on Horst Cassirer.

"I've half-expected it," she said.

"You have?"

"Horst and I were very close." Such statements were now made while boldly looking the inquirer in the eye, to surprise there any moral judgment. The reporter understood.

"Did you live together?"

"Not at present."

"You broke up?"

"No!"

"I know you were his big defender on the committee that turned him down."

"And now I've paid the price."

47

Walter called before she had done her writing stint for the day, but Jessica was glad for the interruption.

"Is there anything I can do?"

He meant for Andrew. She wished there was something she herself could do. From the time Andrew had shown up in her apartment with his incredible story of having picked up the body of Horst Cassirer and dumped it in the street a mile from his apartment, Jessica felt that she had stepped through the looking glass.

"I wish there was."

"What are you doing?"

"Talking on the phone."

"Would you like to talk face to face?"

She would. Walter's calm solidity and unimaginative integrity were just what she needed now.

"Could we go somewhere for a beer?"

"Good idea."

He was there within twenty minutes, and

they went out to his car through a gently falling snow.

"Any ideas?"

"Pat's Pub?"

He smiled. It was there that they had gone on their first date, if that is what it was. Pat's was a sports bar, television sets everywhere, bringing in half a dozen different athletic events, the pictures captioned since the noise level prevented hearing the sound. It looked as if they would have to sit at the bar, but a booth was vacated and they claimed it. A waitress skated up to them.

"Two lites."

"Sixteen or twenty-two."

She meant ounces. "Sixteen?"

Jessica nodded. The twenty-two-ounce beer came in a mug ten inches high, frosted, hard to handle unless you stood up and used a straw.

"What you've been through," Walter said.

"It's not over."

They hunched over the table between them. *How good looking he is,* Jessica thought. Had she ever noticed? He had always been so deferential to her that she found it difficult to take him seriously. Now he seemed everything a girl — a thirty-one-year-old woman, that is — should want.

"This can't help work on your novel."

There had been a message from Thunder, but she had not called him back. His enthusiasm was off-putting, and his emphasis was always on what this novel was going to do. He meant sell and make big money. Well, it had already done that, with the hefty advance he had gotten for it.

"I didn't write a word today," she said to Walter.

"I'm not surprised."

"That was Cassirer who stopped you in the parking lot last week, wasn't it? Bearded, rode a bicycle."

"You noticed."

"I notice everything." She could believe it. "I could see that he annoyed you."

"He was a very annoying man."

She babbled on about the situation at St. Edmund's, the disagreement over tenure for Cassirer, his reaction by declaring war on Andrew. Anne Gogarty had called Jessica about it.

"Why Andrew? I would be the most logical object of his wrath. But Horst just decided that Andrew was the key."

Anne Gogarty wondered again what she could do for Andrew. Why did all his allies seem so ineffectual? Well, how effectual was she? She was sure it had been right to arrange for the meeting between Andrew and

Captain Keegan, sure at the time, more or less sure now. But it would have been infinitely worse had they found out before he told them. And the behavior of Gloria Monday made it clear she would have gone to the police if Andrew hadn't. What a friend. But Andrew hadn't been much of a friend to her, involving her in such an idiotic act. The finding of Andrew's palm top at the spot where Cassirer was struck added an ominous note. For the first time Jessica believed that Andrew would be found guilty. But she could not bring herself to believe he was.

"Why did Cassirer come to you?"

"Oh, he talked to my brother Raymond and my aunt Eleanor too. He seemed to think we would pressure Andrew into voting for him to save the family from scandal."

"Living with that girl?"

Jessica nodded.

"If only Andrew had called the police when he found the body."

"If. Then his darned palm top wouldn't look so bad, being found there."

Walter sipped his beer. Jessica realized that hers was half gone. Maybe she would take up drinking inadvertently.

"I did know why he stopped you there in the parking lot. My sister is secretary of the

English Department at the college."

"She is?"

He nodded. "The stories she tells. She likes Andrew though. And the chair."

"Anne Gogarty."

"Yes. And everyone really hated Cassirer. Well, not everyone. But everyone Wilma likes."

"We're practically related." But she couldn't laugh.

"I wish we were."

She put her hand on his, thankful for the noise, the television sets, the atmosphere of frantic normalcy.

48

The turnout for Horst Cassirer's memorial was disappointing, but Lily put on a brave face. Of course Zalinski came, and Anne Gogarty. How could she refuse to attend the memorial for Horst? And Wilma, the secretary, came, God knows why, but Lily was grateful. That seemed to be it, except for McDivitt, who hovered in the back of the room, in the little group but not of it. The urn with Horst's ashes was bronze, a Grecian shape, an amphora, was it? Lily thought so. In the back of the room McDivitt cleared his throat as if to say no one else would be coming. Students? Not likely. But then the Gorman girl entered, sitting in back, shaking her head when McDivitt urged her forward. She took a seat in the back row of chairs, at the opposite end to Foster, who had entered just before her. Finally, dramatically, Gloria Monday arrived, fresh from the snowy world outside, beautiful. She came to Lily and took her in her arms in an expression of solidarity.

"I am representing the faculty senate,"

she whispered. "And of course myself."

Lily could have wept with gratitude. Gloria had at last seen the light of day as far as Andrew Bernardo was concerned. Even if he hadn't been arrested she was sure Gloria would have ended their relationship and evicted him from the apartment. It seemed a small triumph but infinitely satisfying. Lily went to the podium.

"We have gathered to say good-bye to a man all of us knew as a colleague, some as a friend, some as a dear friend." She dropped her eyes. "It will be said that Horst was not a religious man. And that is true. Unless one wishes to call his unswerving devotion to the truth religious. If so, he would have to be accounted one of the saints."

Gloria Monday's smile seemed to have been put on for the duration, wistful, pensive, unchanging. Zalinski sought a more comfortable position in his chair. Anne Gogarty stared at her hands, which were folded on her lap.

Lily read Catullus's CI ode through in Latin, a short poem but lengthy enough to make her audience uneasy. It had come as a shock to her that Zalinski did not know Latin. After she was done, she put into English "the futility of words over your quiet ashes." Then she stepped back and nodded to Zalinski.

At the podium, Zalinski shuffled his feet and looked at the ceiling. Then, addressing his hands, which gripped the edges of the lectern, he spoke. He told them of Horst's passion for baseball, his head full of statistics. A Mets fan.

"Once I teased him about this, telling him Aristotle had made lists of Olympic winners. Horst glared at me, then said, 'He should have stuck with that.'"

No laughter but an altered key to the discomfort of those gathered there.

Anne Gogarty read from "In Memoriam," a few random quatrains, nothing daring.

> *One writes that "other friends remain,"*
> *That "Loss is common to the race" —*
> *And common is the commonplace,*
> *And vacant chaff well meant for grain*

Gloria followed and spoke briefly but passionately of continuing the fight that Horst Cassirer had begun. The best tribute to his memory would be to bring St. Edmund's College into the second millennium. She looked around. "And then we will push the college into the third."

Lily clapped, bringing her palms together

half a dozen times, but her action was not contagious. The podium was now hers again.

"If I have any regret it is that Horst and I allowed ourselves to be cowed by the medieval regulations of this university. Others defied those regulations." She looked with fierce admiration at Gloria. She avoided Zalinski's skeptical eyes. "Some of you know I wrote my dissertation on the poems of John Clare." She unfolded a sheet and began to declaim.

> I hid my love in field and town
> Till e'en the breeze would
>   knock me down;
> The bees seemed singing ballads o'er.
> The fly's bass turned a lion's roar
> And even silence found a tongue,
> To haunt me all the summer long:
> The riddle nature could not prove
> Was nothing but a secret love.

She paused, then said softly, "Horst, we will never forget you. I will always love you." She stepped back from the podium and let the tears come. Gloria comforted her. Through her tears, Lily cried, *"Atque in perpetuum, frater, ave atque vale."*

Within minutes Lily found herself alone

434

with McDivitt, who took the urn from its stand.

"Come into my office," he said.

Lily followed him, head down, unsure whether the ceremony had been a success. When McDivitt stepped aside to allow her to enter first, Lily saw that a priest was seated there. He rose and put out his hand.

"Father Dowling."

Lily could only take his hand.

He said, "Would you leave us alone, Mr. McDivitt?"

But the door was already closing.

49

"I visited Andrew Bernardo's campus office and learned that you had taken away his palm top."

Lily St. Clair looked startled. "Who told you that?"

"Why did you do it, to throw suspicion on him?"

"Suspicion! He killed him." McDivitt had given Lily the urn of Cassirer's ashes, and she flourished it.

"So you took his palm top and left it in the snow outside his apartment."

"I don't have to answer such questions."

"Not when I put them to you, no. But you will surely be called to testify if there is a trial."

"Have you told the police?"

"I was hoping you would do that. I suspect they may not make too big a thing of it."

"Foster," she said vehemently. "That foul and smelly man."

Father Dowling smiled. "I followed the

memorial ceremony from outside the room. That was a very decent thing for you to do. Obviously you and Cassirer were quite close."

Tears welled in her eyes. "It's all so unjust."

"It's far more unjust to make an innocent man look guilty."

"Innocent? Do you know what he did with Horst's body."

"That was terrible, of course. But Horst was already dead."

"You believe his story that he just came across the body outside the building? Not even Gloria believes that. Andrew hated Horst."

"Wasn't it the other way around?"

"Have you any idea what a negative tenure decision can mean to a junior professor? He is branded for life. Andrew knew that. Andrew, who does not have the credentials of a real professor, was determined to block Horst's advance. Yes, I do indeed think he's guilty, and if they make me testify I will tell that to the jury."

So maybe it had not been a good idea to confront her with what he had learned from his visit to Andrew's campus office. Watching the monitor in the television truck, seeing her interviewed on television when he returned to the rectory, had made him wonder if the attack on Lily had not been staged. And what if her love for Cassirer had been a one-way passion? A woman scorned is a lethal weapon. He had counted on a sense of guilt, at least from being found out, but she had lifted her chin and brazened her way through what should have been an uncomfortable confrontation. Tugging the urn to her bosom she opened the door and stalked out.

After a moment, Father Dowling followed. McDivitt hurried along with him to open the door.

"I hate these pagan rituals, Father."

"Will the urn be buried?"

"She wants to keep it."

"Is that legal?"

"She says she was his common-law wife."

Outside, talking with a spindly girl, was Zalinski. Downwind from them, Foster, rendered innocuous by the cleansing winter air, was lighting a cigar. The girl glanced at Father Dowling and then hurried away.

"That woman is nuts," Zalinski said.

Father Dowling looked after the departing girl. Zalinski continued, "Not her. She's just a student. But Lily, trying to pass herself off as Horst's true love! He never laid a glove on her. He found her a pain in the neck. I mean, it was nice of her to think of a memorial for him, but the weeping widow act is pretty much."

"I understand she was one of his major supporters."

"We both were. Of course it's not altruistic. We needed an ally against the mugwumps."

"Like Andrew?"

Belatedly it occurred to Zalinski that he was standing in the street talking to a priest. A wondrous look came over him.

"I haven't talked to a priest in fifteen years."

"That's a long time." Father Dowling took his pipe from his pocket but decided against filling it. "Are you Catholic?"

"I was."

"What happened?"

"Oh come on, Father. I'm an educated man. None of it adds up."

"We should talk about it sometime."

Zalinski looked wary. "You think you could finagle me back into the Church."

"Good heavens no. What would we do with an educated man?"

Zalinski chuckled. "Okay. Just say I used to be Catholic and am no longer."

"Come see me sometime."

"Maybe I will."

"By the way, who was the student who went away just now?"

Zalinski looked up the street, but the girl was gone. "One of Cassirer's students. Gorman. Mabel Gorman. Your collar probably scared her off."

Halfway to his car, Father Dowling heard puffing behind him and turned to see Foster slipping and sliding across the parking lot toward him.

"What did she say?"

He meant Lily St. Clair. "She more or less denied it."

"I figured she would. But she took it, so she must have planted it outside Andrew's building. She seems to fancy herself Cassirer's great love."

Charity overcame prudence, and he offered Foster a lift.

"No thanks. I've got my car."

God is good. Being in the cramped interior of an automobile with Foster would have called for heroic virtue. Or a bad cold. But it was Foster who snuffled.

"I hate winter."

He continued to a diminutive car, one of the new Volkswagens. Another car was leaving the lot. Lily, in the passenger seat, stared straight ahead. Gloria Monday was at the wheel.

50

Eleanor Wygant had come to Amos Cadbury's office to see if Zwingli really was the best lawyer the firm could provide for the defense of her nephew Andrew.

"He's an excellent young man, Eleanor. I would not have suggested him otherwise. How has he displeased you?"

"It's Andrew who lacks confidence in him. And Raymond too seems puzzled by his evenhandedness."

Were the brothers judges of the way of the world, let alone legal strategy? Of course it was essential that a client have confidence in his attorney, particularly one in Andrew's position.

"I'll talk to him."

"That would give him such a boost, Amos."

He had meant he would talk to Zwingli, but Eleanor's assumption that he had meant Andrew would have been cruel to correct.

Criminal law was foreign to Amos's personal legal experience, and the firm had no reputation in the area, something Amos did not lament. If Zwingli was good, and he would not have been hired if his law school standing had not been astronomically high, he would not stay long with Amos Cadbury, that is, if criminal law should remain his predilection. If Andrew were still in custody, Amos would have taken his young associate along with him. But a call at the Bernardo house was ambiguous enough not to look like second-guessing Zwingli. His associate had arranged bail for Andrew, who had gone to his parents' home.

"I'll meet you there," Eleanor said, when he had declined to ride with her to the house. It was not simply that he preferred to be in command of his own comings and goings but that Eleanor's marital record and continued good looks suggested caution. Was he wrong to detect a speculative look in her eye? What was it like to imagine oneself at square one at her age? Amos's beloved wife had preceded him in death, but her passing had seemed to strengthen their marriage bond rather than end it.

Settling into the backseat of his car, having told George their destination, Amos was beset by thoughts of his long life. He had begun his career in the conviction that the law was the codification of fundamental morality, a set of rules grounded in human nature rather than religious beliefs, but it was his faith that seemed the only bulwark of morality now. The law had become a game practiced by charlatans in catchy costumes who had a knack for misleading juries by pleading their cases to the television cameras. He sighed. What could he say to Andrew? If the young man was guilty, punishment was called for. Amos trusted that Zwingli would use only honest means to defend their client. The firm of Amos Cadbury would continue, as it always had, trusting in the rule of law, no matter the horde of unruly lawyers.

Eleanor was already at the house when he arrived, but then he had instructed George to take a circuitous route. Walking up to the door, he thought of Fulvio Bernardo. The man had made a good end, by all reports, and Amos was glad for that. But the thought of all the money he had purloined from Alfred Wygant was a bitter one. Of course, technically, Eleanor had the right to waive the debt. Now both the one who owed and the one to whom the money was originally owed had gone into that bourne from which no traveler returns. If Eleanor had no wish to reclaim what her late husband had given Fulvio

Bernardo that was the end of it, legally.

The two Bernardo sons were in the house, and Amos spoke briefly to Andrew, assuring him that the firm would do everything possible to defend him.

"I did not kill that man, Mr. Cadbury. I did a stupid thing in getting the body off my doorstep, but he was already dead."

Amos nodded. He was inclined to believe Andrew, but he wondered if a jury would.

Raymond was in his father's home office, and Amos joined him there. They spoke inconsequentially of the college, Amos telling the one-time hope of the Order what St. Edmund's had become.

"It broke Father Bourke's heart," Raymond said.

"You spoke with him."

"Several times."

"How long will you be in town?"

"I'm not sure."

Had the prodigal son returned? Raymond in lay clothes bore little resemblance to the young priest Amos remembered. For almost a decade he had been away, longer than he had been active as a priest. Was it possible to step out of the character one had formed over so many years? Of course it was. Raymond had done it. If Father Bourke's heart had been broken it was Raymond's defection that had done it. Whose heart would he break if he came back?

Before Amos left, having condoled with Margaret Bernardo, Father Dowling arrived. Amos spoke with him in the hallway as he was going.

"You must come for dinner soon, Amos."

"Thank you, Father. I would like that very much." He stepped closer to the priest. "You will find this a house of mourning."

"I want to speak to Andrew."

51

"I hope you don't regret my advice that you tell the police what you had done," Father Dowling said to Andrew.

Eleanor was talking with Mrs. Bernardo, and Raymond had gone upstairs to put through a call to California.

"It was better that they hear it from me."

"I have spoken with Foster. He is certain that Lily St. Clair took the palm top from your desk. I suppose she dropped it outside your building."

Andrew tried to smile. "Even if they believe her, it would make her no more guilty than I am."

"But you will look less guilty."

"If Foster is believed."

"I believe him."

Andrew was absurdly grateful for this assurance.

"There was a memorial service for Horst Cassirer at McDivitt's. Lily arranged it."

"I wonder who was there."

"I was, just outside the room. It was quite

moving. A lovely ode by Catullus. Lily cast herself in the role of quasi widow."

"That's nonsense."

"There was no great love between her and Cassirer?"

Andrew shook his head. "If there were it would have been known." He added ruefully, "Such things always are known."

"There was only one student at the memorial."

"I am surprised there was one."

"A girl named Mabel Gorman."

"Mabel! But she hated Cassirer."

"Hated?"

"You have no idea how he treated students. Mabel is a student of mine as well, a very gifted young woman. She has great talent as a writer."

"And she didn't hate you?"

"Oh, I'm pretty good with students."

That night Father Dowling sat late in his study, smoking his pipe, his mind drifting like the smoke. He had not mentioned to anyone his guess that Lily St. Clair had staged the attack that had gained so much publicity. But why would she do such a thing? It could only have the effect of helping Andrew Bernardo, however equivocally. If there had been an attacker it might have been someone who did want to help Andrew. And then the thought formed like the smoke ring that he sent sailing across the room. He watched it go, and it held its shape until it dissolved. Where do thoughts come from and where do they go?

There was one undeniable fact, and that was that a man whom few had loved was dead. Horst Cassirer. Lily St. Clair, and perhaps Zalinski, had been exceptions. The pathetic memorial service for the fallen scholar induced long thoughts. Gloria Monday had seized the occasion to make ideological points, but there was a certain nobility in Lily St. Clair's effort to save her fallen colleague from oblivion. Andrew seemed to think that her claim to a closer relation with Cassirer had been largely a thing of her imagination. But in dreams begin responsibilities. The more he thought of it, the less plausible it seemed to him that Lily St. Clair had staged the attack that had gained her some minutes of notoriety if not fame. The attack had been too reminiscent of that on Cassirer to be incidental. And the attacker most likely had counted on the similarity being noticed, and serving to exonerate Andrew.

Only one candidate for that role suggested herself. Father Dowling went to bed wondering how he should proceed. Asking Phil Keegan or Cy to pursue his suspicion would entail explanations that, when spoken, might seem far-fetched. He must pursue the matter himself.

The campus was familiar to him after his visit some days before, and once more he was waved through the gate by a deferential guard. But he stopped.

"Is there a list of students?"

"Well, there's the campus phone book."

"Where could I get one?"

For answer, the guard handed him a little booklet. "Better go on through, Father. You can drop it off when you leave."

He parked and walked to the campus church, where he sat in a back pew and opened the directory in the dim light. Mabel Gorman did not live on campus. He jotted down her address and phone number, then closed the directory and got on his knees. The sanctuary was slightly more brightly lit than the nave, and the golden tabernacle glowed. After some minutes of prayer in which he scarcely knew what to ask for, he rose and went out to his car.

Everyone used cell phones now, and not for the first time he wished he had overcome his dislike of them and gotten one of his own. Marie pooh-poohed the idea, perhaps not liking the thought of parish business being conducted out of earshot. At the guard shack he handed back the telephone directory.

"Find what you're looking for, Father?"

He nodded. But what was he looking for?

The address was a huge house a block away. He parked in front of it. As he approached the door, a boy came out and hurried toward him.

"Do you know if Mabel Gorman is in?"

The boy shrugged and kept going. The front door was not locked and he went inside. The house had once been a family residence, but now it bore the marks of a house providing rooms for students. He went through the dining room and heard sounds in the kitchen. When he went in, Mabel Gorman turned and looked at him.

"My name is Father Dowling. I saw you at Professor Cassirer's memorial service."

She said nothing.

"You seemed to be the only student there."

She had been making a sandwich. Now she opened the refrigerator and put a package of cold meat in it.

"Andrew Bernardo tells me you are a

student of his. And that you have great talent."

"What will happen to him?"

"Could we sit?"

She led him into the living room, where he sat on a couch that sank ominously beneath him. The furniture all looked the worse for wear. Mabel sat on the edge of a chair and bit into her sandwich.

"His lawyer is not optimistic."

"He is innocent."

"You're wearing tennis shoes."

She looked at her feet as if to verify this.

"Everybody does."

"Are they the same ones you wore that night?"

This was the moment of truth. Or of denial. She chewed her sandwich, looking at him. There seemed no reason to think that she would confirm his suspicions. He half hoped she would not.

"I hate him," she said. "He was the most hateful man I have ever known."

"But you didn't hate Andrew Bernardo."

"Oh no."

"You have put him in a very difficult spot."

"Why did he have to do what he did?"

"Because he knew what everyone would think." He paused. "What a jury *will* think."

"I don't know what to do."

"I think you do."

Silence.

"What will they do to me?"

"God only knows. But you have to talk to the police."

"No!"

"It would be far worse if Andrew Bernardo is found guilty of what you did."

She stared at him, a pathetic girl on a straight-back chair, her tennis shoes flat on the worn carpet. She looked at her sandwich and then at Father Dowling.

"I'm not sorry for what I did."

"That will come with time, I think. Would you like me to come with you?"

"Where?"

"To the police."

All she had to tell him was to go, to leave her alone. But he could not really hope that she would refuse him.

"Or I could have them come to you. We could go to my rectory, and they could come talk to you there."

How passive she seemed. Perhaps she had used up all her strength in attacking Horst Cassirer. But twenty minutes passed before they left for St. Hilary's, minutes during which he insisted gently that there was only one thing she could do. It was the thought that she had put Andrew in jeopardy that proved decisive. When she went upstairs for her coat, Father Dowling had the fear that she would flee, but she did not. She came slowly down the stairs, and they went out to the car. Outside, she pulled the hood of her coat over her head.

Epilogue

Christmas came and went, and the new year began. Amos Cadbury returned from Florida, bronzed and hearty, and stopped by the rectory to report on Zwingli's defense of Mabel Gorman. Amos's young associate had been transferred from Andrew Bernardo's defense, all charges against whom had been dropped somewhat to the indignation of Tetzel, the local reporter, to Mabel Gorman's.

"He has entered a plea of insanity," Amos said mournfully. It was clear that he did not approve of efforts to establish that people had not done what they had done.

"I suppose *insanity* has become a term of art," Father Dowling said.

"Like so many other terms."

Poor Mabel. Father Dowling had continued to visit her, and something like remorse for what she had done was beginning to emerge. But she had difficulty letting go of the idea that in wielding that baseball bat she had been striking a blow for justice.

"And Professor St. Clair?"

"I did not mean to injure her. And I didn't."

Amos said, "There will be a parole hearing for Earl Hospers in a month's time."

Edna of course was elated by this. There seemed some prospect that Earl would be released from Joliet, where he had been a model prisoner. There was however one negative effect of this good news.

"Janet tells me that Rudy Berg avoids her now."

On campus, a romance had sprung up between Janet Hospers and the student entrepreneur who had contracted to paint the rectory trim next summer. But the publicity about Janet's father, and the rehearsal of the events that had led to his conviction, had cooled Rudy's ardor.

"I'm sorry to hear that."

"Janet is glad to know his reaction. She herself told him about Earl before all this publicity broke. He seemed to take it in stride, but the newspaper stories were too much for him."

"And if Earl is released on parole?"

Edna shook her head.

The sins of the fathers continue to be visited on their children. When Raymond and Andrew heard of the money Fulvio had taken from Alfred Wygant, they insisted that it must be repaid before the estate was settled. But Eleanor would not hear of it.

"It was an investment he freely entered into."

"But he received nothing in return."

"That was the risk he took."

The manner of Alfred Wygant's death came up, and Eleanor grew angry.

"McDivitt told me he had a snootful when he fell," Marie said. "The phrase was his, and he ought to know. But Alfred Wygant was a teetotaler."

Phil Keegan entered into speculation with Marie, imagining Eleanor getting her husband drunk and pushing him over the upstairs railing in their house. Father Dowling held his peace, remembering Fulvio's confession in the hospital. But even without the barrier of confidentiality he would not have joined in constructing the lugubrious scenario Marie and Phil imagined. Only a fraction of the misdeeds done in this world receive their just punishment, in any case, and Fulvio had received the grace of going into the next world absolved of his sins. And he had been at most a secondary cause of Alfred Wygant's death.

"If Eleanor will not claim the money, that is an end of it," Amos said. So perhaps even the justice of this world was satisfied.

Andrew had moved into his mother's house and, the estate having been probated, Raymond's duties in Fox River were done. He had formed the habit of accompanying his mother to the noon Mass, and one day Father Dowling asked him to come back for lunch after he had taken his mother home.

Marie outdid herself, overcoming her aversion to feeding a runaway priest. At table they talked only of the Bernardo family, but when they adjourned to the study Father Dowling asked Raymond what he intended to do.

"I will go back to California."

"To resume your work as counselor?"

"To wind it up. Phyllis has formed another attachment, and I am free."

"Free."

"Free to return to the Edmundites."

"And will you?"

Raymond fell silent for a time. "It's all too easy, Father. I came home expecting to be excoriated, but only my father treated me as I deserve. As far as the other Edmundites are concerned, I can just move back in and take up where I left off."

"And will you?"

"As I say, it is too easy. My father's judgment was the right one. I betrayed my vocation. Coming home made me realize that as I never had before. Then I thought I faced the dilemma of continuing the betrayal or of betraying Phyllis. Now she has removed that difficulty. Everything is far too easy."

"So what will you do?"

"When I have taken care of things in California, I am going on an extended retreat with the Benedictines in Manchester, New Hampshire. St. Anselm's Abbey. They will let me live a community life with them. A time of penance. When my inner house is in order, I will go back to the Edmundites." He looked around the study. "I almost long to have someone accuse me, call me a Judas as my father did."

"Your own judgment is severe enough, I think."

When he rose to go, Father Dowling accompanied him to the front door. Before they went outside, Raymond asked for his blessing, and Roger Dowling was happy to give it. "Now you must give me yours."

Raymond hesitated. "When I return from St. Anselm's."

Father Dowling watched him go out to the family car. He doubted that things were as easy for Raymond as he said.

"Is he gone?" Marie asked when he came down the hall.

"Yes."

"He seems such a nice man."

"I think he is."

"But what he did!"

"You should have said something."

Marie was shocked. She stepped back, eyes wide, her mouth agape.

"Oh, I would never do that."

"That was his complaint."

Jessica's novel had been finished. She dedicated it to Walter, and her Raymond character ended quite differently than did her brother. Her hero, if that is what he was, returned to his beloved, happy to escape again what the Church had become. But as he walked along the Pacific shore with the waves rolling inexorably in, his mind was troubled by memories of the faith he had lost. Time would take its toll on him, he realized that. After all, even in California people were mortal. The Four Last Things tumbled like breakers in his mind.

"I'm surprised she knew of them," Amos said. "The Four Last Things."

"She reads Dante, you know. She and Walter are taking Italian and intend to read the *Comedy* only in the original."

"Perhaps Western civilization will survive after all," Amos said.

"Stranger things have happened," said Father Dowling, and began to fill his pipe.

Ralph McInerny is the author of over thirty books and has taught for over forty years at the University of Notre Dame, where he is the director of the Jacques Maritain Center. He has been awarded the Bouchercon Lifetime Achievement Award and was recently appointed to the President's Committee on the Arts and Humanities. He lives in South Bend, Indiana.

The employees of Thorndike Press hope you have enjoyed this Large Print book. All our Thorndike and Wheeler Large Print titles are designed for easy reading, and all our books are made to last. Other Thorndike Press Large Print books are available at your library, through selected bookstores, or directly from us.

For information about titles, please call:

(800) 223-1244

or visit our Web site at:

www.gale.com/thorndike
www.gale.com/wheeler

To share your comments, please write:

Publisher
Thorndike Press
295 Kennedy Memorial Drive
Waterville, ME 04901